DOUBLEDAY
CELEBRATES
100 YEARS OF
EXCELLENCE

FLESH WOUNDS

MICK COCHRANE

NAN A. TALESE

DOUBLEDAY

NEW YORK · LONDON · TORONTO · SYDNEY · AUCKLAND

PUBLISHED BY NAN A. TALESE
an imprint of Doubleday
a division of Bantam Doubleday Dell Publishing Group, Inc.
1540 Broadway, New York, New York 10036

DOUBLEDAY is a trademark of Doubleday, a division of
Bantam Doubleday Dell Publishing Group, Inc.

Book design by Jessica Shatan

Library of Congress Cataloging-in-Publication Data
Cochrane, Mick.
Flesh wounds / Mick Cochrane. — 1st ed.
p.   cm.
I. Title.
PS3553.O267F58   1997
813'.54—dc20   96-42558   CIP

ISBN 0-385-48661-8

ACKNOWLEDGMENTS

I would like to thank Lon Otto and Lance Wilcox for their wonderfully smart and sympathetic readings of the book, for their advice, and above all for their generous and constant friendship. For encouragement and acts of kindness too many and various to catalog, I am grateful to Ron and Marlys Ousky, Paul Schmidt and Holly Haugerud, Fred Von Drasek, Paul and Lisa Von Drasek, Michael O'Connell, Tom and Virginia Gilmore, Jack Foran and Nancy Schiller, Nancy Rosenbloom and Larry Jones, Dave Lauerman, and Rita Capezzi. I am especially grateful to Nan A. Talese, Jesse Cohen, and Jay Mandel for their confidence in me and the careful attention they've given my work.

For Mary

GENEALOGY

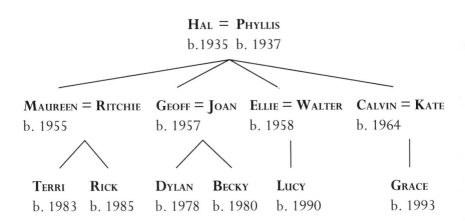

HAL = PHYLLIS
b.1935 b. 1937

MAUREEN = RITCHIE   GEOFF = JOAN   ELLIE = WALTER   CALVIN = KATE
b. 1955   b. 1957   b. 1958   b. 1964

TERRI   RICK   DYLAN   BECKY   LUCY   GRACE
b. 1983 b. 1985   b. 1978 b. 1980 b. 1990   b. 1993

PART I

FALL

1

MR. LAMM

THE POLICE CAME JUST AFTER EIGHT. HAL WAS SITTING IN HIS CHAIR watching the "Today" show when he saw the car pull up, a shiny black Plymouth with a big antenna jutting off the back like a deep-sea fishing rod. There were two guys in dark suits and ties—they weren't Jehovah's Witnesses. He got the hell out. Grabbed his keys and his wallet off the microwave, slipped past the laundry room where Phyllis was folding towels, out the back door, over the deck, down the stairs, across the lawn, and into his Town Car, backed, as always, into its spot. He moved like the teacher in a fire drill, swift and purposeful, but not panicked. Not what he planned so much as what he half-expected from himself. Wearing slippers and a white T-shirt and golf slacks with a hole in the crotch. The fear rising in his chest, noxious and sour, like heartburn. He started the car and eased down the alley, where the kids used to play softball and kick the can, waved to Leonard Kruk in an orange slicker carrying trash bags, stopped at the sign, and gunned it onto Dillard.

He made the light on Fifty-fourth, but was held up at the on-ramp of 35W behind a blonde applying mascara in the rearview mirror. Finally, he got on the freeway. He headed north, against the rush hour traffic, into the Minneapolis suburbs—Coon Rapids, Anoka, Elk River, where he used to stop for pancakes with Geoff on their way up to Mille Lacs to go fishing. He turned on the radio and set the cruise control and tried to think. What was happening?

One fine day there had been a gray-haired policewoman in pants at the door, a uniformed stranger with a spiral notebook. She sat on the couch and smiled demurely, like the Avon lady. She cleared her throat and talked about agencies and reports, authorities and procedures, a preliminary investigation, so roundabout at first he thought his granddaughter was dead. And then she told him it was him. The more they talked—how many ways can you say, I don't know what you're talking about?—the more she treated him like a criminal. She didn't know the first thing about him. And when she finally left, her eyes scanning the room, studying the photos on the mantel, looking for something suspicious, promising she would be back, his heart was beating in his chest like an angry fist.

His daughter Eleanor was making accusations now, too. She had always been an imaginative child. She used to play alone in her room for hours and hours, inventing names and personalities for all her dolls and stuffed animals. She had a flair for the dramatic, was a sidesplitting mimic of her teachers, easily slipped into the speech and mannerisms of the people she was around. And she loved to perform—dances, puppet shows, and especially plays—which she would write and direct and star in, drafting her brothers and sister and him, too, into supporting roles, handing them neatly typed scripts complete with stage directions and pauses for laughter and applause. He could remember roaring and rattling tire chains as Marley's ghost one Christmas. And now her life was not turning out the way that she wanted—whose did?—and she needed a villain, and she'd assigned him the part.

He spotted a strip of service stations and restaurants and retail outlets—golden arches and the orange Union 76 ball, Hardware Hank and winking Mr. Donut. He exited, made a right onto a frontage road, and pulled into the big lot of a Target. It was the sort of store that bought his line: some movie tie-ins but mostly professional sports souvenirs, bobbing head dolls, playing cards, key chains, buttons with computer chips that played "Take Me Out to the Ball Game," so time-sensitive—it was cheap, crummy stuff, all of it, he had to be first on the shelves—that in the case of a big upset, he would be saddled with sweatshirts and pennants commemorating nonexistent champions, Super Bowls and World Series that were never played.

The store was just opening, and inside, a busy team of employees was getting ready for business. They were the kind of grown-ups who work days at kids' jobs, lifers, dressed in red uniforms, like Santa's helping elves, mopping, pulling trays of cookies from the bakery ovens, flipping on overhead lights and inserting cash trays at the checkouts, retracting the metal cage from the florist's.

There was a bank of pay phones just inside the door. He

fished a quarter from his pocket and punched in the number. "It's me," he said.

"They're gone now," Phyllis said. "They were going to arrest you. Where are you?"

"What did you tell them?"

"I told them the truth," Phyllis said. "I said you were here a minute ago and then you were gone. I don't know where he went, I said. No idea when you would be back. They weren't happy, let's just say that. I thought maybe they would want to search the place—you know, pull out drawers and throw papers around, just like on TV. The chubby one asked to use the phone and the other one just scowled. Finally, they left. For all I know, I'm staked out. Wiretapped. Watch what you say."

"Okay," he said.

"What are you going to do now?"

"I don't know."

"Call Calvin. He'll know what to do."

"Maybe."

"And Hal," she said.

"What?" he said. A guy walked in the store carrying a walkie-talkie. "What?"

"Don't come back here. Please."

He set the phone down. The guy with the walkie-talkie was talking to another fellow about towels in the ladies' room. He was cleaning service.

Hal wheeled a big cart through the store, past the car batteries and the sweet-smelling new tires in Automotive, past the bins of footballs and closed-out baseball mitts in Sporting Goods, past Records and Tapes, into Menswear. He picked out a turtleneck, a shiny black warm-up suit, a pair of Reeboks, and a bag of tube socks. In Notions he grabbed some miniature toiletries from a bin of sample-sized products: Crest, Listerine, Speed Stick, Foamy. He dropped a pack of disposable razors in the cart, a toothbrush, a comb. At the counter he threw down some magazines and chocolate bars. He paid with his Visa card.

He carried the bag into the men's room and put on his new clothes, slipped into a pair of socks and the sneakers. Combed his hair and brushed his teeth. Zipped up the jacket and inspected himself in the mirror. He looked fine. He folded his old clothes in the big shopping bag, stepped outside, and headed for the dumpster in the parking lot. He lifted the lid and stuffed the bag inside. And kept walking. Wondering if anyone was watching him. Thinking of the serial murderers who leave their victims' body parts scattered in garbage cans across town.

He got into his car and drove slowly out of the parking lot. Now what? What he would like to do would be to get a flight to Vegas. Take a couple of days with Rita and get some breathing room. He could spend some time at the tables (he played blackjack and, having years ago mastered a streamlined system of counting cards, did all right). They could take in a show. He loved Vegas, the lights and the free drinks and the chips and new cards and the nice hotel rooms and yes, the aroma of sex. It was legal there, the girls like models, all wet lips and bare shoulders in their little black dresses, Lord knows how much they cost. Last time Rita went with him to a topless club, and while they watched a girl working on stage with a fireman's pole, she touched him under the table. The dancer was looking into a bank of bright lights. Hal could see little beads of sweat running down between her breasts, but she couldn't see him. He was hard as a rock.

————

Hal found a parking spot near the entrance to Dayton's in Rosedale and took the escalator to the second floor. Rita's office was located down a hall lined with travel posters. She was sitting at her desk, her back to the door, looking out a sliver of a window, like a sniper's outpost in an old-time western fort, with only the top of her brilliant red hair visible above the back of her black executive's chair. When he knocked, Rita swiveled around to face him, a slim telephone receiver cradled on her shoulder and a stack of pink invoices resting on her lap. She waved him in. She was wearing a green dress, the color of an avocado, cut almost like a coat, adorned in front with a double row of big black buttons. "Good," she said into the phone, and rolled her eyes. "Very good." She smiled, the most photogenic person he had ever known, every single snapshot like a studio portrait, the same perfect teeth proudly displayed, though he knew for a fact that after her ex-husband Albert, the drunken real estate developer, had slapped her around, she had needed some serious dental work. She looked terrific. She was in her late forties, fifty tops. (Once, when he playfully tried to wrestle her driver's license away from her just to have a peek, she jabbed him so hard in the solar plexus, he realized right then that the mystery of her age was no joke—she was dead serious.) She took good care of herself, aerobics every morning, salads for lunch, every Friday at the beauty shop to have her hair and nails done.

He took a seat. Rita had transformed her office, a cubicle, really—there were no ceilings and you could sometimes overhear the other buyers and even the travel agents down the hall—into something warm and inviting, like a room in a magazine. She'd covered the beige institutional carpeting with an

oriental rug and hung the walls with a framed brass rubbing—
a somber, bearded young man with a dog curled around his
feet—and a black Georgia O'Keeffe flower. The credenza,
covered with a floral runner, was filled with photos of Rita's
daughter, Jessica, holding a dance trophy, in her cap and
gown, dressed for the prom. A brass lamp cast a soft light
across her desk, and there was classical music playing.

They'd met in this office, two years before, Hal in the same
chair with a big box of World Series paraphernalia on his lap.
She was a hard sell. "Are these licensed?" she'd sniffed at his
Homer Hankies. But in the end, she bought a bundle, and
then they went down to the food court for ice cream. The
next week, back at her apartment on Lyndale in the middle of
the afternoon, they made love on her overstuffed couch.

"Thank you," Rita was saying into the phone. "You don't
know how much I appreciate this. You're a lifesaver." It was
vintage Rita. Hal loved her capacity for gratitude, which she
worked at like a second job. She wrote thank-yous constantly—she kept a big pack of blank cards in her purse to
compose during lulls in her day—for things you would never
think of thanking someone for, at least not in writing, a dinner, a movie, a nice walk, and once, really, a kind remark.
Hal earned her gratitude with little gifts, at first especially,
just trinkets for her, some samples for Jessica, but underneath
it all, what she must have appreciated so ferociously was that
he wasn't Albert, that he had no taste for booze, that he
didn't yell or hit.

Rita hung up the phone and made a note in her datebook.
"Hal," she said. "You look slick. Hal opts for a day of leisure
or an evening of pleasure in his spiffy Members Only jacket
and beautiful new"—she craned around the desk and stared at

his foot—"Reebok sneakers. That's what your ad copy would be. Except that I never seem to opt for anything myself in real life. How about you? Maybe only people in catalogs opt. I thought you were on the road this week."

"Change of plans," he said.

"I wish I could change my plans today," she said. "I'm swamped. And I'm still stiff from sleeping on the lumpy bed in Jessica's dorm room. How do they do it? But we got her moved in, all her clothes and her stereo and books. And her roommates are dears, Aileen and Tanya, one from Duluth, the other from St. Cloud, I can't remember which is which. But how about you? How was your weekend?"

"I washed storm windows," he said.

"Well," Rita said.

"And I watched the telethon."

"How was Jerry? Did he sing that little song at the end, 'You'll Never Walk Alone,' is that it? Did he cry?"

"He's gotten mean," he said. "Have you noticed? I used to like him, when he was just a goof, but now the way he sweats and snarls and yells at people, it's like he's taking it all personally. Like muscular dystrophy is our fault. It's spooky."

Rita's phone blipped, and she was on again, chatting about silk blouses. Jammed into his small chair, feeling his new pants cutting his waist and tugging at his thighs, staring across Rita's imposing desk, full of accessories, a Rolodex, paperweights, a cup of pens, the clock facing her, Hal felt both diminished somehow, like a schoolboy in the principal's office or a troubled patient with a shrink, and also inappropriately large, bloated and awkward, like a Macy's balloon. Something scratched the back of his neck and he swatted at it. It was a store tag from his new turtleneck that he hadn't removed. He yanked it and got the paper tag, which he rolled in his palm and jammed in his pocket, but half of the plastic string disappeared down the back of his shirt.

She put the phone down. "Sorry," she said.

"Look, Rita," Hal said. "I've got to tell you something."

"What?" she said. "What is it?"

"The police." Rita knew something was up. He had told her that Becky was telling stories. Generally, not necessarily just him. She needed attention, that's what Rita thought, girls are like that at that age. Jessica used to talk about monsters and slashers and the psycho in lover's lane with a hook as if they were real, too. She got over it.

The police came when he was out, Hal told her. They wanted to arrest him. Rita stared at him, her face suddenly stony and blank, somehow impaired or disabled, as if it had been shot with Novocain. But there was something working behind the eyes, he could tell. Like the policewoman. She was making calculations.

"So now you've come here, to my office? Jesus, Hal. You're wanted. You're some kind of fugitive. The cops are probably talking on the radio about you, looking for your car. I can't protect you, Hal."

"I don't want you to protect me," Hal said.

"What do you want then?"

Hal stood up and walked out. Past a framed Scottish castle and the Alps, down the escalator. Not this.

He bought a ticket for the four o'clock showing of *In the Line of Fire*. He had to say it twice. The girl behind the Plexiglas at the box office, who talked into a microphone and took money and shoved tickets through a slit in the bottom, like a cashier at the track, cocked her head and touched her ear. She didn't quite get it the first time. There were six features. His voice wasn't working right, his throat was dry. He read the lettering above her head and said it again. *In the Line of Fire.*

He had been driving for a couple of hours, had gone through a quarter of a tank of gas, and wanted just to lose himself now in the dark. He'd driven around the lakes on the parkway, Harriet and Calhoun and Lake of the Isles, watching the joggers and bladers and race walkers, mostly women during the day, their firm butts in brightly colored outfits, wearing headphones, sometimes walking a dog or pushing a kid in a stroller. He drove up and down Dillard, slowing at Gibbon to look at his house, Phyllis's Taurus parked in front, the rake on the porch where he'd left it the day before, the curtains drawn, and the black front door giving the illusion somehow it was opening every time he drove by. Circling again and again, stupidly returning to the scene, but mesmerized by the vision of the life he'd been dislodged from—the lawn he watered and the windows he washed, his newspaper on the step, the lamp in the living room running on electricity he paid for—as though he were returning from the dead to discover that everything looked just the same without him.

He bought himself a box of popcorn and a Coke and headed inside. The movie had already started, and he stood for a moment in the aisle, letting his eyes adjust. The theater was almost empty. A group to his right, crinkling paper and whispering, the dry combustible voices of elderly women, and two solitary heads in front. He rarely went to the movies anymore, never by himself. He believed there was something wrong with people who did. He sat down in the back, where he could rest his head on a wall, and hear the hum of the projector above him.

Clint Eastwood was a Secret Service man who'd been in Dallas, old now, and out of shape, puffing along the presidential limo, ashen and gasping, like the last guy in a marathon, looking for redemption. His voice, to Hal, who was familiar only with imitations, who'd heard Rich Little and Robin Williams and a million others on Carson say, "Make my day," but never Eastwood himself, sounded like a so-so impression, a mediocre parody.

The bad guy was John Malkovich, a cunning assassin, determined to take out the President. He was protean, now bald, now bearded, sometimes puffy and sometimes lean, a clean-cut businessman one minute, a shaggy bagman the next. He taunted Eastwood on the phone, his voice an icy, knowing whisper, surgically exploring old wounds. He saw everything, studied his face under a magnifying glass in old photographs, fixed him in the crosshairs of his scope. He was pure evil, and he never slept.

When Malkovich was in the house of a bank officer, a chatty fat girl who maybe knew too much, edging closer and closer to her, smiling, polite and menacing, Hal got up and pushed the doors aside and stepped into the lobby. He got another Coke—he was still dry—and asked about a telephone. Down the hall, past the rest rooms.

He found the number in the yellow pages and got put through to Cal's secretary. "Who may I tell him is calling?" she wanted to know.

"His father," he said. Cal was on in a flash, and Hal knew that he knew.

"Dad," he said.

"Hi, Cal. What's up?"

"You tell me."

"You heard."

"Sure I heard. I came back from a deposition this morning and found a pile of messages from Mom. Where are you?"

"At the movies."

"At the movies. Are you okay?"

"I'm fine."

"You shouldn't have run."

Another show got out, and a slow stream of people moved past him toward the exit, more elderly women, a tiny oriental couple, a guy wearing work boots and a down vest, all of them bleary and stiff, as if they'd sat too long in the same position. They pushed the steel double doors open and Hal got a glimpse of the parking lot and the gray sky, a street lamp flickering on, the wind ruffling the old ladies' hair.

"I guess not," Hal said.

"I don't think you get it, Dad. You're in big trouble. This isn't a traffic ticket. I can't call the county clerk and fix it for you. You can't just mail in a check and forget about it. You can't go to ding-dong school for two Saturdays and clear your record."

"I'm sorry. Is that what you want me to say? Okay. I'm sorry. I wasn't thinking. If I had to do it over again, I would do it different."

"Forget it."

"Now what?"

"Here's what you do. Go to the downtown station; it's in city hall, the main floor. Go now. It's dinnertime, it's quiet, you'll be in and out. Tell them who you are, and they'll book you. It's a formality."

Cal was using his attorney's voice with him. It was the way

Hal had heard him speak to clients when they'd call him at home, people who'd just been evicted or harassed or denied visitation. Kate would whisper the name and Cal would get up from the dinner table and clear his throat and take it in the kitchen, stretching the long cord into the pantry, a bit hushed, earnest and confident, someone who knew what to do.

"Do I have to plead? Innocent or whatever?"

"Later. At the hearing."

"Do I get to make a call?"

"Like in the movies? Who do you want to call?"

"I don't know," Hal said. It seemed important to be able to make a call. "Will you meet me down there?"

There was a pause. Hal could hear paper rustling on Cal's end, the hum of a machine, a computer or a fan. "Dad," Cal said, a sad reprimand.

"I would rather not do this alone."

"Kate and I have Lamaze tonight. It's our first class. I'm meeting her at the hospital. I've got the pillows in my car."

Cal was going to be a perfect father. He was reading books already, planning on taking a paternity leave. He would carry the baby around in a pouch.

"That's okay," Hal said. "Don't worry about it."

Hal had been to the downtown precinct only once, years before, to drop off a gift for Santas Anonymous with one of the girls—Maureen probably, who had a big heart and used to fret during the holidays about orphans and cripples and shut-ins. He remembered holding her up while she tossed something, a coloring book, a puzzle, into a big blue bin, like a dumpster, full of brand-new Barbies and shiny toy trucks.

He parked a block down from the station and put four

quarters in the meter. He locked the car. He was good for two hours. There was a gust of wind, weirdly warm, like something artificial, created by a machine, as he walked down the sidewalk past two men in overcoats carrying umbrellas and briefcases. He could smell exhaust fumes and feel a blister forming on the heel of his left foot. There were lights blazing on every floor, city government or police, offices or cells, you couldn't tell.

Hal pushed through the revolving doors, into the lobby, past the elevators. There was a sign with an arrow. He pulled open a heavy glass door and entered the precinct house, where a man and a woman, his age, maybe a little older, gray-haired, bundled in heavy sweaters, stood at the desk listening to an officer. The woman, wearing tennis shoes and brown anklets, the backs of her legs mapped with varicose veins, yanked the leash of a white toy poodle at her feet. The man had a gauze patch taped to his forehead. They looked stupidly stunned, slack-jawed.

"I know you don't want to go home tonight," the officer was saying. His skin was pock-marked, and he had a bristly red mustache. His name was stitched above his breast pocket, Skinner, and he wore the American flag on one shoulder, the emblem of the city's police on the other, a lake. His silver badge glittered in the fluorescent light but it seemed flimsy, like a toy. "We're trying to come up with something. But City Mission only takes men."

The dog sniffed Hal's feet, and looked up at him, its big eyes watery and bewildered. "Mickey," the woman hissed, and gave another sharp pull on the chain.

Behind Skinner, another officer was sitting at a desk spooning up what looked like rice pudding from a Styrofoam carton and reading a folded newspaper. The top two buttons of his uniform shirt were opened to reveal a white T-shirt and an extravagant shock of black chest hair, like an animal's winter coat. "Senior Services," he said, without looking up.

"What's her name there?" Skinner said. "Edith? Ethel? It's one of those waitress names. Edna?"

"Esther."

The dog was back, nibbling at Hal's shoelaces. "Just take a seat, Mr. and Mrs. Maki," Skinner said. "I'm going to make a few more calls and see what I can do." They shuffled away from the counter and sat down heavily on a wooden bench against the wall. The woman reeled in the dog, hand over hand, and it hopped onto the bench and curled up between them. The man pulled a can of Copenhagen from his pocket and took a pinch. Skinner disappeared in the back, around a corner.

Hal stepped up to the counter. He was ready. The other officer—Eddy, his shirt read—was still bent over the newspaper, still working on the pudding. Hal cleared his throat. They were ten, no more than twelve feet apart. Hal could see flakes of dandruff on the shoulder of his blue shirt, hear the plastic spoon scraping the carton. He was reading the comics. Hal cleared his throat again, but Eddy didn't even look up. It was like the post office or worse, the department of motor vehicles. If there were a bell, Hal would have rung it.

Hal knocked twice on the counter, good solid raps, but Eddy didn't move a muscle. It was ridiculous. Hal knocked again, harder. "Excuse me," he said.

Eddy wiped his mouth on a napkin. He put the napkin and spoon in the carton and dropped the carton in a plastic wastebasket. He stood and ran a hand along the side of his head, smoothed his hair down in back. He walked toward Hal slowly, a deliberate waddle, swaying from side to side, his arms away from his body, as if the piece he wore on his belt were a tremendous burden. He stared at Hal. His left eye was blue, the other, something else, hazel. "Hi, asshole," he said. "What can I do for you?"

Hal introduced himself. Explained why he was there. "You're turning yourself in," Eddy said. Skinner was back, a piece of paper in his hand, and the old couple came off the bench and rushed the desk, the dog scrabbling across the floor behind them.

"You're out of luck," Skinner said.

"Come with me," Eddy said.

He led Hal into the back, down a long hallway, past a row of vending machines, into a room with a table and chairs. "Sit down," he said, and ducked out. There was a blackboard on one wall, a telephone and phone books piled on a typing table on the other. On the tabletop in front of Hal, someone had carved a lopsided heart with an arrow, and some jagged initials, G.D.

Eddy returned with a clipboard and some files. The top folder was fat with documents, and when Eddy opened it, Hal could see papers full of single-spaced type. About him?

"Legal name," Eddy said.

"Excuse me?" Hal said.

Eddy was holding a fat four-color pen poised over his clipboard, circling. "First, middle, and last name," Eddy said. "Say it and spell it," and Hal did. Eddy bit his lip and squeezed the big pen, serious and awkward as a grade school kid with his first pencil. "Address," he said, and Hal recited it. "Slower," Eddy said.

Eddy moved from form to form, asking Hal the same questions again and again. It was like his army physical, forty years ago, when he had stood in the armory for hours in his jockey shorts, compliant and covered with goose pimples.

"You're a good candidate for ROR, Harold," Eddy said. "But we're going to have to detain you until Neil gets here. If you want to use the phone, go ahead."

"Who's Neil?"

"He makes a recommendation about bail, yes or no, how much, whether you get released on your own recognizance."

"When?"

Eddy shrugged. Hal got up and walked over to the phone, a fancy new model full of lights and buttons. Next to it there was a dirty typed list of lawyers' names covered in plastic. He turned his back to Eddy and picked up the receiver. He pushed the first three numbers and got a shrill alternating mechanical tone, like an ambulance blasting through an intersection. He hit another button and it came blaring out of a speaker.

"Dial nine," Eddy said.

Phyllis answered on the first ring.

"I'm downtown," Hal said. "At the police station."

"Are you okay?" Phyllis asked.

"I think so," Hal said. He'd eaten nothing but candy and popcorn all day and felt sick to his stomach. He had a headache. His shoes didn't fit right. He didn't feel like himself. "They're keeping me here until the bail guy comes."

"Do you need money? Do you want me to come down?"

"I don't know," Hal said. "Maybe. If you want."

Eddy took Hal across the hall, where there was another officer sitting on a stool. They told him to empty his pockets into a tray. His billfold, creased and fat with credit cards and photographs. His keys. A handful of change. A Snickers wrapper. A pencil stub. A wad of tissue. They told him to put his thumb in the ink. There and there. They told him to put his heels on the marks and look straight ahead. Turn to the right. To the left. They made him sign for his possessions, in triplicate, a faint photocopied form full of barely legible disclaimers. "Okay," they said.

"Thank you," he said.

They led him down the hall into a holding cell. It was a big open room with a concrete floor and wooden benches and a wall clock, like a church basement, except for the bars. There was one other white guy, youngish but almost completely bald, rail-thin, the bones of his skull visible beneath his skin. He was leaning on the bars, his arms crossed and the sleeves of his denim shirt rolled up, his forearms covered with diseased skin, layers and layers of white flakes. An Hispanic kid with a chin beard was slumped on a bench, his head bowed and his eyes closed, and two black guys in big unlaced sneakers were sitting on the floor across the room. One was chewing something, and the other was shaking his head slowly from side to side as if in sad disbelief.

They weren't friendly, they weren't threatening. They were just there. Nobody said anything. Hal sat down and minded his own business. He watched the clock's red second hand sweep the face, once, twice, three times. It was after nine. He considered the possibility of his being stuck there all night. What about the car, parked at an expired meter? How could he sleep in a room with benches and four other men? And what was he going to do with his partial? He needed a glass of water.

It smelled smoky and stale, like a barroom. From time to time the Hispanic boy raised his head and looked around, his eyes red and heavy-lidded, like somebody on a bus checking to see if he'd missed his stop. One of the black guys talked softly on and off, maybe to himself, maybe to the guy next to him, but except for the profanity Hal couldn't make out many of the words, just the singsong melody of question and complaint. *The fuck he doing?* The other white guy paced some and cracked his knuckles and chewed his nails.

Finally somebody called Hal's name. "Mr. Lamm?" It was a kid with a wispy mustache wearing jeans and sneakers and a corduroy jacket. "I'm a bail officer," he said. He wasn't old enough. He had a tiny diamond in his left ear. He squatted outside the cell and talked to Hal through the bars, a clipboard balanced on his knee, like a kid calling a play in a backyard football game. "Just a few questions," he said. Name and address, again. Social Security number. Criminal history. Any prior convictions? arrests? Hal said, "no," and "none," and the kid drew lines through whole big blanks on his form and turned the page. After that, it was like a credit card application. Employment history. Years at his current job, at his current address. "That's all," the kid said, and then he got up and walked away.

A few minutes later Officer Skinner came back and opened the cell door. "Harold?" he said, and Hal got up, like it was his turn at the dentist, and headed out. Skinner took him back to the room where he had been photographed and brought out a big manila envelope. He spilled Hal's things on the desktop. Thrown together under the bright lights, his brown wallet with a couple of worn fives sticking out and his Swiss Army knife key chain and a few quarters and dimes and scraps of paper, they made a sad, lifeless heap. But as he stored them away, straightened the bills and put the wallet in his hip pocket, keys in the right front, silver jingling in the left, he felt stronger, loaded somehow, properly equipped and identified and ready, reconnected. Skinner told him that he would be arraigned the next morning at ten o'clock, same building, second floor. Don't be late. Hal waited. ''That's all,'' Skinner said. ''You can go home now.''

Hal walked out the door and down the long hallway. He could see Phyllis standing on tiptoe and squinting, looking for him. He walked slowly, with his head down, rubbing his wrists. He stepped through the double doors and they embraced, rough with longing, bone on bone, like a hostage home at last, like lovers in a film.

2

LARGE GARBAGE DAY

TUESDAY, THE DAY AFTER THE LONG LABOR DAY WEEKEND. LARGE Garbage Day in the city of Buffalo. On the way home from dropping Lucy off at nursery school (suddenly and inexplicably delighted today, after weeks of screaming trauma, to part: ''Bye, Mama,'' she'd said, dismissively, almost impatiently, and headed off in the direction of the paints and Play-Doh), Ellie drove her Escort wagon slowly up and down promising side streets with the flashers on, like a great teal-colored predatory fish, searching with an experienced eye among the doorless refrigerators and obscenely stained mattresses and rolls of threadbare carpeting for what she liked to call treasures.

Walter didn't entirely approve of her garbage-snatching, she was quite sure, so she was glad to be alone. On the few occasions she had asked him to pull over in order to allow her to examine something, he never joined her curbside. He waited guiltily in the car with the motor running, sneaking glances in the rearview mirror, like an accomplice afraid to be identified. He would never say anything critical, but he always looked glum when he discovered another of her projects in the garage—he loved open spaces, emptiness really, dreaded a house crammed with hulking hutches and couches, the decor of grandmothers. He thought the garage was for automobiles and a lawn mower. So she had sworn off bringing furniture home, at least until she'd redone the pieces she had already accumulated, but she couldn't seem to stop.

On Highland she spotted a well-dressed woman tottering down a steep driveway in high heels carrying a child-sized Adirondack chair piled high with paperback books. Ellie pulled over. The woman dropped the chair, books and all, into a considerable heap of belongings on the boulevard, an upright Hoover, a dented toaster, two reclining lawn chairs, a stack of boxed board games and jigsaw puzzles, a mounted moose head staring dolefully up into the sky—enough for a respectable garage sale. The woman patted her elaborately coifed hair, straightened the jacket of her navy suit, and headed back up the drive.

Ellie got out and examined the chair. It was dirty. One leg was scarred, chewed, apparently, by a dog. The paint on the back was peeling like the bark of a diseased tree. Otherwise, it was in fine condition. The joints were strong, the wood was in good shape.

The woman returned, carrying an enormous jingling bird-cage, and smiled at Ellie, who was still holding the chair. ''Take whatever you want, honey,'' she said.

''Thank you,'' Ellie said. ''It's a lovely chair.''

"Honey," the woman said, giving the moose head a nudge with her foot, "I've got a garage full of lovely. Do you want to see?"

Ellie slid the chair in the back of the wagon and followed the woman up the driveway.

The side door was propped open, and leaning against the house were dozens of blue-and-gold lawn signs, their stakes still covered with dirt: RE-ELECT JUDGE JIM BOWIE. "The judge and I just got ourselves married, and I'm moving in. But only, I told him, if we clean up. Just look at this."

"Congratulations," said Ellie, who didn't know what kind of judges exactly campaigned for office, who couldn't recall ever having voted for a judge herself, certainly not for Jim Bowie.

Mrs. Bowie bent down and lifted the garage door with both hands, jiggled it halfway up to keep the runner on its track, and pushed the door back overhead with an explosive grunt. "Here you be," she said. "Help yourself."

It was dark inside, full of dim shapes and shadows, and smelled of gasoline and old newspapers. Ellie forced herself to go slow, let her eyes adjust, not get carried away. She took a deep breath. She studied a row of framed certificates of appreciation—from the PTA, the Rotary Club, the state bar association—hanging on the wall above her next to a 1983 calendar and several framed black-and-white photographs of men in caps and flannel shirts holding cans of beer and stringers of fish.

She moved cautiously around a tremendous pile of magazines and two sawhorses toward the back of the garage, where she spotted some furniture. There was a plaid recliner, its seat decorated with iron-on patches; a coffee table into which holes had been drilled to create an oversized cribbage board; a Formica kitchen table covered on one side only by cigarette burns, like an army of brown caterpillars. Ellie settled finally on just one thing: a wooden school desk, which, like the little chair, when painted, would be just right for Lucy.

Ellie drove home, pleased with her finds, proud of her self-restraint—if Walt could only see what she had passed up—and determined to begin work on the chair immediately. In the past year she had found a kind of engrossing satisfaction and almost guilty pleasure working with furniture. Every Tuesday evening for two full community-education semesters, from October through May, Ellie had filled her purse with wire brushes and steel wool, and driven to her furniture restoration class at the local middle school. Under the supervision of Otto Kreutzner, the district's retired shop teacher, and his strapping son Karl, Ellie worked on her oak console table alongside a handful of other students whom she grew inarticulately, irrationally, embarrassingly fond of. There was an elderly couple redoing a dining room set, one chair at a time. They had three beautiful grandchildren on the West Coast and seemingly infinite reserves of patience and gentle concern for one another. They took turns: while one painstakingly worked on one of the chair's ornate spindles, the other would sit by, cheering, complimenting, declaring it time to take a break. Another fellow, in his fifties, always arrived just a few minutes late, his hair slicked back and wearing a fresh short-sleeved sport shirt—he dressed up for class, Ellie suspected. He softly whistled show tunes while he worked on his rolltop—"Oklahoma," "Easter Parade"—in his own distinctively jazzy arrangements. A group of three or four women who seemed to know each other already attended class on and off, rarely all of them in the same week, and gathered together outside during breaks to smoke and crack loud jokes about their diets and ex-husbands. They didn't make much progress with their pieces and didn't seem to mind. And there was an overweight high school boy with bad skin who arrived early and stayed late to work on some sort of keyboard instrument, a pump organ maybe, Ellie couldn't say for sure, that folded up into a neat little box. He listened to jangling rock music on headphones but always smiled at Ellie when she'd look up from her work. They were oddballs, all of them, Ellie knew that. Who else would spend six weeks sanding something? But she loved them anyway. She was an oddball, too, she supposed. So what?

Otto himself moved from worktable to worktable, where they competed for his attention like reporters at a presidential press conference. He would spend a whole class helping one or two students, regluing joints, filling cracks with plastic wood, replacing broken dowels, his thick, short fingers—he told the class he had lost the tip of one in an accident but Ellie could never tell which one—working abrasive string into tiny crevices as precisely as a dental hygienist with floss. He would talk the whole time, about his woods, which he named with affection and loved equally, like a good father, in their rich variety—softwoods and hardwoods—for their beautiful differences—cherry and gumwood—in their strength and flexibility—maple and pine and poplar, a solid oak and even a well-crafted veneer.

Ellie so loved Otto's workshop that even though the smell of chemicals, the Zip-Strip and polyurethane and stains, made her dizzy, she retreated outside for fresh air only reluctantly and returned as soon as her head cleared. It was the act of restoration above all that fascinated her: scraping and burning and sanding away layer after layer and discovering finally the wood beneath, smelling it, letting it breathe, after all those coats of paint and stain and shellac and God knows what. When she used a rented heat gun on a bookcase for Lucy and watched thirty years of paint peel away in seconds like a skin, she was thrilled. But when she told Walt that she wanted her own gun for Christmas, he thought she was kidding. Recently she had heard of dipping things, a commercial process by which big pieces—doors, say, window frames, a mantelpiece—were plunged into powerful chemicals and stripped to the grain, and she had even dreamed once of being dipped herself, burned pink as a newborn in a frothy cauldron and emerging clean and raw.

Ellie could hear the telephone ringing as she put the key in the front door. By the time she made it to the phone, the answering machine had clicked on and someone was already talking. It was Maureen. In the past, Mo had taken it upon herself to organize gifts for their parents, a winter coat or microwave for their mother, a string trimmer or a putter for their father, buying whatever it was and calling to tell Ellie what each kid's share was. Now, since what Mo called ''this thing with Dad and Becky''—she couldn't bring herself to use the real words—she called to keep her informed. Ellie stared at the machine's glowing green light and listened. Two plainclothes cops had come for their father, Mo said. That's all she knew. She promised to stay in touch.

"And, Ellie," she said. "It's not your fault."

In July, the Minneapolis police had called. Ellie had been in the kitchen, heating soup for Lucy's lunch. ''I just want to ask you a few questions about your father,'' said a Sergeant Jenson, who sounded so sweet and elderly, like Miss Marple, that it was impossible to conceive of her in uniform, at a desk in a busy station.

Geoff's daughter, Becky, had talked to her sixth-grade teacher after a program about good and bad touch. Who? Mrs. Reed wanted to know. Who did it? but Becky wasn't going to say. Finally she wrote it down on a piece of looseleaf paper. *Grandpa.*

''If you don't mind, we're going to tape-record what you say, so we'll get it exactly right,'' Sergeant Jenson had said. Ellie felt awkward at first, self-conscious, aware of the slightly false pitch in her voice. She sounded as if she were answering a question from the floor, that formal and deliberate. It was strange, talking to someone she had never met and couldn't see, a policewoman, a thousand miles away, being taped, but some of these sentences she had already formed, put together and rehearsed over the years while she was doing laundry or taking a shower or digging in the garden, imagining conversations with—whom? The Authorities. After a while, she no longer felt nervous. (Maureen had agonized about whether to talk, what to say, worried about the consequences, implications. ''It's simple,'' Walt told Ellie. ''Tell the truth.'')

Lucy had played quietly in the living room the whole time. Ellie watched her standing at the coffee table with her three bears—two stuffed teddies she won at a carnival and a buffalo wearing a baseball cap who stood in for Papa Bear—and a plastic farmhouse, which served as their cottage. She moved them intently up and down, in and out, talking quietly to herself all the while.

Ellie had told Sergeant Jenson that she didn't know anything about Becky and what might have happened to her. She was a sweet girl, her favorite niece. The last time she had seen her was three years ago at a resort in northern Michigan, where they'd joined her brother and his family for a week's vacation. Becky had been fascinated by Lucy, just a newborn then, and used to stand above her bassinet holding up and describing interesting objects for her consideration—an apple, a pine cone, a fishing lure. She always sat next to Ellie in the paddle boat, loved to play cards—Hearts, wild variations of Crazy Eights, Double Solitaire—and was intent on becoming an archaeologist. Now it was probably something else. She reminded Ellie of herself at that age. Ellie mailed her a birthday card every year and sent her art supplies from time to time. Her Christmas picture was on the refrigerator. That was it.

But, yes, Ellie had some information about her father. She was ten years old, maybe eleven. They were in the house on Gibbon by then, and her mother was still drinking. It was 1969, 1970 maybe. She was sitting on his lap in his chair watching television. It was a cowboy show called ''High Chaparral,'' no one remembers it now but her. It was on Sunday night, right after ''Bonanza.'' Her mother must have been in bed already and the other kids might have been outside playing. Anyway, it was just the two of them. While they were watching he slipped his hand slowly down the front of her jeans. He just kept looking at the television the whole time, as if nothing was happening, as if he were in a trance. His hand was warm and sweaty. And then he started to touch her. That was the first time.

While she talked, Ellie looked out the window into the backyard at Lucy's toys, her Sesame Street pool, her turtle sandbox. She could hear a high-pitched tone sound on the telephone line every minute or so, a signal she was being recorded. She felt lightheaded, as if she'd been blowing up balloons, and her scalp was tingling, but she just kept talking.

There were other things. Her father coming into the bathroom while she was in the shower, seeing his lurking silhouette through the opaque glass door. His bursting into her bedroom at the exact moment—how did he know?—she had her pants around her ankles, so that she dressed herself always as she did at camp, fast as a firefighter, learned to take her bra off with her blouse on, slept in layers of sweats. Mo's friend Shelly, who spent the night once and never came back. Her father walking through the house with his robe open, pretending he didn't notice. His hands, like vermin, clamped onto your arm while he held forth about some damn thing, nuzzling your shoulders, nibbling at your back. Listening for his footsteps at night. The magazines he kept in the house and took no pains to conceal. It wasn't illegal, just creepy. His girlfriends and his trips to Las Vegas.

''Is there anything else?'' Sergeant Jenson had wanted to know. ''Have you anything to add?'' she asked, sounding not exactly disappointed, but close. Ellie knew it didn't make a good story. But it was her story, and now Becky's, too.

''Do I want to add anything? What is there to add? I've been expecting this for years. I'm not surprised. It's the other shoe and it's finally dropped. I almost feel relieved. I hope something comes of this. I hope steps are taken. Do something, Sergeant Jenson, that's what I want to say. Don't just ask questions. Do something about him.''

Several days later Ellie received a fat manila envelope in the mail. Inside were two copies of her statement, twenty-one typewritten pages, heavy as a congressional report. She thought of whoever it was, a man or a woman, who had transcribed it all, who must have sat for a good long time hunched over a keyboard, listening to Ellie's voice on those little headphones. It was a job, and they did it eight hours a day, and no doubt had heard it all in their time and after a while probably just listened to sounds, and might have stood after it all and stretched and yawned and thought about lunch.

Ellie started to read with a pencil in hand, but she stopped somewhere on the second page. She couldn't say exactly where or why she stopped. After a while she just wasn't reading anymore. She signed one copy and put it in the mail the next day. The other, she stuffed in the back of a file cabinet, like an old term paper, where she could find it if she ever needed it. Something like that cost too much to throw away, and someday, years later, you might pull it out and look at it again and learn something.

Ellie sat down. She called Mavis, her friend from college, and got her machine. "Hi there," Mavis's voice said with such startling clarity that as often as not Ellie answered her. "I can't come to the phone right now," Mavis said. "Leave a message at the beep." And then Ellie remembered, Mavis was off on one of her spur-of-the-moment jaunts, to New England this time. "It's me," Ellie said. "How about coffee sometime? When you get back?" Mavis knew about her father, she would have something to say. She would know what to do.

In the kitchen Ellie washed the breakfast dishes and wiped

the counters. She thought about her father under arrest, tried to imagine what it must have been like. He might have been lying awake, alone in his king-sized bed, her mother long ago having retreated down the hall into Mo's old room. He would have been able to hear the car turn off Dillard and onto Gibbon, slowing down to read the numbers. The purr of a big engine in the driveway. Two doors slamming and leather shoes scuffling through leaves. Feet on the stairs. A pause, long enough for the officers to read the sign across the bell, check their equipment, take a deep breath, just long enough for him to think that maybe it was nothing, the neighbor's kid coming in late. And then the machine-gun knock on the door like holy hell breaking loose.

By the time Ellie finished in the kitchen, it was almost noon. Where did the time go? Once she had confided to her neighbor Angie how difficult it seemed to her that life had become, not to achieve anything noteworthy, not even to be good, but just to perform the basics, to keep yourself clean, properly fed and clothed, legal, all the equipment it required, clippers and files and razor blades, floss and brushes, creams and deodorant, mothballs and shoe trees, irons, spray starch, and soap— dish soap, hand soap, laundry soap, and deodorant soap—all the appointments, to change the oil and rotate the tires, clean your teeth, cut your hair, tighten your glasses, all the paperwork, inspection stickers and insurance forms and canceled checks and stamps and envelopes and warranties and receipts for everything. And Angie, who taught management workshops and sewed her twins' adorable outfits and grew her own vegetables and wrote letters on behalf of prisoners all over the world, just looked at her as if she were crazy. There were so many things Ellie wanted to do—frame photographs, finish Lucy's baby book, write letters. She wanted to cook, not that Walt cared if she didn't (his taste and Lucy's were identical, phosphorescent Kraft dinner, endless peanut butter and jam on Wonder bread, canned ravioli, fish sticks), but because preparing interesting meals was something that grown-up people did.

Ellie drove down Delaware to Lucy's school. She stayed off the side streets and kept her eyes on the road. It was a dark day, and Ellie was afraid that the interminably gray Buffalo winter was already closing in. She had come to Western New York more than fifteen years ago to attend the university, sight unseen, because it was listed as a best-buy college in the counselor's handbook and had a strong art department. Because she loved snow. Because going to college in New York, however far it turned out to be from the city, seemed glamorous, and no one else from her school applied there. Because her brother Calvin loved the Bills, and the little buffalo on their helmets was kind of cute. Because it was a thousand miles away from her father.

At first she hated the city. It was dirty, and the sun rarely shone from November to April. The mayor looked like a crook, and nobody took checks. On the local television newscasts they offered bowling tips. (She tried to explain it to her roommate, a girl from Cheektowaga, "Advice on the 6–10 split," she told her, "a diagram, for God's sake," but she didn't get it. "There's no 6–10 split," she told Ellie, and that was that.) You couldn't get spring water or whole-wheat bread in the cafeteria.

It was a stupid, scruffy city, but slowly she developed a

passion for it. Not for the stuff people talked about. The Falls bored her and so did the Bills. Chicken wings gave her indigestion, and Beef on Weck made her gag.

In her first years at UB, dazed with loneliness, she found her own way around. She spent hours and hours in the Albright-Knox, at first researching her papers, and then just because she felt comfortable there. She enjoyed the modern stuff, Rauschenberg and Warhol and Clyfford Still, but she spent most of her time in the little room devoted to the unfashionable eighteenth century, where even the guards rarely ventured, staring at the Hogarth and Reynolds and Gainsborough.

She used to ride her ten-speed through the neighborhoods on the west and east sides, through other people's lives as though she were invisible, watching the kids in the street and the old people on the porches and the bad boys on the corner, listening to the music and hollering, smelling the cooking from the kitchens. She would stop to eat at the Saigon on Bailey, where, as often as not, she was the only customer. She'd point to something on the menu, chat with the couple who ran the place, and settle in with them in front of the television to eat her noodles and watch something, *The Hustler, I Confess,* always an old movie. She visited the magnificent old train depot on Paderewski Drive. She bought Cokes and the *New York Times* at a newsstand on Hertel Avenue where a fellow named Tony made book on the phone, very loud, nothing furtive about it. She fed the ducks at Forest Lawn and searched out Millard Fillmore, Red Jacket, all the people who shared her birthday. So after she graduated, there was no question about moving back. For better or worse, Buffalo was her home.

As she pulled into the parking lot, Ellie spotted Lucy standing on the top rung of the big slide. She was calmly surveying the playground in her jeans and Little Mermaid sweatshirt, with Silky, the tattered remnant of her pink baby blanket, preserved like a sacred relic, pinned to her chest with a safety pin like a first-prize ribbon. She was fearless, a beautiful little discoverer. On the way home, Lucy sipped a cup of juice and stared silently out the window. "What did you do today?" Ellie asked.

"Play," she said, a bit annoyed, as if to say, "You have to ask?"

While Lucy napped, Ellie worked at the computer in the spare bedroom that served as her office. Having settled on a major in graphic design—she loved her studio courses, throwing pots especially, but her work was eccentric and she worried about making a living—Ellie worked for a while with an agency downtown and then, after Lucy was born, did freelance work. She was good and had a core of loyal clients, but she never made much money because she was meticulous and spent so much time on each job that she never had the guts to bill anything like the real number of hours she worked.

Ellie called up a photograph of a young couple sitting in front of a balding man in a dark suit who was bent stiffly over a big pile of forms. The man did not look at all friendly or efficient nor did the loan application process look especially easy, as the text of the bank pamphlet promised. Powerful as her photo retouching software was, Ellie wasn't at all sure that she could tidy up the desk and cheer up this loan officer.

She stared at the photograph. There was something wrong

with the man's right hand, which rested, clawlike, atop the paperwork. Either it was artificial or he was so terrified of the camera, he was hanging on for dear life. When the screensaver kicked in, she started to straighten her own desk. She sorted through her in-basket, restacking an invoice from the printer, the new community education catalog, a crayon drawing of Lucy's. At the very bottom was the birthday card her mother had sent her the month before. Phyllis had underscored "lovely daughter" three times and "special day" twice. On the back she'd scribbled a short note. She wrote that the weather was awful, the coldest, wettest summer on record. The tomatoes were rotting on the vine. Maureen was taking a night class, she said, and just loved it. If she knew that Ellie had talked to the police, she didn't mention it.

Ellie wondered how her mother was taking it. Wrapped in a terry cloth bathrobe and heavy wool socks, Phyllis would slip down the stairs and into the kitchen. She would fill the back of the coffeemaker with water and deliberate in front of the cupboard—red or green Folgers? regular or decaffeinated? She would take a few spoons of each, lean against the radiator cover, and watch the carafe slowly fill. She would look at the photos on the refrigerator: Lucy in her sandbox, Calvin smiling under his mortarboard at his law school graduation, Maureen's kids sitting skeptically on a department store Santa's lap, spit-and-polished school portraits of Dylan and Becky, her crooked grin revealing metal braces adorned with neon bands. Phyllis would listen to the voices in the next room, low and insistent. They might have been insurance salesmen or a couple of Hal's reps going over monthly receipts. If Maureen were there, she could maybe make a joke. How do they take their coffee down at the station? I wish I had some doughnuts.

Her father was a good talker. He would have had something to say. He was in sales, something to say was his stock in trade. Do I look like a criminal? he'd ask. I have gray hair, and look, these are trifocals. I'm a grandfather. I subscribe to *Reader's Digest*. And sometimes I even read it. He would laugh. He would want them to like him. I pay my taxes, I observe the speed limit, I always come to a complete stop. I return my library books on time. I'm an usher. I've been married forty years, raised four children, lived in this house since 1959. Can't you fellows see? Somebody's making a big, big mistake.

To a police sergeant, an Irishman from St. Paul, call him O'Connell, he would have looked like an ordinary guy, a little bit like his own father-in-law maybe, the same jowls, the same lines around the eyes, like any old guy, really, you might see in the barbershop or in the park walking his dog. Except that he smiled too much. And his name was on the warrant.

He would have kept talking as long as they let him. I know what she said, but, look, she's twelve years old. She says a lot of things, believes a lot of things. She's in seventh grade; she reads comic books. For all I know, she still believes in Santa Claus. She believes that the good guys always win and that someday her prince will come. Do you know what she asked me last month? Always keep them engaged, he told her once years ago, bury them with detail, specifics, features and benefits, when she was only selling candy bars door to door, don't give them a chance to say no, his whole philosophy of sales, the foundation of his entire life, which struck her—by then, she knew all about him—as a crock of shit, nothing more than greasy insincerity and manipulation. Who are you going to believe, for chrissake?

Finally, enough. They wouldn't buy it, not this time. Mr.

Lamm, one would say, not the guy from St. Paul, but another, a lieutenant maybe. You've heard about the bad cop? Well, I'm him. The discussion period is over. You have two minutes to get yourself dressed and come with us downtown. Or we can cuff your ass and take you kicking and screaming in your PJ's. You decide.

Phyllis would stand on the porch and wave at the taillights, watching until the car braked at the corner and disappeared onto Dillard, the way she used to watch Grandma and Grandpa's old Chevy drive off after their annual visits, the way she used to watch the kids head back to school, except they had bikes tied to the back, mattresses on the roof like Okies, and hung out the window—the boys, anyway—waving and shouting the whole way. It was a private superstition and a blessing, as if no harm could come to them as long as she guided them safely out of her space, like an air traffic controller.

In the dark Phyllis would move from room to room, her coffee in hand, from window to window. The wooden scarecrow suspended from the neighbor's porch roof turned and flipped in the wind, double-jointed, like an Olympic gymnast on the parallel bars. Their floodlight, activated by motion, turned on and off, on and off again. A cat or a garbage lid. Across the street, Mrs. T.'s kitchen light would be on. She'd be making tea, toasting an English muffin, listening for the weather on the radio. She might have noticed the commotion.

It must have been like riding in a taxi. The driver on a beaded cushion that clicked and rattled when he shifted his weight as he turned the wheel. The scratchy voice of the dispatcher on the radio, vaguely irritated, a woman wearing headphones and smoking cigarettes and staring at a stained map, reciting intersections and addresses, maybe talking to your guy, maybe not. And the backs of their heads, brush-cut, on-duty and indifferent.

Ellie was in the kitchen chopping onions, a slice of whole-wheat bread clamped between her teeth, something suggested in a newspaper column, but her eyes were stinging anyway. She heard Walt's Duster rumble into the drive, the oldies station on his car radio blaring Sam Cooke singing about the cha-cha-cha. She felt something in herself tighten up.

Lately he just seemed to occupy more space, to take up too much room, to fill the kitchen, say, as he made a sandwich, not just with his physical presence, but with his noise too (why are men so loud?), rattling silver, squeaky shoes, heavy breathing through his nose like someone with adenoids (Had she not noticed this before? Was it something he'd developed?), and such repulsive wet smacking and clicking while he ate that she would have to leave the room. And lately she'd heard him talking to himself. "Okay," he would say, almost under his breath as he stamped a letter or pulled off his shoes, "okay," as if he were checking an item off his private to-do list and was now pondering his next move. And when Ellie would say, "What?" or ask, "Did you say something?" and tell him, "You're talking to yourself again," he would just look up, disoriented and innocently baffled, like someone who'd been shaken awake for snoring.

But how could she complain? He was a good man, gener-ous, gentle, optimistic, professionally unflappable. He was nice. When they were first dating, before he had his own car, he had talked with a representative of AAA on the phone for forty minutes one night and finally bought a membership. She had to call the next day to get him out of it. He felt sorry for the woman, he'd said, and besides, there were discounts and those maps.

And he'd been good when she told him about her father, what he had done to her. It was the week of their wedding, at the county fair, they were sitting on a picnic table, right outside the van holding Little Irvy, the giant whale. "If he's not real, you can keep the truck," the man on the loudspeaker said, and they considered why anyone would want a forty-foot refrigerated van that reeked of formaldehyde. "There's something about me that you need to know," she said, and then she told him, and he held her for the longest time, right at the picnic table, and said it was okay.

But lately it was different. Here it is, Ellie told Mavis. He's a man who fixes a big vat of oatmeal on Sunday night and warms little servings of it in the microwave the rest of the week. And what's wrong with that? Mavis had wanted to know. Nothing, Ellie said. Except that sometimes I just want to dump the goddamn oatmeal on his head.

Walt opened the back door and strode up the stairs and into the kitchen, with a newspaper under one arm and a plastic-covered bundle of shirts on hangers from the cleaners draped over his shoulder. He was a big man, a former football player, some kind of guard, surprisingly agile—he was a good dancer—and, though he'd grown a little soft, still imposing in his uniform. He was only a paramedic, but he was in the house so fast, so big, and with his name tag and shoulder patches and shiny black shoes, so officially, it felt like a raid.

Ellie dropped the bread and turned to him, red-eyed, flustered, the big knife still in her hand.

"What's the matter?" Walt said.

"Nothing," she said. "Onions."

Lucy streaked into the room, sliding on the linoleum floor in her socks, chanting, "Daddy, Daddy, Daddy," and Walt set down his paper and his shirts and hoisted her up above his head, dangerously close to the door frame, and then upside down, by her ankles, like a goose in the butcher's window, and then she disappeared behind his back for a moment and emerged unimaginably at last, like his partner in an Olympic skating dance team, grinning, from between his legs.

"Big Bird is building a sand castle with the Honkers," Lucy said, pulling him toward the living room. "Come see."

"In a minute," Walt said. "Let me say hello to Mommy first." He put his arm around her. "Hello, Mommy," he said. He nodded toward the mounds of chopped vegetables on the cutting board: onions, carrots, eggplant, mushrooms, potatoes, celery. "Looks good," he said, and popped a slice of carrot in his mouth.

"It's vegetarian stew," Ellie said. "Something new." She wiggled free of Walt's grasp. She moved to the stove and turned on a burner. "How was work?" she said.

"Slow," Walt said. "A girl with a broken ankle at the tennis courts in Delaware Park and a guy in East Amherst who had a stroke, very minor. A great big fat guy, not that old. He was taking a shower and thought his face had fallen asleep. Can you imagine? Your face falling asleep? When we got there, he seemed embarrassed and kept offering us these giant homemade chocolate chip cookies."

He scooped up a handful of celery, while Ellie dropped a pat of butter into a big frying pan. "How about you? How was Lucy at school?"

"Happy as can be," she said. "And after the long weekend. Go figure."

Ellie considered telling Walt about her father's arrest. She knew she would tell him eventually. But it was all so complicated, the edge in Mo's voice—It's not your fault, what in the hell was that supposed to mean?—and the birthday card from her mother, and the judge's wife, she was a part of it somehow, too, her image of the cops pounding at the door, it was all connected, but where do you begin? Walt would be calm and sensible and say all the right things. But she didn't want to hear the right things, not tonight.

"Hey, Ellie," Walt said. "I almost forgot to tell you. Kenny Clayton's offering us one of Misty's puppies. There's two females and a male left, yellow labs. They're purebred, they just don't have the right papers is all. He's asking twenty-five dollars, which is what the shots cost him. What do you think? You know Misty, she's great with kids. Lucy's ready for a dog, don't you think?"

Ellie threw a handful of onions in the pan. To her, a dog suggested drool, muddy footprints, loose hair, stains. Her grandmother's dog, an arthritic, foul-smelling cocker spaniel full of tumors, used to terrify her with its seizures, which were treated with generous doses of Christian Brothers brandy, both for Grandma Rose and the dog. Later Geoff brought home a mutt he named Ed, which bit Calvin and made their mother break out with hives and disappeared one day while they were at school.

"I don't know," she said. She stared into the cookbook, propped open with a ketchup bottle, squinting at the recipe, which was printed in tiny fancy script. Walter, it occurred to Ellie, was a big puppy, a Newfoundland maybe, with big webbed feet, playful and loyal and a little bit clumsy. "Burgundy," she said. "Tamari. Shit."

"What's the matter?"

"When I try to cook something besides Rice-a-Roni or chicken pot pies for dinner, I don't have the right ingredients. So it ends up tasting like Swanson's anyway."

She moved over to the cupboard and peered around him into the spice rack. "This kitchen is too small. I'm sick of it." Walt stepped aside. He smelled like pepperoni and shoe polish.

"Stop looking at me. I don't want an audience. Go watch 'Sesame Street.' Maybe Big Bird can make stew."

"Okay," Walt said, with a kind of infuriatingly studied calm, "okay," and he backed out of the room slowly, as if she were a dangerous person.

At dinner, Walt ate two bowls of stew doused with pepper and talked about what he'd read in the newspaper while Lucy fished the little pieces of eggplant out of her bowl one by one, patient and precise as a scientist, and piled them on her place mat. Afterward, Walt did the dishes while Ellie read to Lucy from a fat illustrated collection of fairy tales she had pulled from a curb on Parkside along with a set of vintage Nancy Drew mysteries. The book included the familiar classics—"Cinderella," "Hansel and Gretel," "Rapunzel," and "Little Red Riding Hood," here called little Red Cap—but there were many others too that she had never heard of before, often quite strange, full of gnomes and hedgehogs and simpletons, wishes and inexplicable wickedness, and sometimes grotesque and grisly punishments meted out in the end, which

Ellie tended to edit as she read, abridging, summarizing, paraphrasing.

Not that Lucy seemed to mind. She would sit through it all in silent rapt attention, leaning into Ellie on the old couch on the front porch, her chubby legs extended straight out onto the cushion, and always something clasped in her hand, a toy necklace, a Fisher-Price man, a rubber bug. She examined the busy and sometimes surreal engraved illustrations with wary fascination, as if they too were magic, and upon the completion of one tale, asked promptly for another. She had always been that way, even as a baby, watchful, intense, capable of remarkable stretches of concentrated stillness, whether watching a movie or studying birds at the feeder or listening to books.

Tonight Ellie began with "Snow White," Lucy's favorite. (It had already been decided that Lucy would be a princess come Halloween, and Angie had been contracted to sew a costume.) She filled the queen's lines with cackling wickedness and lingered over an illustration of the dwarfs, here unnamed, not at all cute, but real dwarfs, haggard little men with tiny hooflike feet, gathered around Snow White's glass coffin in seven postures of despair.

At seven-thirty, Ellie searched through the book for one more, relatively short tale. (Some of them she had discovered—"The Two Brothers" was one, a story of fraternal treachery involving a golden bird, talking forest animals, a virgin-eating dragon, and a magic root—went madly on and on, page after page of dizzying elaborations in the plot which first baffled and then annoyed her, though Lucy never complained.) She settled on a five-page story called "The Girl with No Hands." Once upon a time there was a miller who accepts riches from a mysterious stranger in exchange for whatever is standing behind his mill—as it turns out, the miller's beautiful daughter. When the stranger, now identified as the Evil One, returns in three years for the girl, he is thwarted first by her washing herself clean and drawing a circle around herself with chalk, and then, by her washing her hands with her own tears. When the Evil One demands that the miller cut off her hands, he asks, "How can I cut off my own child's hands?" But he does it.

Ellie felt pressure building behind her eyes, something welling up in her chest, but she kept reading. The girl binds her maimed arms, leaves home, and comes across a beautiful orchard surrounded by water. " 'And as she had walked the whole day and not eaten one mouthful,' " Ellie read, the page starting to wobble before her eyes, " 'and hunger tormented her, she thought: "Ah, if I were but inside, that I might eat of the fruit, else must I die of hunger." ' " And suddenly Ellie was convulsed with sobbing, overcome by a deep shuddering grief, like a seizure.

Lucy stared up at her, stunned, her eyes wide in horrified astonishment. And then she started to cry, too, sudden and shrill as a fire alarm. Ellie reached down and pulled Lucy toward her. She tried to say something but couldn't. She held her tight, and that's how Walt, who heard the wailing and rushed in from the kitchen, found them: embracing on the couch, their chests heaving, both of them gasping for air, their faces wet with each other's tears.

Walt gathered Ellie up firmly, all trembling dead weight, like one of the shapeless burlap bundles he'd toted during his physical training, his hand on her wrist, checking her vitals while he spoke calmly to Lucy, a steady stream of sonorous reassurance. It's okay, honey. Mom's okay. Don't cry. It's all right.

Even though she was still shaking, incapable of speech, it seemed to Ellie as if part of her remained completely rational, seeing now with a startling, almost hallucinogenic clarity. She could smell the sweet scent of fabric softener on Walt's flannel shirt, feel for all his gently hypnotic, calming talk, the strength of his hands, the force they could exert. She understood then that he handled other people's emergencies so well, with such dispatch—he stamped them out like fires—because he feared them so much himself. She wanted to tell Walt not to worry. You don't have to treat for shock, she wanted to say. I'm not going to swallow my tongue, for God's sake. I'm sad, that's all, it's a sad story. Don't be so squeamish.

Finally calmed, and having drunk a tall glass of water and eaten several soda crackers at Walt's insistence, her face washed and hair combed, she lay on their queen-sized bed covered by an afghan, while Walt put Lucy to bed. She felt like a child home from school with something contagious, listening miserably to the after-school laughter below her window. She could hear Walt singing to Lucy—no more stories tonight—wretchedly off-key but sincere, the songs he knew, "Wheels on the Bus," "This Old Man," "Froggie Went A'Courtin'," and then, his children's repertoire exhausted and Lucy wide awake, cuts from his Johnny Cash records, "Folsom Prison Blues," "Big River," "Ring of Fire." They said good night and blessed Lucy's entire roster of important friends, people and animals, real and fictional, kids at nursery school and the big brown dog down the street and the woman at the corner store and her baby-sitter and Peter Rabbit.

Afterward, Ellie and Walt sat at the kitchen table and talked

about it. What could she say? It was embarrassing. "It's probably just PMS or something," she told him. "A hormone
surge." He was doggedly concerned. Ellie assured him that
she was fine. There was nothing wrong with her, she said.

That night Ellie dreamed about him. She is sitting on his lap in
their living room, and he is cutting her fingernails with a
grotesquely oversized clipper, like a big nutcracker or a wire
cutter. There's classical music playing and some kind of party
going on—balloons, plates of hors d'oeuvres, grown-ups talking in groups. She looks down and sees that he is paring not
her nails but her fingers, her whole hand—the clipper is biting
into her flesh, chewing it like a hungry animal. There's blood
on her hands, on her dress, on the chair. She tries to scream,
but can't. Her father smiles serenely.

3

THE BURDEN OF PROOF

CALVIN AND KATE SAT ON THE FLOOR, SURROUNDED BY PREGNANT women and their coaches, watching Patty, their instructor, working a dirty-pink, hand-knit uterus back and forth in mock contractions as she described the process of childbirth with an absolutely frank and unself-conscious vocabulary. "Mucous plug," she said. "Bloody show." She tugged harder and harder at the uterus—the labor was in transition now, contractions coming just seconds apart—and then suddenly she paused, released her grip, and out slid a baby doll, headfirst, a chubby little girl with a thick head of black hair and wildly rolling orange eyes.

"I'm not his lawyer," he whispered to Kate. "So why does he call me? What am I supposed to do?" He had told her, in bits and snatches, in the few minutes before class began and during lulls in their get-acquainted exercises, about his father's escape.

Patty dimmed the lights and ran a videotape showing a young couple preparing for the birth of their first child. The tape showed them painting a bedroom, shopping for baby things, packing an overnight bag. The woman ate fruits and vegetables and the man rubbed her back. They spoke into the camera about their hopes and fears.

"This is going to cost," Calvin said. "I don't think they realize that. Byron Burke is good, but he's not cheap." Kate kept her eyes on the screen, like the good kid in school, always paying attention. The man on the tape was saying, "It's a miraculous thing, it really is. A miracle." And then the couple on the tape was at the hospital, in a little room with a bed, the doctor, in green scrubs, standing alongside the woman with the husband and a nurse, giving encouragement, the woman pushing and groaning, and then there was a little cry, and a tiny bloody baby held aloft like a prize, wailing like mad. When the lights came up, Kate was wiping a tear from her eye, and she wasn't the only one.

At the break, the expectant mothers lined up outside the ladies' room and their coaches, men mostly, but at least one older woman, a mother presumably, and two younger, sisters or girlfriends, hovered around the snack table, loading their napkins with crackers and cheese cubes and pouring juice into paper cups hardly bigger than the rinse cup at the dentist's. Kate came back, her hair brushed, smiling, long-legged and graceful still, wearing one of Calvin's button-down dress shirts over black stretch slacks, her big white sneakers—new today, a half-size larger to relieve her swelling feet and ankles—

squeaking across the auditorium floor. She took two Triscuits and a piece of cheese from Calvin's napkin and made a little sandwich.

"Can you see it?" he said. "My dad in the police station with a bunch of dope dealers and crackheads and drive-by shootists? He's probably chatting up the felons, you know, working the crowd like it was the St. Mark's parking lot on Sunday morning. It's almost funny."

Kate took one bite and dropped her crackers in a wastebasket. "I feel queasy," she said.

Patty flicked the lights, and they returned to their spot on the floor. In the last half hour, Kate assumed different positions, standing, leaning on a chair, down on all fours, and practiced breathing, while Calvin kept track of time. On the way out, they picked up a bag full of literature and samples, baby wipes, lotion and shampoo, a little first-aid kit.

At home, propped up in bed with her copy of *What to Expect,* Kate asked Calvin what was going to happen.

"It probably won't ever come to trial," he said. "You've got the testimony of a twelve-year-old, which is always iffy. You can find experts to say anything you want. And Ellie's talking about stuff from twenty years ago. At worst, I suppose, Byron could always cut some kind of deal for him. There could be a fine or some sort of court-ordered treatment. Maybe the workhouse. It depends on the judge."

"Did he do it?" Kate asked. "Is he guilty?"

"There's different definitions of guilt," he said. "Burdens of proof."

"Come on," Kate said. "Cut the crap."

"I don't know," he said.

Sunday morning, using a master key he found in the receptionist's desk, Calvin let himself into Byron Burke's office. He was
the senior partner who did criminal work, a pale man with
perfect hair and slits for eyes, like Roy Rogers. (He was from
southern Ohio, a guy in the mail room told Calvin, where
everybody looks like that.) Two months earlier, when he had
approached Byron about the possibility of his representing his
father, Byron shut the door and listened and nodded and then
shook his hand and afterward, when they passed in the hall or
met in the library, he would give Calvin a knowing look, his
manner not so much confidential as conspiratorial.

Byron was a collector, and his office was full of African art,
a herd of ivory elephants stampeding across his desk, a small
arsenal of primitive weapons in a glass case, ghoulish masks
lining the wall. Calvin turned on the light. He searched
through Byron's desktop, his credenza, and finally found his
father's file in a small stack of folders piled on the floor in the
corner.

He felt furtive and nervous—Byron never came in on Sun-
days, but what if?—a bit appalled with himself, but also
strangely alive, full of adrenaline. He had always relished research, academic and professional, and was rarely as happy as
he was in a library with an old book and a pencil and a yellow
pad. He was drawn especially to what he thought of as secret
history, loved to investigate, to ferret out what was concealed,
obscure, hidden. As an undergraduate, he especially loved his
course on the Soviet Union, with its tangle of plots and shifting allegiances and the workings of the KGB and the bundle of
secrets locked away in the Kremlin. In Catholic grade school
he had heard the story of Fatima, and couldn't let go of it: for

a short time, much to the amusement of his family, he told people that he wanted to be pope when he grew up. He never quite explained that it was because he wanted to know the terrible secret, too.

And he could still recall vividly when he was in junior high school, searching through bureau drawers one rainy afternoon, looking for nothing in particular, pure research, for its own sake, and discovering, among the old photos and coffee-stained report cards, his parents' marriage certificate. He read the date on it—they celebrated their anniversary but never mentioned years—and counted on his fingers, and realized that Maureen had been conceived out of wedlock. When his mother was married, Calvin realized, she was eighteen years old and five months pregnant.

He sat in Byron's chair and opened the file. There was a pink message slip with his mother's name on it; ''worried about Hal—depressed?'' Byron had scrawled across the bottom with his blue fountain pen. There was a copy of a letter to his father acknowledging the receipt of his retainer—two thousand dollars.

He found a copy of the statement his sister Ellie had made to the police when they called during the summer. They called both girls, his mother had said, but only Ellie had anything to say. He skimmed it—it was long—and read passages here and there. She talked about the lousy marriage their parents had, about their father's affairs. She called him an addict (nowadays, everything was an addiction or a disease). There were pages about their mother's drinking, about bottles stashed in the basement, about Ellie helping her into bed when their father was on the road, particular scenes rendered in excruciating detail—their mother, drunk, in a red flannel nightgown at dinnertime, burning a pan of tomato soup black on the stove top, stumbling on the stairs, unable to write a legible permission slip for Ellie's school trip to the science museum. He found his own name too, as if he were a character in her book, and he didn't like it. To hear Ellie tell it, he was still a kid that she had raised herself.

Calvin found her description of the first abuse, on their father's lap, watching a television program, the rest of them mysteriously absent. Then he heard a noise, and put every-thing back—it was the elevator rumbling below—and killed the lights and closed the door behind him. He headed down the hall and turned into the men's room. The elevator rattled by their floor without stopping, and he looked at himself in the mirror—unshaven and a little red-eyed, his contacts were acting up—and splashed some water on his face and combed his hair.

Back at his own desk, he paged through the Sunday *Times* he had picked up on the way in and thought about them, his family. Ellie, with her tortured little pencil drawings and in-delible memory for injury. His father, the souvenir salesman, the middle-aged Casanova. They were all freaks, he used to joke with Kate. Maureen, who hadn't completed one of her own sentences since her husband packed up two years ago. Geoff, the cable magnate, who had a car phone and sounded just like a TV anchor making happy talk, all the time now, even at home. That's why, he'd told Kate, as a kid his favorite television programs were "The Munsters" and "The Addams Family"—Fred Gwynne staggering through the house with those little nodes in his neck, Uncle Fester with a lightbulb in his mouth—why he identified with the Munsters' son, a boy surrounded by freaks. But even though he joked about him, he took his father's shortcomings seriously. He feared them. He quite consciously constructed his own life and character in such a way as to exclude them, the way he caulked and weather-stripped and insulated to keep the cold air out of his house.

His father liked things better than people, his car, the crap he sold, the attic and garage full of "collectibles," old *Life* magazines green with mildew, coffee cans of bottle caps and marbles, shoe boxes full of ticket stubs and old coins and scorecards. And especially, his television, a new model now, with a larger screen and stereo speakers, the centerpiece of the living room, like a sacred shrine. He was addicted to that, and clung to his remote like a life support, never turned it off anymore, not even during Thanksgiving dinner. (Calvin often thought that was why his brother Geoff got into cable in the first place—he got his start doing a movie review show on public access—just to get the old man's attention: hey, Dad, look at me.) During one of those grim Sunday dinners, when Calvin was still in law school and used to park his car on the street with the wheels turned out so he could leave that much faster, it occurred to him that his father never laughed anymore. He could sit in his chair stone-faced while the laugh track of a sitcom washed over him, all the mad cackling and whoops of delight, and never crack a smile. Like a zombie. Calvin had become something of a crank on the subject of television: he didn't own one, and prided himself on never having seen shows that everyone else was crazy about, "The Simpsons," or "Twin Peaks" or the latest Barbara Walters interview. He liked the radio.

Of course, he knew about his father's affairs, too, that was nothing new. He had joked about them with the other kids for

years. "Dad's going out of town 'on business,' " Maureen or
Geoff would say and supply the quotation marks with their
fingers like their teachers did. "He's going to the Vikings
game with a 'client.' " They even learned their names,
Wendy, who lived in Mankato, and Mindy, whose name was
spelled out on the vanity plates of her pink Mary Kay car. His
latest, the redhead, Calvin had seen with his father at Sears, in
Housewares. He didn't want to know what they were buying.
His mother knew, too, of course, and Calvin always figured
that for her it was something, like hunting or fishing, that kept
his father out of the house, and she was relieved as much as
anything.

So Calvin had vowed to be faithful, not just at the altar in
front of the priest, but to himself, to make fidelity mean
something. That's what he knew. He clung to his simple
rules—stay home, don't fool around, don't get hooked on
television, keep the attic clean. It sounded crazy if you just
said them, but they were something, and Calvin was grateful
for that much.

In the *Times* there was a story about John Demjanjuk. He
had just been allowed back into the country but there was
some question now about somebody in the State Department concealing evidence. There was a picture of him with
his son. Calvin studied the old man's face, and it was like
the drawing of the duck-rabbit he remembered from his
psychology textbook: sometimes he saw Ivan the Terrible, a
killer's cold eyes, the sadist's brutal mouth, and sometimes
he saw an autoworker from Cleveland who loved the
Browns, somebody's grandpa. Always one or the other, back
and forth, never both at the same time, as if the mind
couldn't hold the two at once. And just when you had it

figured out, the right image fixed in mind, you blinked, and
it changed.

The next Saturday morning, Calvin took Dylan and Becky to
Al's Breakfast in Dinkytown near the university: thirteen
stools, two surly waitresses, a cook who looked downright
dangerous, and fantastic blueberry pancakes. It opened at six
and was always crowded. You stood in line behind someone's
stool and waited for an opening. If you needed three seats in a
row, you had to execute some complicated maneuvering—a
little negotiating, a little lobbying, maybe some hard looks at a
dawdler—but it was worth it. Al's had become a Saturday
morning religion for him when he was an undergraduate, and
he had started taking first Dylan and then Becky, too, from
time to time back when they were so little that he used to
worry that they might topple off their stools. (They made no
concessions to cuteness at Al's: the waitresses snarled at the
kids, too, and snatched their menus back, same as always.)

Dylan was a sophomore in high school now and affected a
breezy, worldly wise manner. He peppered his speech with
mild obscenities, and called him just "Cal," now, having
dropped the uncle, which was fine. He wanted to order coffee
but settled instead for dousing Calvin's cup with cream and
sugar and stealing sips.

Becky drank hot chocolate. She was at an awkward age. She
carried a little handbag now but didn't quite know what to do
with it. Her face was starting to break out. She talked about
going out trick-or-treating on Halloween with a pal from her
old neighborhood—just for the loot—but was having a hard
time coming up with a costume. "Be a hobo," Calvin told

her. "Put something black on your face and carry a pillow case, a big one, king-sized. And give me all your peanut butter cups." Becky still loved her pancakes, but with braces now, she ate with great delicacy, and after the last bite, she headed immediately into the bathroom with her miniature toothbrush.

This was the first time he had seen her since he had looked over the papers in his father's file a second time. He had gone back into Byron's office early on Wednesday, before seven, when the all-night cleaning people were still in the lounge having a last cigarette. He'd rolled Byron's chair over to the window to catch the gray light of dawn, and sat with the file on his lap, the grinning masks glimmering in the half-darkness. He was looking for something, he would know it when he saw it, he figured. Evidence.

He was skeptical about sexual abuse prosecutions—post-traumatic stress disorder and flashbacks and celebrity victims in the tabloids like Oprah and Roseanne. He had just finished reading a magazine article about an entire organization—they had an annual convention and a newsletter and an articulate spokesman—made up entirely of people who believed they had visited and, in some cases, made friends with extraterrestrial creatures, experiences that nearly all of them "remembered" while under hypnosis, a favorite technique of sexual abuse therapists, he knew.

In a neatly handwritten letter on lined paper, Becky's teacher went to great lengths to explain that Becky had come forward with "utmost reluctance" and named her grandfather only after considerable encouragement. (Byron could seize on this, no doubt: one teacher's encouragement is a defense attorney's coercement.)

He had searched through the folder for a statement by

Becky. She had to have spoken to the police at some point, and Byron would have received a copy. Calvin wanted, if not to hear her own words, then to read them himself, in black and white. But all he could find was a form completed by a school counselor, with little numbers circled, like a survey, evaluating her moods, appetite, attention span. Byron could have taken it home. Calvin looked into Byron's desk drawers—they were perfectly arranged, big paper clips, little paper clips, a coin purse full of quarters, a pack of breath mints—and then he heard voices outside, and he bundled the papers up again and left the office. He double-checked to make sure Byron's door was locked and slipped the key back in Sandy's desk.

Becky returned from the bathroom with peppermint on her breath. She seemed pretty much the same. But there might have been something about her lately, Calvin couldn't put his finger on it exactly, nothing he could prove. A kind of wariness. She was always on guard. There was just a slight pause, like a tape delay on the radio, between the time you said something and the time she responded, as if she were considering and preparing. He couldn't remember her being that way. She still smiled and laughed, but so carefully now, as if she'd been practicing, her mouth covered, polite little controlled syllables of appreciation and amusement, not the raucous belly laughs he remembered. Maybe it was just adolescence. But maybe not.

On the sidewalk outside they ran into a fellow Calvin knew from high school. He had a neat beard now and some gray hair and was wearing sweats and wraparound eye goggles, but Calvin still recognized him. His name was Paul Powell, and he used to be on the student council and drive a red Camaro, the envy of their class. Calvin introduced him to Dylan, who pumped his hand manfully, and Becky, who smiled and said she was pleased to meet him. After ten years, it turned out, they had practically nothing to say to each other. Paul worked for 3M and was headed to the armory for a racquetball game with his brother-in-law, who was a lawyer, just like Calvin. "What's new with you?" he asked, and Calvin for a moment was stopped short. He couldn't think.

A woman walked by pulling a slavering bulldog, and they stepped aside. "I'm going to be a father," Calvin said finally, and having said it so often, he felt as if he were parroting a phrase in a foreign language: his pronunciation was perfect but for the life of him, he couldn't say what it meant.

Calvin asked Paul about the car, and he said that he didn't know what he was talking about, he never had a car, much less a Camaro. He took the bus. He wasn't kidding, Calvin was almost certain. It made you think.

He held the flashlight while his mother peered into boxes. "Photographs," she said, and held up a handful of snapshots. She had her reading glasses perched on her nose but still held the photos at arm's length. "Uncle Charlie with a mustache," she said. "Ellie's first communion."

They were down in the basement, next to his father's office in what they used to call the fruit cellar, a damp side room with wooden shelves, searching for a wicker bassinet. It was just what Calvin and Kate needed, Phyllis told him on the phone. It had little wheels and with a coat of paint, it would be as good as new. Stop by and get it. She knew right where it was, she said. They had been looking for almost an hour. And even though Calvin thought that he had long ago removed all his belongings from the house, they had so far discovered an unopened box of Wheaties his father bought for him in 1987, his first guitar, and a stash of tissue-thin letters he'd written home during his semester in France, his tiny, lonely handwriting running to the edge of the page and spilling onto the flap of the mailers. But no bassinet.

He came closer and shone the light into his mother's hand. Ellie was standing in front of St. Mark's Church, wearing a white dress and squinting into the sun. Either the image had faded over time, or the technology back then was primitive, but the colors—the blue sky, the yellow flowers in Ellie's hand—looked washed out, artificial, like a colorized movie. Only Ellie's jet-black hair and her dark eyes seemed right. In some way, she looked the same then as she always did: intense, a little stern even in her innocent holiness, a fierce little saint.

"Ellie," Calvin said. She used to sit on the edge of his bed and sing him to sleep.

"She was a middle child and just too quiet, too well behaved," his mother said. "When she was a baby, I would forget to feed her because she never cried. Maureen was rowdy and wild, Geoff was the oldest boy, and you were the baby, always so cute and so smart, and poor Ellie got lost in the shuffle. I think she's still mad about that."

Calvin tested the bottom rung of a step stool and sat down. His mother moved a box and settled herself on a wooden chest. He scanned the floor with his flashlight—a pile of battered board games, a pyramid of paint cans in the corner, a box of ice skates—and then turned it off. "Did you suspect anything?" he said. "Ever? Did Ellie ever say anything to you?"

Calvin could see his mother in outline, bent slightly, her

arms wrapped around herself. The furnace buzzed and clicked on. Once in Calvin's windowless Con Law seminar, when there had been a power outage, their gravel-voiced professor just kept lecturing into the darkness, and then, as if he finally noticed, he stopped. "Is there any question you've been afraid to ask until now?" he had wanted to know.

"It's cold down here," she said.

"And damp," Calvin said. "And full of garbage. Nothing wrong with this basement that a can of gasoline and a Bic lighter couldn't fix."

"How do you suspect something like that?" she said.

The sump pump gurgled. "I don't know," Calvin said.

"Once," she said.

"Once what?"

"She came into the kitchen and told me that Hal did something to her."

"What did you do?"

"I went into the living room and asked him. 'No,' he said. 'Absolutely not.' I told her never to talk like that again."

"Jesus," Calvin said.

Upstairs there was the sound of a key turning in the side door lock. The door opening. Steps creaking across the floor into the kitchen, right above them. He was supposed to be gone for the day. Calvin could hear the refrigerator door opening and water running in the sink. Then more footsteps. And the television.

They sat there in the dark, silent, listening, as if they were in hiding, like Anne Frank's family. There was the pounding bass of rock music above them, then the sounds of an argument, laughter and applause, then a dull mechanical whine.

"Ellie came home at Christmas," Phyllis whispered, "after

her first semester at college and talked to me. She'd been seeing a counselor. I didn't believe her. Maureen thought she was on medication. She was so angry, just spoiling for a fight. She told me she wanted to confront Hal.''

''Did she?''

''I wouldn't allow it. Not during the holiday, I said. Not with the tree in the living room. Not in my house, I told her. It would kill him.''

Calvin flicked the flashlight back on. He shone it on the floor, his sneakers, his mother's scuffed leather bedroom slippers. He swept it across the shelves like a searchlight. He held it on an oversized Raggedy Andy doll, big as a toddler, slumped in a corner, its checked shirt buttonless, with a big red heart on its chest like a fencer's. He hadn't seen his father since the arrest, and he didn't have to now. He could slip out the side door and drive away.

''I did my best,'' his mother said. ''But still. So many mistakes. So much heartache. If you only knew.''

It was not the first time his mother had hinted darkly about the past. I know, he wanted to tell her. I know about the drinking. I know why there're no wedding pictures of you and Dad.

Calvin let the light play on the shelves. A stack of jigsaw puzzles, more games. ''There it is,'' his mother said, and sprang up from where she was sitting and pulled down a cardboard box. ''The baptismal gown,'' she said. She slowly lifted the top of the box. ''I wore this. And you did, too. All the grandchildren except Lucy.'' She held it up, a long, shapeless garment with some lace at the collar. It was shiny, satin Calvin supposed, but yellowed now, like old newspaper. ''What do you think?'' she said.

"I'm going to talk to him," he said, and stood up. "I've got to ask. It won't kill him." He turned and left his mother in the darkness, fumbling with the gown, trying to force it back into the box, making low noises of protest or alarm, but he didn't look back.

Hal was in his chair, his feet elevated, his eyes closed, his hands crossed on his chest, white and puffy, perfectly reposed, like a dead man's. There was an automobile race on the television.

"Dad," Calvin said. His father's eyes opened so immediately and so easily, Calvin knew that he hadn't really been asleep.

"Calvin," his father said, bluff and apparently delighted, surprised, as if he hadn't seen his car at the curb out front. Calvin pulled a rocker over and sat at his father's side.

"I want to know, Dad," Calvin said. "I know what Becky and Ellie are saying. I want to know what you have to say. Tell me. What happened? What did you do?"

"I love my children," he said, his eyes fixed on the television, the cars roaring around and around the banked track. "And I love my grandchildren." His voice was flat, as if he were drugged, absolutely without affect, like a hostage on videotape. "My life is an open book," he said, and he looked up at Calvin.

"Okay," said Calvin. "I know." He said, "I know it is," and his father shifted himself, his hands on the arms of the chair, desperate claws, like an invalid's, trying to pull himself up, and Calvin felt sick with fear that his father was going to touch him.

4

HIGH FIDELITY

IN SEPTEMBER BECKY STOPPED EATING MEAT. SHE WAS SITTING AT the dinner table, a big slice of her mother's meat loaf in front of her, when she announced she was a vegetarian. Dylan either didn't notice or didn't care, but her father seemed flustered. "What do you mean?" he wanted to know. "What's wrong with meat?"

Her father liked family dinners to be harmonious, without incident. He fought with her mother afterward, their arguments a controlled, acrimonious murmur, like insidious Muzak, which Becky heard in her room if she didn't play her tapes. He was a big shot in the local cable franchise. He wore a suit and worked late most nights and occasionally brought home promotional pencils and notepads and helium balloons. He smoked two packs of Kents a day. Because of his job, they had a new house and a huge cable box on top of their television with red lights that never went off. They got every channel, something like a hundred, movies and sports and a priest sitting under a hanging plant twenty-four hours a day. Once she found ''Mr. Ed'' on three channels at the same time, different episodes. They got all the premium channels and pay-per-view without paying. At Sheila's house, they stayed up and watched the adult stations even though they were scrambled, and they saw—or imagined they saw—torsos and legs and bare rumps separated and recombined like a Picasso, in livid shades of green and blue, shifting like a kaleidoscope. At Becky's house, it was right there all the time, unscrambled.

''It's gross,'' Becky told her father. ''That's what's wrong with meat.''

''Joan,'' her father said. ''Talk to her.''

''Leave her alone,'' her mother said, and scooped the meat loaf off Becky's plate. ''If I were a vegetarian, maybe I'd drop a few pounds.'' She had been trying to drop a few pounds for as long as Becky could remember. She went to Weight Watchers on Monday nights, and got on her doctor's scale every morning, edging the weight slowly to the right and groaning in alarm. In the past she had tried Overeaters Anonymous and Nutri-Systems. She used to drink ten glasses of water a day and write down everything she would eat before she ate it on little pieces of papers that Becky still found around the house. She bought lite everything—cream cheese, salad dressing, mayonnaise, cheese—and she used to water down the orange juice until Becky's father made a scene. She counted calories and grams of fat and spent food exchanges like hard-earned cash. (''Think about it,'' Becky told Sheila. ''She's got this huge new kitchen, two ovens, two sinks, a center island, a shelf full of cookbooks, a million pots and pans hanging from the ceiling, and a fancy food processor. And she's always on a diet.'')

"What about milk?'' Dylan wanted to know. He was fifteen, a smart-ass. "Spaghetti in meat sauce? Did you know that McDonald's french fries are cooked in beef fat? I guess this just means more for me.''

Her parents exchanged glances. Dylan shoveled up a big mouthful of meat loaf.

"What if I become a carnivore,'' he said, still chewing, "and just eat gobs and gobs of bloody meat? Like a lion. And no peas or brussels sprouts.''

"Shut up, Dylan,'' her mother said, and for once he did.

Becky decided eventually that she would eat yogurt and cheese, but not eggs and fish, which she didn't really like anyway. At McDonald's she ordered salads, and she still ate desserts. When they ordered out for pizza, she got her own small one with mushrooms. Dylan didn't rag her anymore, and her mother went out of her way to prepare nutritious meatless dishes, rice and beans, a peanut butter stew, stir-fried vegetables. When her father barbecued hamburgers, her mother made Becky grilled cheese. Her parents were so accommodating, so deliberately nice lately, she sometimes felt as if she was getting away with something.

Every Tuesday afternoon her mother picked Becky up at school and drove her into St. Paul, where, in the back bedroom of a converted Victorian mansion on Summit Avenue, she met with a psychologist who had been recommended by her school counselor. Her mother sat in the waiting room, smoking and reading magazines which she sometimes slipped in her purse and finished at home, while Becky sat on a floral couch in Dr. Reston's office, with a candy dish and a box of tissues on the table in front of her, as if she were required to sniffle and sob. Dr. Reston sat in a cane rocking chair and always wore bright outfits complemented by dramatic scarves and shawls and belts, dangling earrings, pins as big as cookie cutters.

They started slowly. "So what do you think about all this rain?" Dr. Reston might say. Becky would pull a string from the padded arm of the couch and study the framed diplomas on the wall above Dr. Reston's head, her full name, Eudora Anne Reston, magnificent in the calligrapher's stately black letters.

"I hate it," Becky would say. "I just hate it."

Eventually, though, she realized that she could talk about anything at all, and that Dr. Reston never told her mother anything, and that she didn't contradict her or encourage her to look on the bright side. She loosened up. She talked about the nerds in her class, why she hated Dylan, the weird way Sheila was doing her hair. Dr. Reston didn't say much, but she was interested, you could tell. She leaned forward and smiled and remembered names. And she didn't make Becky talk about anything she didn't want to.

One sunny afternoon in October, Becky told her about their new house in Eagan. "Dad tells people he built it," she said, "but he can't even hammer a nail straight." Everything was new—windows, carpets, fixtures. They had moved in late in June, but the whole house still smelled like fresh paint and glue. Even the lawn was brand new, having arrived one morning in a flat-bed truck, rolls and rolls of vivid green sod unfurled and stamped in place by two shirtless men in just a few hours. Becky hated it.

The place was huge. Everyone had their own bedroom. Her father had an office in the basement, and her mother had a sewing room on the third floor, even though she never sewed. There were three bathrooms. "So we all hole up in our separate little rooms," Becky said, "like the prairie dogs at the zoo."

Dr. Reston nodded and wrote something down, and Becky, who had recently received instruction in note-taking, learned to distinguish major points and identify key words and phrases, couldn't help but wonder what—"like prairie dogs"? "new house sucks"?

"We need an intercom so we can talk to each other. My mom calls in my room when I'm doing my homework. 'Becky,' she says, so loud I practically drop my pencil, out of nowhere, like God talking, but then she never has anything to say. 'How are you doing?' she says. 'Are you okay?' Like I'm this crazy person or something."

Becky might have said more but stopped. The digital clock on the bookcase read five minutes to, so she paused and waited for Dr. Reston to declare them out of time and then stood up. She always felt awkward at their leave-taking. Her father had given her and Dylan lessons in the art of the handshake—firm and confident, no dead fish—but that would be too weird. And Dr. Reston was not the hugging type. So she just said, "See you next week," and backed out the door with a little wave.

In the waiting room, her mother looked up from a wrinkled copy of *People*. "Ready, honey?" she said, rumpled and tired-looking, and Becky felt bad for talking about her. They walked out to the car and got in. Her mother asked if she wanted to stop for ice cream.

She never asked her what happened during her appointments, but Becky knew that her mother liked her to tell her things, who said what at school, even after the orthodontist's, what got adjusted, whether or not she got a new wire or rubber bands. What was there to say? Becky turned on the radio, found her station, adjusted the balance on the rear speakers, and after her mother gave her a look, brought the volume down, and then up again, just a little.

At Bridgeman's, they sat at the counter on stools. Becky ordered a hot fudge malt and her mother got coffee, black. She found a bent tin ashtray behind a napkin holder and lit up. The place was almost empty, just a few older people eating an early dinner, little toasted sandwiches with toothpicks and potato chips, and a couple of guys hunched over coffee and the newspaper.

Her mother smoked and watched her drink her malt. Becky loaded up her spoon, a big chunk of ice cream and some whipped cream, and extended it toward her mother. "No thanks," her mother said, halfheartedly.

"Oh, come on, Mom. Just a spoonful, I'll never tell."

"All right," her mother said, and slurped it up. "That's ten minutes on the bike," she said, and lit another cigarette. "No more."

Becky spun slowly on her stool and watched her mother in the mirror behind the counter above the sparkling soda glasses and silver malt cups, the spigots of hot fudge and butterscotch, the bins of nuts and candy sprinkles, a basket of overripe bananas. She blew her mother a kiss, but she didn't see, she was staring off somewhere. She pulled so hard on her low-tar cigarette that lines formed on her forehead and around her mouth, deep ugly furrows, and Becky wondered again, Why does she always look so mad?

That evening they knocked on her bedroom door like a committee, her father with his paisley tie loosened around his neck and his left eyelid drooping the way it did when he was tired, her mother in the blue sweats she liked to wear after dinner, watching him, waiting for him to begin. Something was up.

Becky had been lying on her bed, listening to Pearl Jam on her boom box and staring at an illustration in her life science text: two giraffes standing under a tree, one, typically long-necked, chewing leaves, the other, with a short, stubby neck, like no animal she'd ever seen, an angular, graceful zebra maybe, sadly looking up at the lower branches. The point was something about natural selection.

Her mother sat at the foot of her bed and her father leaned on the desk. He turned off her music. "How's school?" he said.

"Fine," Becky said.

"She's squinting again," her mother said. "We need to get your eyes checked."

"My eyes are fine, Mom," Becky said. "I just got them checked."

"Okay," her mother said.

"My hearing is good, too."

"I'm glad," her mother said.

"So what's up?" Becky asked. "What did I do wrong?"

"Nothing," her mother said. She picked up Brambles,

Becky's eyeless bunny, and held it on her knee. "You didn't do anything wrong."

"We've got something to tell you," her father said, and Becky knew it, they were getting divorced.

"Grandpa met with the judge today," he said. He lit a cigarette. "He's going to get help. When he's better, you can see him again."

"If you want to," her mother said.

"If you want to," her father said. "Now he's on probation—"

"If he does what he is supposed to for a certain period of time," her mother said, "then there's no other punishment."

"Mom, I know what probation means," Becky said. She felt okay, she wasn't going to cry. "Denise is on probation."

"Denise Wetterland?"

"Academic probation. She got three D's on her last report card."

"So it's over now," her father said. "Finally."

"Is that it?" Becky asked.

"Not quite," he said. "There's something else we want to talk about."

"What?" Becky said. "What?"

"Someone's got a birthday coming up," her mother said. It was eighteen days away, two weeks from Saturday.

"We want to do something different," her father said. "Something special." The ash on his cigarette was getting longer and longer, but he didn't seem to notice.

"What's wrong with the Ground Round?" Becky asked. A group of waiters there, most of them college boys, would gather at their booth and sing "Happy Birthday." It was embarrassing but fun. Afterward they would go home and eat cake and open her presents, and then she would have cake again for breakfast the next morning.

"It's just hamburgers and steaks there, honey," her mother said.

Her father cupped his left hand and tapped the ash into it. "We want to have people over now that we've got the room," he said. "An open house."

"A party," her mother said. "So you can invite Sheila and your friends from school."

"I don't have any friends from school," Becky said.

"What about Jennifer?"

"I hate Jennifer. She's a nerd."

"Karen?"

"Nerd-deluxe."

"Okay," her father said. "I'll leave the guest list to you two." He leaned over to give Becky a kiss, but she pulled back ever so slightly, like a fighter dodging a jab, and he stopped just short of her cheek, and it landed in midair, a loud, stale-smelling smack.

That night she dreamed about him again. She is slamming windows, fumbling with door locks, breathless and awkward. He keeps coming. It's not even his face, it's a movie villain's, like Nicholson's or De Niro's, but she knows it's him. Then he's framed in the doorway of her room, all shadowy menace. He whispers her name. *Becky*.

In homeroom Becky handed out invitations, little cards with balloons saying "You are invited," which she and her mother had filled in and addressed at the kitchen table the night before. Most of the girls were reading for a first-hour English quiz, bent over their paperback *Scarlet Letter*s, trying to get through Chapter 11, so she just set the envelopes down silently on Karen's and Nikki's and Allison's desks (Jennifer she would see at lunch). She looked over Karen's shoulder and saw a page full of underlining, highlighting, little notations in the margin, just like Sister Kathleen's book.

Becky was reasonably well prepared herself—she had read carefully if not as meticulously as Karen—but nervous. She felt pressure anyway, and it didn't seem fair. If Karen blew the test, she wouldn't be yanked into the counselor's office and interrogated. Or if she sat alone at lunch one day—or skipped a class or got caught daydreaming or just had a bad day—no one would flip out. But Becky knew that she had to be unrelentingly normal or else her parents would find out and there would be consequences. She could do it, but it was exhausting.

Sheila, on the other hand, her best friend from the old neighborhood, still going to public school, junior high this year, rarely even took books home. And already she seemed different. She was hanging at the mall after school and had just gotten her ears pierced again, three holes in each ear now, and was wearing her hair teased and sprayed stiff—big hair, they called it.

Becky had come here in September, a Catholic girls' school, because they'd moved and it was closer to their new house and because private education was more "rigorous," her father thought. (You think it's a good school because it costs a lot, Becky didn't tell him.) And because after the big flap last spring at her old school—the counselors and conferences and phone calls, getting pulled out of social studies to talk to a police detective—it was supposed to be a fresh start. But they knew about it here too, Becky could sense it, the teachers, anyway. They were watching her. She didn't like it. It wasn't even a school, it was a convent, for crying out loud, that's what it was, the sign out front said so, and they wore black wool uniforms like nuns.

The English quiz was easy, ten identifications, and Becky knew them all. When they exchanged papers, Becky got Lisa Sorentelli's, who got a hundred, too, except that she spelled Arthur's name "Dummsdale." Becky wrote "ha ha," next to it in the margin, very small, but then she had second thoughts and scratched it out. In math, she went to the board and got chalk all over the sleeve of her blouse, but she solved the equation, no sweat, and sat down. X equaled four. In World Civilization, all she had to do was look interested while Mr. Hassett talked. He wore suspenders and a big black mustache that was shiny and stiff-looking, like he really put wax on it. When he got to the end of one of his famous stories—"So don't put all your Basques in one exit"—she laughed, even though she couldn't say what came before, didn't know what was so funny, and she would bet that none of the other girls did either. But they laughed anyway.

The worst part of Becky's day was noon in the cafeteria, a carton of milk and her brown bag on an orange plastic tray, moving slowly from the cashier toward the lunch tables, scanning the room, circling, like a plane in a holding pattern, looking for a place to sit. She spotted an open chair across from Jennifer and two girls she knew from volleyball. Becky sat down, and they kept talking while they watched her open the brown bag. The girls knew that Becky bypassed hot lunch, the turkey with gravy and the tacos and chicken fingers. They were interested in her food, still checking her out, having suspended judgment so far as to whether she and her little bags of vegetables and wedges of cheese and dried fruit were exotically different, the next big thing maybe, or just weird. I'm on probation, Becky thought.

Becky sliced her pear into little pieces with a plastic knife and listened to Jennifer talk about a pair of winter boots she was maybe going to get. She was tall and athletic—she had a wicked spike and her own knee pads. She was pretty. Her father was a state legislator who was coming to speak on Career Day.

When the other girls got up to bus their dishes, Jennifer lingered a little, brushing the crumbs from her hands.

"Hey, Jen," Becky said. She pulled the last invitation from her purse and held it on her lap under the table, smoothing the edges of the envelope. "I want to give you something."

"I'm busy that Saturday," Jennifer said. "My dad is taking me to a play."

Becky closed the invitation in her fist. "That's okay," she said.

"Sorry," Jennifer said, but she wasn't.

It had been impulsive, almost as much a surprise to her as it had been to her parents. Now she was stuck. "I'm Becky the vegetarian now," she said. "That's who I am. You know what I mean? It's like my identity. And I like it, sort of. Except sometimes, when I'd kill for a Big Mac."

Dr. Reston nodded. "I know what you mean," she said.

And then there was this party. "I know what it's about," Becky said. "I'm not stupid. I'm getting a big bash, like I'm a hero or something." She checked the clock. "Don't you think it's strange?" she asked. And Dr. Reston nodded some more.

On the morning of Becky's birthday, her mother placed a small bundle of birthday mail—a half-dozen brightly colored envelopes and a brown padded mailer—next to her cereal bowl. Dylan was watching "Sports Center" in the family room, and her father was outside. Her mother watched as Becky worked her way through the cards, reading the messages aloud, looking for cash, and lining them up on the table. There was a card from her godparents, the Hutchinsons, who had moved to Seattle years ago and whom Becky could barely remember. There was another card—a kitten, a rocking chair, and a ball of yarn, in pastels, with old-fashioned lettering, "To a special girl on her special day," and a check for thirteen dollars—signed Grandma and Grandpa in Grandma's loopy handwriting.

The package was from Aunt Ellie in Buffalo. She always remembered. There was a homemade card with a watercolor sunflower, a pale delicate yellow, on the front and a big black-ink HAPPY BIRTHDAY inside, signed by all of them, Aunt Ellie and Uncle Walt, who printed his name, and even Lucy too, who made a big shaky "L" and some other scratches that looked like her name. Becky knew that Ellie had talked to the police last summer, that she had backed her up. There was a piece of school art paper with a painting, big splotches of fall colors, orange and yellow and red, and "For Becky from Lucy" neatly written in the bottom corner. There were two small wrapped presents. One was a little green book with soft leather covers, like a Gideon Bible, but darker, combat green, with gold lettering on the cover: MY DIARY. The other was a jewelry box. Inside was a pair of earrings, brilliant blue droplets with small round beads of purple. There was a printed card explaining that these were Princess Earrings, lapis lazuli and amethyst, adapted from originals belonging to Princess Sithathoryunet, daughter of the Twelfth Dynasty King Sesostris II, who ruled Egypt during its golden age. They were dazzling, with gold clips, Aunt Ellie knowing somehow that she was practically the only girl her age without pierced ears, not because her mother minded—she offered to pay for it, even to do it herself—but just because Becky, who'd seen it done at slumber parties, the ice cubes and needles and bubbling drops of blood, couldn't stand the thought of it, the stabbing. She picked them up and held them in the palm of her hand and showed her mother. They were beautiful. Princess Earrings.

Her father came in the side door humming "Happy Birthday." He was wearing a gray sweatshirt and khaki pants, his weekend clothes. "Happy birthday, honey," he said. He looked over her booty. "Come on outside," he said. "I want to show you something."

She put on her mother's pea coat over her pajamas and slipped into a pair of Dylan's high-tops that were parked at the door. It was chilly outside; only the sixth of November, but she could see her breath. She followed her father into the front yard, where, in the middle of the lawn, there was a huge metal sign on a trailer hitch with big black tires and the plastic letters you slide into place, the kind of sign garden centers use to advertise specials.

*   *   *   *   *   *   *

HAPPY BIRTHDAY BECKY!!

LUCKY THIRTEEN!

*   *   *   *   *   *   *

She walked around it. There were big yellow bulbs flashing at the corners and an orange extension cord snaking from the heavy black base across the frosty lawn up to the front door and through the mail-box slot. A gray minivan drove by, slowed in front of the sign, and then honked the horn. Her father waved.

"Well," he said. "What do you think?"

"It's something," Becky said. "Unbelievable."

The rest of the day was devoted to getting ready. Her father and Dylan raked leaves and straightened the garage and went to the store for soft drinks and ice. Her mother fixed two huge pans of lasagna, one with meat, one with spinach. Then she started to clean. Once she got started, she was a furious housekeeper, wearing rubber gloves and a kerchief on her head, with a bucketful of hot suds and a rag, scrubbing, scraping, polishing. She was in her own world. Early in the afternoon, when Becky came into the kitchen for a glass of water, her mother looked up at her—she was on her knees, washing the baseboards—almost annoyed, suspicious, as if she were responsible for all the dirt, as if she were just another mess waiting to happen. Becky filled a paper cup and got out.

Becky got dressed in her room. She put on her new earrings first and looked at them from different angles, admiring their sparkle and the graceful way they swung when she turned her head. She went into the bathroom and stood on the ledge of the tub and inspected her stockings in the mirror. She tried her hair a couple of different ways, with and without barrettes, and, in desperation, with a black velvet bow, which was ludicrous. She searched through her mother's closet, looking for something, some accessory, the sort of thing Dr. Reston wore, a scarf maybe, but she couldn't find anything that was her style, whatever that was. Her school friends dressed like J. Crew models, and Sheila was into grunge. Everybody had an angle, it seemed, but her. She settled on her outfit from last spring's piano recital, before she had quit her lessons, a flowered skirt with her white turtleneck and a long black cardigan. It was okay.

Finally, just before four, they came down from their rooms one by one, Becky and Dylan, her father and then her mother, showered and dressed, and they sat together on the couch in the living room, a little shy, their hair combed and their shoes shined, smelling of Ivory and aftershave and perfume, a perfect, untouched plate of cheese and crackers in front of them on the coffee table. Nobody said anything. There was just that moment, a delicious pause, like holding your breath, after her mother had put away the vacuum and before her father picked up the camcorder, when they were neither preparing nor remembering, when they were just there together, living, like a real family. Her father touched her hand. Her mother smiled. Then the doorbell rang.

It was Aunt Maureen in a black jumpsuit and a thick leather belt, like a weight lifter's, cinched around her tiny waist, disorganized and bubbly, kissing cheeks, while Becky's cousins, Terri and Rick, stood in the front yard fiddling with the birthday sign. Then her father's boss, Michael Jackson—that was his name and he didn't like jokes about it—arrived wearing a tweed sport coat and aviator sunglasses and carrying a bottle of wine, and her father took him on a tour. Sheila showed up in blue eyeliner and a new leather jacket covered with zippers, smelling of Aqua-Net, her hair bigger than ever. Then, their new next-door neighbors, Jodi and Anton, who were married but had different last names and played in the chamber orchestra. The convent girls came in together, Allison, Nikki, and Karen, dressed in muted earth tones with matching hair bands, like the Magi, each one carrying a little gift. They solemnly placed them on the dining room table and then headed for the soft drinks and dip.

Before long, after its slow beginning, the awkward introductions and greetings in the front hall (''Where's the birthday girl?''), the taking of jackets and the getting of drinks, the party swelled into a crowded and chaotic buzz. Becky's mother shuttled back and forth between the kitchen and dining room wearing an apron and hot pads, bringing first stuffed mushrooms and baked brie, then, the main course, the lasagna and salad and bread. People sat where they could and balanced their plates on their laps and went back for more. Her father got the camera and taped a little, the obnoxious red light blinking, narrating the whole time, like always, announcing the date and occasion and guests, even the menu, as if he were doing some big historical documentary.

Sheila ended up outside in the driveway playing basketball with Dylan and two of his neighborhood buddies. Becky stood in the dining room window with Allison and Nikki and watched her dribbling around Dylan, past his friends, in for a layup. ''Nice hair,'' Nikki said. Michael Jackson got bumped and spilled his white wine on the living room rug and dabbed at it timidly with a pile of Happy Birthday napkins, and her mother told him, forget it, don't worry about it. Becky couldn't believe it.

Uncle Calvin and Aunt Kate stopped in for a minute, on their way somewhere else, Calvin, handsome as a movie star in his blue suit, and Kate, looking painfully pregnant in a denim jumper and moving through doorways as slowly and deliberately as a semi or a bus turning a tight corner. Kate gave Becky a sideways hug, and Becky tried not to stare at her stomach. Calvin gave her a kiss and told her she looked ravishing and snitched a cherry tomato from her plate and shouted thank you to her mother and father, who were busy with something in the kitchen, and then they were gone.

Dylan got hold of the camera and zoomed in on Becky for a mock interview. "What does it feel like to be thirteen?"

"Knock it off, creep," she said, and put her hand over the lens. They had enough horse-faced footage of her, grotesque enlarged explorations of her imperfect complexion.

Then her mother burst into the room, carrying a big cake. She set it down on the table and lit the candles, while everyone gathered around and sang. It was a chocolate sheet cake decorated with pink and green roses and white lettering, "HAPPY BIRTHDAY, BECKY," same as always, except in the left corner there was a face, an oval of flesh-colored icing with blue eyes and red lips and light brown hair, even a pink hair band, just like hers, all in the inhumanly bright shades of the Sunday comics, the girl's frosting features greasily thick, but it looked like her, sort of, it really did. Becky bent over the cake, blew as hard as she could, and nailed all thirteen in one pass. She forgot to wish for anything.

Everybody marveled at the likeness. They couldn't get over it. On a cake. "You just bring them a snapshot," her mother said. Who's going to eat that? that's what Becky wanted to know, but her mother worked around it, cut enough little squares for everyone there plus a few extras, and left Becky's face intact, just smudged a little, a hole in her hair and a few drops of wax on her forehead.

They made her open presents right then, while everyone

watched. She did it the way she was supposed to, read the cards and passed them around, took her time with the packages, noticed the paper and saved the bows. Her mother took notes on who gave what. A necklace from Sheila. Bath oil and scented soaps and powder from her school friends. A peach turtleneck with no tags from Aunt Maureen, who was broke now, everybody knew it, the same sweater Becky remembered her wearing last Christmas. A Dayton's gift certificate from Michael Jackson and a fancy leather bookmark from Anton and Jodi.

Then her father disappeared with Dylan and Michael Jackson. "One more," her mother said.

"What?" Becky said. "What is it?" She was tired of smiling.

"You'll see," her mother said.

They were back, carrying five or six big boxes, all wrapped in shiny silver paper, like fancy aluminum foil. They piled them at her feet.

"Go ahead," her mother said. Becky felt funny. Not like a birthday.

"Come on," Dylan said.

Becky tore the paper on the first package and saw something printed in another language, German maybe. She looked up at her father and Dylan, both grinning like idiots. She gave the box a half turn, tore back more paper, and saw the words "HIGH FIDELITY." It was a stereo.

And what a stereo. All the components, a tuner and an amplifier and a tape player, with two decks, for dubbing. A five-disc, programmable CD player. Two huge speakers, almost as tall as she was, not boxes, but thin, delicate towers.

Her mother and father smiled at Becky, their arms wrapped

around each other, looking happy and shy, like newlyweds. "Thanks," Becky said. "Thanks and thanks."

Her father sliced open the cardboard cartons with a kitchen knife, then removed the Styrofoam corner pieces and lifted the components out as gently as a doctor welcoming a newborn baby. Sheila was making low, moaning sounds. "Oh God," she said. "Oh God." There was a bundle of wires, antennae, headphones, two remotes, all in plastic bags, and another box with a cabinet, wood shelves and a glass door and a million screws.

Finally, an hour or so later, once it had been wired and plugged in, the sleek black components stacked in the rack and encased behind the glass door, once Anton returned from next door with a disc, an eerie minor-key cello sonata, and it had been turned on and the green power light was glowing and the output needle flickering, they sat on the floor, listening and watching, and it seemed to Becky to possess, like some robot in a science fiction movie, a monstrous, malignant intelligence.

"It's like a bribe," Becky said.

"What do you mean?" Dr. Reston said. "What makes it a bribe?"

"A bribe," Becky said; she could do this, she was good at definitions. "A bribe is when you give somebody something, money, whatever, it doesn't matter, to do something."

"To do what?"

"To do something bad, like bribing a judge to let a crook off. Or a politician to vote for something. Maybe just to do something you wouldn't do otherwise. Or not to do something you would do otherwise. Like hush money. Black-mail.''

''So what do they want you to do?''

''I don't know. Be happy. Stop hanging around Sheila. Like school. Be perfect. Act like everything's fine. Turn the volume way up so I don't hear them fighting. No more nightmares.''

''What about the hush money? What are you supposed to be quiet about?''

Becky looked down at the candy dish on the table, the same foil-wrapped toffee that had been sitting there for weeks, all disgusting flavors—coffee, maple nougat, mocha mint. She felt dizzy, like the room was trembling, what she imagined an earthquake to be like. ''You know, don't you?'' she said.

''Tell me.''

''He's afraid.'' Her legs were shaking now, crazy spastic bouncing, but she couldn't stop.

''Of what?''

''That I'm going to tell.''

''Tell what?''

''It wasn't just Grandpa.'' She was crying now, hot tears flying off her face. ''It was him too,'' she said, and then her throat seemed to close, and she couldn't speak another word.

PART II

WINTER

5

YOU NEVER KNOW

AFTER ELLIE HEARD THAT HER FATHER HAD GOTTEN OFF WITH A SLAP on the wrist, a small fine and probation, she called her friend Mavis, back finally from her travels. They met that night for coffee at a Perkins restaurant, where, Ellie used to joke with Walter, all her major life decisions and crises seemed to take place. She broke up with her college boyfriend at a Perkins, and eight years ago, at a Perkins in Harrisburg, Pennsylvania, after nearly two hundred miles of sullen misunderstanding on the road in her old Maverick, she and Walt had decided once and for all to get married. After they closed on their house and both felt almost physically ill with debt, they went to Perkins. Mavis and Ellie had started going as seniors in their studio seminar: they'd order sundaes and fill the place mats with excited drawings, sculpt miniature models in whipped cream. Not that there really was anything special about Perkins. But it was always open, that was important, and they gave you the whole coffeepot and real half-and-half, no chemical creamer, and they never rushed you. It was like a good family kitchen.

Ellie pulled into the parking lot next to Mavis's ancient blue Toyota, which was rotted with rust and plastered with bumper stickers: SUPPORT YOUR LOCAL POET. KILL YOUR TELEVISION. NIXON EATS LETTUCE. Dried leaves were blowing across the pavement and piling up in the corners of the lot. Winter was closing in. It was just after six o'clock but already dark. A chance of scattered flurries overnight, the radio said.

Inside, Mavis waved her down from a corner booth, where she already had a pot of decaf on the table and two cups poured. Mavis was a jewelry maker, who sold her work—complicated metal pins and earrings she soldered and glued in her studio—at art fairs and a few little shops on Elmwood Avenue and in Toronto, and she looked, to Ellie at least, like a real artist. Her hair was a wild black mane, streaked with gray, and she wore tunics and big embroidered smocks and long homemade print skirts. She loved jewelry, but never wore any of her own pieces, Ellie never asked why. Tonight she wore a glossy blue and red pin on her beige sweater, oval-shaped at one end, narrow and elongated at the other, like a stylized tennis racket, one of several Spanish charms she wore from time to time, this one, she claimed, to protect her from those who were insensitive to art.

"You sounded a little quaky on the phone," Mavis said as Ellie slid into the booth.

"I've been quaky for weeks," Ellie said. "Quaky is my middle name."

Mavis pushed a steaming white cup across the table. Mavis had been around. She'd done some things. To hear her tell it, she'd once been a spoiled rich kid, a dropout, a kleptomaniac (her specialty was lingerie—teddies and camisoles and bras and panties and fancy garter belts and hose that she never wore—brought home and crammed in a suitcase, stolen for no reason, because it was there), and a drug addict—a chain-smoking, pill-popping, shoplifting mess.

It was hard for Ellie to believe. Now Mavis was utterly responsible. She took good care of herself, didn't eat meat or sugar or white flour. She was independent and successful. She took violin lessons and volunteered at Hospice. She was great with kids. She would walk into Ellie's house, get down on the floor with Lucy, and ten minutes later, they'd be blowing homemade kazoos or building the Great Pyramid out of Legos or singing a French duet.

Still, there were things about her. She believed in reincarnation. Or at least said she did. She read books about self-hypnosis and crystals. Walt thought she was a character, a charming eccentric. Ellie wasn't always sure what she thought.

"So what's making you quaky?" Mavis said, and Ellie started in. She told her everything: her father's sentence, the messages from Maureen, her dreams, Mrs. Jim Bowie and the little Adirondack chair, the fit of crying or whatever it was that had overtaken her while she was reading to Lucy. Mavis never said a word. She listened in a kind of Zen-like state, with an intensity Ellie used to find unnerving. With her back absolutely straight and her shoulders square, her hands flat on her lap, Mavis never nodded, made no little noises of encouragement, and when Ellie teared up, didn't pat her hand or offer her tissues. She just listened.

"Think of the harm he's done," Ellie said. "These ripples of misery and confusion, they just don't stop. Now Becky. And me, and Mo, and my mother, too. And who knows who else? I'm afraid for Lucy. And he sits in the middle of it. Like a storm, Hurricane Hal. He's touched down again, and we're all left to pick up the pieces. He's a bad man. He's evil. And he's my father."

Ellie took a deep breath and stared into her cup. "And my mother, his sidekick. I hold her responsible, too. I talked to her years ago, and she wouldn't listen. She's still living with him, still standing by her man. It makes me sick to my stomach."

Ellie looked out the window. There was a man in a knit cap tapping the side of a newspaper machine with his gloved fist. In the light of a street lamp she could see a fine mist falling.

"So there," Ellie said.

"What are you going to do about it?" Mavis said.

"Why do I have to *do* something? Besides, what is there to do? Buy a gun and shoot them? Come on. What difference would it make? The past is past."

"Do you pray for them?"

"Pray for them?" Ellie said. "Why should I pray for them? I'd like to boil my son-of-a-bitch father in oil. I'd like to bury a hatchet in his smiling, lying, hypocritical face. I'd like to watch him dance in red-hot shoes until he drops dead."

"Red-hot shoes?" Mavis said. She smiled. "Listen," she said. "It's a technique. To free yourself. You pray for the person that you resent. Pray that they are granted all the good things you want for yourself, success, peace of mind, whatever. Do it every day for a month. Thirty days. It always works."

"My mother, maybe. I can almost imagine it. But I'll be damned if I'll pray for him," Ellie said.

"That's okay," Mavis said. "Maybe you don't want to be free right now. I understand."

But she tried it that night, who prayed only before dinner and at bedtime with her daughter, cute rhymes she brought home from nursery school, who hadn't prayed in earnest for years, not since she was a little girl, not even in childbirth. She checked on Lucy in what she still called her big girl bed, surrounded by a menagerie of stuffed animals, angelic in the yellow glow of her night light. And then, with Walter already in bed, asleep, snoring faintly, she went into the bathroom and closed the door. She kneeled down and rested her elbows on the lip of the pedestal sink, like a cold white communion rail. She could remember picking the sink out with Walt when she was pregnant, agonizing over their decision much longer than they'd ever considered a wedding ring, watching with delight as the man she called Fred the Happy Plumber, a beaming young father of two, installed it while extolling the joys of parenthood. "It's all new," he said. "Everything like the first time." Ellie closed her eyes. Dear God. She could see her mother's face, her sunken eyes and wrinkles, a face blasted with sorrow. God bless her. She could see her father, too, his round face, like a boy's, eager to please, scared, too, somehow. Bless him.

Ellie kept it up. She prayed the next day, and the next day, and the next. Before long, she had a full-blown, secret prayer life. Because she felt, however foolishly, that she ought to assume a posture of prayer, hands folded, kneeling, eyes closed, she found it necessary sometimes to sneak away, which was never easy. The bathroom was fine, but Lucy, only reluctantly respectful of closed doors, would stand outside jabbering, trying to talk her out, asking impossible questions: "Where does the moon go?" "What's higher than the sky?" "Are you old?"

One morning Walter, having forgotten something in the bedroom, walked in unexpectedly and discovered Ellie kneeling at the bedside. He didn't say anything but it was clear he saw that something unusual was going on. She was caught, but couldn't begin to explain. She got up, flustered, flushed with shame, and did her best to feign the motions of deep cleaning.

At the library, she stole away from Lucy in the Bear's Den long enough to look up prayer in the card catalog and grab two books—*The Power of Prayer* and the *Spiritual Exercises* of St. Ignatius—which she guiltily checked out and kept concealed in her purse, lest Walter think she'd flipped altogether. She paged through them when Walter worked and Lucy was at school. The *Exercises* were all severely numbered paragraphs and rules, spiritual statutes in fine print. *The Power of Prayer* was a pamphlet published by the Mormon Church, just questions and answers. "How can you know your prayer is answered?" There was a whole paragraph of qualification, but finally they just said it, "You never know." Ellie felt inexplicably heartened that the Latter-day Saints invoked the very same motto as the New York State Lottery. *Hey,* it said on the sides of buses, in full-page newspaper ads, on the incessant radio spots, *You Never Know.*

Her prayers were so haphazard, so amateurish and childish,

they seemed hardly worthy of the term. They involved self-conscious recitations of half-remembered formulas, free associative nonsense, and chatty insincere good wishes, like something you write in a greeting card. It was a funny business. She dutifully said things she didn't mean to someone whose existence she doubted, repeatedly asked favors she never expected to be granted. But she was *doing* something at last, and however ridiculous her inner life, she told herself, at least she had one.

Those quiet moments began to matter to her in ways she didn't fully understand. Sometimes, when she could think of no more words to say, she recollected and remembered pieces of her parents that had been lost or misplaced over the years. Untidy scraps of memory. Her father's starched white shirts fresh from the cleaners in boxes, which she plundered for the cardboard. Her mother's strong hands braiding her hair. Their vacant smiles in holiday photographs, beaming bland goodwill at the camera. The time her father brought her saltwater taffy for no reason, a whole bag. Another time he stood up on his chair during Thanksgiving dinner, the turkey on the table, and dusted the chandelier with his napkin. The drunken set of her mother's shoulders that Ellie could read before she put down her schoolbooks and know her father was out of town. Her mother's lipstick-stained filtered cigarettes. The way he strangled the steering wheel in traffic. The pleasure he took in his paper, the newsprint on his hands. Her mother at the wheel of a stalled car full of kids in the middle of a busy intersection, helpless and afraid, smoke seeping from the hood. His crabbed, shuffling usher's walk up the aisle every Sunday at St. Mark's, his long-handled basket and his awkward genuflection, her own little envelope and insane desire to claw his face, right there before the congregation. Her mother's black veil, her shyly sweet voice singing sacred songs. Her father's white face in the dark, his hands on her, an impassive thief, robbing her while she looked on from afar. Everything was true, every bit of it, she was almost certain, and none of it simple, and all important somehow.

Ellie counted the days with tiny marks she made on the kitchen calendar. By the time she had accumulated fifteen days, she believed in it, somewhat, a little bit, the power of prayer. She felt more serene, maybe. It lowered her blood pressure, probably, like meditation or yoga. Neutralized bad cholesterol or something. But nothing had happened, really. Nothing had changed. She was the same, still distracted, still a baffled, alien inhabitant of her own life. Haunted still by dreams full of grinning menace and black smoke. Walter was still suffocating her with his big benignity. And, according to Maureen's reports, her family in Minneapolis, all were remaining true to character, doing what they always did. Her father was on the road, selling a new line. Her mother got her hair done. Ellie didn't expect anything to change, wasn't sure that people changed, really changed, down to the roots, ever. But she kept them up anyway, her harmless, clandestine, oddball prayers, in neither hope nor despair, like a crank's relentless unanswered, unpublished letters to the editor, the unacknowledged, unrequited babble of a passionate idiot.

6

LOVE ON THE RUN

THE WOMEN SAT IN A CIRCLE, ON FOLDING CHAIRS, IN THE BASEMENT of an Episcopal church, ten Partners of Offenders and a facilitator with a clipboard. There were bright banners on the wall——HE IS RISEN! REJOICE!——and a bulletin board full of Sunday school crayon drawings, all of them depicting the Annunciation: Gabriel wearing magnificent feathery wings in some and little batlike appendages in others, sometimes tall and stately, sometimes small, tugging at Mary in one drawing like a pesky child, and Mary herself, always in blue, her head encircled with yellow light, amazed, a little fearful, her eyebrows raised, her hands clasped together, her mouth round with surprise.

Phyllis had arrived early and sat in her car in the parking lot with the motor idling, watching a few wet snowflakes land and

melt on her windshield, so big they looked fake, like Hollywood snow. She was not a group person. It depressed her to
have to listen to a long litany of someone else's problems, and
it was not her way to cry on anybody's shoulder. But it was
part of the deal. Byron Burke had explained to them that Hal
could take it or leave it, probation and outpatient treatment. If
not, there would be a trial. It would cost thousands, and no
guarantees. "It's up to you," he had said, "but I know what I
would do." He folded his milky white hands and waited, patient as a priest.

The name bothered her. She understood that they wanted
to include both wives and girlfriends too, but Partners of Offenders sounded too much like Partners in Crime, as if she
were implicated, too, as if she were Bonnie to his Clyde. But
Hal's counselor said she should go, so that night she had eaten
an early dinner and got dressed and drove off, as if she were
headed to PTA or Craft Club.

The leader was a frail-looking woman named Ann. She introduced Phyllis to the group, and the other women leaned
forward and peered at her and said, "Welcome," mindlessly,
in unison, as though she were a new kid in school. Ann explained the procedure. First names only. "What you say
here," she said, "stays here when you leave here." She passed
the clipboard around so everyone could sign up for time to
talk. If more time was requested than was available, they
would negotiate. Newcomers were expected to tell their stories within the first month of their joining the group. Phyllis
never thought of her life as a story. It was just what she did
every day. If anything, her life was a list.

First to speak was a heavyset girl in blue jeans and a gray
sweatshirt with a plaid scarf draped over her shoulders like a

stole. There was a covered baby carrier at her feet, pointed toward her. She rocked it gently with her foot and said that she was worried about money. Keith was trying, she said, he really was, but they kept calling and making threats, and the mail was all bad. There was a little catlike cry from beneath the blue canopy, and the girl looked down and made a face of exaggerated surprise. She smiled and smacked her lips and made clicking sounds with her tongue, but there were tears running down her cheeks. "I'm afraid," she said, "that's all." "It's simple as that," she said, and someone handed her a tissue.

One after another they talked, moving clockwise around the circle toward Phyllis. Such complicated misery, such involved histories of turmoil, so full of problems that Phyllis couldn't follow it all. Ray had a relapse, one woman said, something involving the telephone and a Visa bill. Another woman was concerned about her daughter, who wasn't eating. Half an orange, that's lunch. Nagging only made it worse. What was she supposed to do about it? The woman next to Phyllis, wearing fingerless black gloves and a pillowy round hat, like a Dutch painter's, stared at her blue rubber boots and murmured about her husband. He had disappeared, Phyllis was almost certain that's what she said, but none of the other women commented or looked to be in the least bit alarmed, as if a disappearing husband were unremarkable, as if it happened all the time. Phyllis felt overwhelmed. It was like switching from soap to soap or reading the crazy weekly summaries in the *TV Guide*. The leader made notes on her clipboard.

Finally it was her turn. "My name is Phyllis," she said. She hated speaking in public. "I'm here for my husband," she said. The women leaned forward and smiled at her and said "Welcome," again, as if it were a social club.

"Phyllis," Ann said, studying her, "what would you like to get from the group?"

"What would I like?" she said. "That's a good question. I don't know. To be honest, I'm not thrilled about being here. I never imagined I would end up here, in a church basement, nothing personal, with Partners of Offenders."

The women nodded and smiled, and the woman to her right, the one who had lost her husband, reached out and patted Phyllis with a gloved hand.

"I want things to be the way they used to be," she said. "But they're never the same again, are they? That's what your faces say. Besides, I know they never were the way they used to be." She laughed, but she was the only one. "So here I am."

At the end of the meeting, the women joined hands and recited something. "Keep coming back," they said to each other. While they hugged and chatted in little circles, Phyllis edged toward the card table filled with literature. She scooped up a couple of pamphlets and slipped out the door.

The day that Hal had pleaded, she had ironed a white shirt for him and laid out his best tie. She touched his sleeve as he headed out the door—he insisted that he go alone—and wished him luck. Maybe someone could blame her for that. But luck, that was all she wished him. Didn't they all need some luck?

Afterward, he sat at the kitchen table with his tie loosened and top button undone, as if it had been a hard day at work, and explained the terms, what was expected of him. He had to attend treatment and get a letter upon completion. He had to stay away from his female grandchildren until they were eighteen years old. He had to pay a fine, a thousand bucks. She would have liked something else from him, not a confession, but some emotion, not remorse necessarily or tears even, but something. Instead it was all strategy, facts and analysis, the way it was with the IRS the year before. Then he changed his clothes and drove off, and Phyllis was alone again, just like that. It was like a death in the family, and now that the official words had been pronounced, and the formal clothes hung in the closet, that was supposed to be the end of it. Things were supposed to return to normal.

The morning after her meeting, Phyllis sat at the kitchen table with a cup of coffee, staring mindlessly out into the darkness. She and Hal were moving in separate orbits again. They had their own rooms, their own cars, their own checking accounts. They kept different hours, Phyllis up before dawn, listening to corny jokes and the farm report on the radio, and Hal, the night owl. Their natural incompatibility exaggerated into caricature, like so much of their marriage. (When they used to argue, the louder Hal got, the quieter Phyllis became, until she was barely moving her lips. In restaurants, he tipped big, and she pocketed loose bills when he wasn't looking. He liked it cool, and she turned the heat up, a contrarian reflex so ingrained she no longer knew for sure whether she liked it warm or not.) They might not see each other for days at a time, though Phyllis would find signs of him around the house:

a bowl in the sink encrusted with soggy cereal, a wet towel in the bathroom, crumbs on the kitchen table.

An old clunker roared to life down the block, sputtering and rattling, and she wondered why it was, without fail, that between five and six in the morning, nearly every car on the street was some big rumbling wreck. And suddenly she was almost doubled over with a pain so searingly specific, so exactly placed, she could imagine her innards being probed by a red-hot instrument. She grabbed the table with both hands and took a deep breath and then it passed.

Later she consulted her medical companion, which was a mistake, of course. It was a fat red volume she'd bought at a grocery store, probably hopelessly out-of-date by now. She would pull it down from time to time, when Maureen, say, needed to know how long her kids' chicken pox were going to be contagious. But lately she had been browsing, maybe because she felt herself wearing down just like an old car herself, starting slow, the transmission slipping. She propped the book in front of her while she ate her toast. It was indexed by symptom and nearly all of them—stomach pain was no exception—led to something horrible.

It was probably just indigestion. Phyllis chewed a couple of lemon-flavored tablets she found in the cupboard and resolved to cut back on coffee. Her stomach rumbled a bit, but mostly she felt all right.

She had lots to do. She got dressed, and just as she heard Hal starting to stir upstairs, headed out the door. It was a freakishly mild December day, the sky a brilliant blue, melting icicles dripping from the eaves onto the driveway. The streets were greasy, and the boulevards lined with mounds of dirty snow, tiny crystals sparkling in the sunshine like sequins.

There was a humpbacked snowman at the corner, two black charcoal briquette eyes lying on the ground, its head caving in from beneath a jaunty blue beret and a plaid scarf, like the last sad scene from a children's story.

Phyllis decided to stop first at the car wash. The kids laughed at her, but she worried about rust. She would see all the salt on the road and imagine her undercarriage being eaten away, the metal slowly corroding, dark spots forming.

She pulled in, found a coupon in the glove box, and paid a boy in the little booth for the works. He was scruffy—a blue bandana tied on his head and an earring, like a pirate—but polite. She pulled in line behind a red sports car, and thought about her Geoff, who, after dropping out of college the day of a big exam, had worked at this same car wash for exactly one day. She had spoken to him only once since Hal's arrest, a short, tense conversation on the phone. Maureen still cut Joan's hair, and she thought there was trouble, not just Becky, but their marriage. Phyllis told Maureen that she would be willing to do anything to help, but, face it, what did she know about marriage?

When she was next, they directed her in and hooked up the car. She liked the sensation of being pulled through the wash in neutral, her hands off the wheel, folded on her lap, the mechanical spray guns appearing like snipers to shoot their soapy stream, the woolly buffers and rollers pressed flat against the windshield. It was like taking a hot bath without getting wet.

In the sunshine outside, steam rose from her hood while two boys in jeans and rubber boots dried and buffed the car with their snapping towels, swift and stylish, like a professional pit crew. She waved and pulled out into the street, feeling, for the moment, clean and invulnerable beneath her new layer of hot wax.

At Maureen's, Phyllis rang the bell at the back door and let herself in. Maureen was in the kitchen, scissors in hand, dressed in a long black smock, like a cassock, standing over someone in a kitchen chair, lifting little strands of the woman's hair, letting them go, considering, testing. She tilted her head and caught sight of Phyllis in the mirror propped above the kitchen sink. "Hi, Mom," she said.

Maybe it was just the habit of hairdressers, but Phyllis found it unnerving that Maureen would speak to an image in the mirror rather than address the real face in front of her, not just when she was doing her hair but other times too, like now, sometimes even in restaurants. She knew all the angles. Phyllis would then have to duck down or lean to the side in order to find her in the mirror.

There was a semicircle of auburn hair on the floor bunched in springy curls and the counter was littered with Maureen's equipment—rubber gloves, conditioner, shampoo, mousse, boxes of color, an electric trimmer, a curling iron, fashion magazines full of new hairdos. The kitchen smelled sweet, the fruity fragrance of expensive shampoo, coconut and peaches, like a fancy mixed drink.

Phyllis took off her coat and helped herself to a mug in the cupboard. She picked up the glass carafe from the stove. The spout was broken, so she poured a half a cup slowly over the side and managed not to spill.

Maureen kept talking, a mile a minute, her chatter part of the job, a happy noise, the sound if not the substance of female friendship, lively and gossipy and requiring nothing but a nod or a smile. She was saying something about a man who wanted his hair colored. "And then, after a couple times, he unbuttons his shirt and shows me this wild patch of silver hair on his chest, and he sort of looks around and says, 'Do you think you could, you know, color this too?' 'Well,' I say. 'I stop at the navel, okay? Nothing below the waist.' So he comes into the shop every five weeks or so—he was paranoid about roots—and we go upstairs and sort of turn toward the wall and he unbuttons and I get out my spatula and I do him."

Phyllis took her coffee into the den and sat down on the couch across from Ritchie's hi-fi and his wall-to-wall record collection. They'd been divorced for almost two years, but Maureen kept his things around, records and books and big black boxes full of musical equipment in the basement, as if he were just away at school.

Now Ritchie sent the children postcards once in a while and called them from time to time, usually late at night, past their bedtimes, sometimes collect. Once or twice a year, he would drive up in his van, painted with the name of his old band, LOVE ON THE RUN, with some wildly impractical gift for the kids, a pogo stick, a unicycle, a scrawny yellow puppy named Freedog. He would stay for a few days, maybe a week, and even though Maureen feigned exasperation—he was like a teenager, a whirlwind of ashtrays and beer bottles, loud music and broken lamps—Phyllis knew that Maureen lived for those days: the rest was waiting. Phyllis could hear Ritchie in her voice on the phone even before she announced that he was back. Love, whatever it was, what all these songs were about, no matter how foolish or irresponsible or destructive, whether or not it was on the run, Maureen felt it for Ritchie and always would.

But still she needed money, and Phyllis did what she could.

For Christmas, Maureen said, Terri had her heart set on Samantha, the American Girl, which cost eighty-five dollars, and Rick wanted a football shirt with his name on it. She took the check for Maureen from her purse and held it in her hand. In the kitchen, there was a burst of laughter, and then the sound of a blower. At Phyllis's feet on the floor was an open Monopoly board, what looked like a game in progress: a few houses scattered across the board, a red hotel looming on Marvin Gardens, the metal terrier in jail, the little iron resting on the B&O, neat piles of brightly colored money tucked under the board.

Maureen came into the room, her smock flapping behind her, the long red nails on both hands raking through her own hair like sharp glossy combs. "I still have to give her highlights," she said. "Did you go last night? How was it?"

"Fine," Phyllis said. She stood up. "It was sort of huggy. Like a Tupperware party without the Tupperware." What could she say? She'd been thinking about that girl and her baby, who needed to be held, not rocked with a dirty sneaker, but what was the point of that?

"I still don't see why you have to do time for Dad," Maureen said.

"I'm not doing time," Phyllis said. "Prisoners do time. It's not jail. I'm being supportive. We're a family, and we're all in this together." She handed Maureen the check. "You would do the same for Ritchie."

"Ritchie," Maureen said. "Don't get me started." She folded the check and slipped it in the pocket of her smock. "Being supportive is all well and good, Mom, but what about Rita Redhead? Calvin saw them together at the mall, you know. They were probably picking out curtains. Why doesn't she go?"

Phyllis didn't have an answer. Maureen peered around the corner into the kitchen. "I gotta go, Mom," she said. "Come by next week and I'll give you a perm for the holidays. You're starting to look limp."

Next she stopped at the baby store to pick up something for Kate's shower. She moved slowly up and down the crowded aisles, astounded by the ingenuity, the complexity, the technology: wind-up silent swings, nursery walkie-talkies, electric bottle warmers, a big-wheeled collapsible buggy that a saleswoman was demonstrating to a young couple like a soldier performing the manual of arms. Everything was bright and sturdy, portable playpens, canvas backpacks strung over shiny aluminum tubes, padded car seats with heavy buckles plastered with stickers attesting to their safety.

In the front of the store there was a big shelf of how-to books and videos on every subject imaginable—baby names, the art of breast-feeding, bathing, potty training, bringing your child up in the Christian faith. Calvin and Kate, she knew, were reading like crazy, cramming for the baby as though it were a big exam. Phyllis herself had never looked at *Dr. Spock* or any book about babies for that matter—who had time back then? Someone was always crying, the television blaring, something boiling on the stove—but she wished she had. When Terri had colic and Maureen was almost beside herself with sleeplessness and frustration, Phyllis had given her the only bit of advice she possessed: "Try something," she told Maureen. "And if that doesn't work, try something else." She picked up one heavy paperback and flipped through the pages: there were short chapters, common questions in boldface and one-paragraph answers, and big black-and-white photos of such beautiful babies, being bathed and fed and swaddled by perfectly calm and confident young women, their faces aglow in happy adoration.

Phyllis wasn't sure what she was looking for exactly. She followed a winding path through the bedroom furniture, whole rooms full of dressers and changing tables and cribs, made up with waterproof sheets and colorful bumper pads. There was a plush teddy bear tucked under a quilt in one, a mobile suspended above its head. Phyllis wound it and sent Pooh and Piglet and the others floating in a circle to the melody of Brahms' "Lullaby," their arms outstretched and eyes bulging, like frightened parachutists.

She sat down in a wooden glider and moved slowly back and forth. She could remember sitting in Aunt Alma's rickety old rocker in the middle of the night, comforted by the hiss of steam heat and quiet breathing. She closed her eyes, and just for that moment, she could feel the warm weight of a baby on her shoulder. It was as if her skin remembered. When she finally opened her eyes, there was a woman staring at her. She wore glasses on a string around her neck and looked tight-faced and strict, like an unhappy schoolteacher.

"Can I help you?" she said.

"Oh no," Phyllis said, embarrassed. She stood up awkwardly, her foot tangled for an instant with the runner, and she almost lost her balance. "I don't think so," she said, steady again. "Just looking."

Back in the aisles of accessories, she hefted a bath set—a heavy blue tub with a detachable plug, baby washcloths, a hooded towel, shampoo, a nail clipper—but put it back finally, discouraged by the prospect of wrapping something so bulky and oddly shaped. She looked at books that squeaked and popped up and played music. She tried on bath puppets, a

terry cloth elephant, a lion, a giraffe. She dialed a toy telephone. She shook rattles.

She fingered bedding, satin-edged flannel baby blankets and
miniature quilts, stitched with the ABC's and little yellow
ducks. On the lower shelf she found a stack of crosshatched
cotton blankets—waffle blankets, Maureen called them—the
kind they used at the hospital nursery and sent home with the
babies. It was Geoff, she thought, who later wore his little
blanket draped over his shoulder as Superman's cape, and Ellie
who slept with hers until it was a frayed and knotted rag. She
held one to her face. It was impossible, she knew, but it
smelled like a baby. They came in white, blue, and pink. And
then it hit her. If Calvin and Kate had a girl, Hal would not be
allowed to see her. It was part of the bargain. Her stomach
sunk with the weight of so many more excuses, so many more
lies, so much more knowing silence. Embarrassed special arrangements into the next century. It felt like remembering
something she had endured in the distant past, like Latin
grammar or cavities drilled without Novocain, something she
could not imagine going through again, never again. She
couldn't do it. It was that simple.

Phyllis put the blanket down and walked out, past a bar-
rel of stuffed animals, past the racks of lullabies on cassette,
past the stern saleswoman, at the checkout now, painstakingly
extracting the white store hangers from a pile of baby
clothes, ringing them up. She gave Phyllis a look as she
walked by, suspicious, but just then, Phyllis didn't give a
damn.

Later, at Mr. Oil Change, waiting for her car, with snow
melting from her boots into dirty puddles on the tile floor and

only torn automotive and hunting magazines on the table in front of her, she pulled the Offenders literature from her purse and started reading. One pamphlet talked about rebuilding what had been destroyed. Trust. Intimacy. It talked about the need for partners to express feelings, to communicate. It occurred to her that Maureen was right, she wasn't the one who should be reading this. It really wasn't for her. I'm not his partner, she thought.

There was another pamphlet entitled *Making Amends.* It was necessary and right, it said, that they, too, strive to clear away "the wreckage of the past." Phyllis thought of an auto wreck, crumpled metal, a wheel spinning in the air, black smoke and sirens, a body slumped against the wheel. She thought about Becky, who was a victim, that's the word the pamphlet used, a little girl who wore braces and loved stuffed animals and hot chocolate with marshmallows. And she thought about Ellie, the picture she'd found in the basement and had been carrying in her billfold, her dark angel in white lace, her first communion, those burning brown eyes. How old had she been? It was essential that everyone make amends, the pamphlet said, "essential" written in all capital letters, like someone shouting. Okay. But it didn't say how.

There was a boy standing over her with something in his hand. "Doesn't look good," he said, and held it out to her, a dirty webbed ring. It was not like anything she had ever seen before, soft fiber bulging with black sludge, a perfect circle of poisonous filth. Phyllis just stared, as if she were in a trance. "Ma'am?" he said. "You want a new one?" he said.

"Yes," she said finally. "By all means. Throw that thing away," she said, but she still couldn't take her eyes off it.

Back home, she dialed slowly, and on the third ring, someone picked up the phone. There was some fumbling and clunking and light breathing on the other end, and then a squeaky little voice said, "Hello," not so much a greeting as a triumphant proclamation. Phyllis could see little hands wrapped around a heavy receiver. "Hello," she said, and the tiny voice said, "Hello," still delighted. It was Ellie's voice, and she was a little girl again.

7

GRACE

KATE'S WATER BROKE AT SIX IN THE MORNING. CALVIN WAS STANDING in front of the bathroom mirror, his chin in the air, a razor poised over his Adam's apple. He had been up and into the office early every day for the past two weeks, hoping to clear the decks before the baby came. He had only Roach to worry about, a messy custody case that he hoped to settle soon or at worst, get continued—this was no time for a trial.

He heard Kate stirring in the bedroom. "Calvin," she said. Her voice sounded peculiar, flattened with shock. He rushed into the room, little flecks of shaving cream spraying onto the hardwood floor. She was sitting on the side of the bed, rubbing her basketball stomach like a good-luck charm. "This is it," she said. "Junior is ready to make his entrance."

He helped her to the bathroom, hovering uselessly at her

elbow like the elderly Red Cross volunteers who lead hulking blood donors to the sugar cookies. He waited outside the door until she said she was all right. He called the office and left a message for his secretary.

While Kate got dressed, Calvin pulled the Lamaze bag from the bottom of her closet. It was his high school gym bag really, red and yellow vinyl, school colors, emblazoned with the somber head of an Indian chief, smelling vaguely of sneakers and bulging now with Kate's nightgown, robe, and slippers. He threw in the two green tennis balls that had been rolling around the bedroom floor for the past two weeks and the cassette tapes he had recorded for the stereo system built into every birthing room, Mozart violin sonatas.

He carried the bag downstairs and made toast and herbal tea. Kate came into the kitchen smiling, a canvas tote bag slung over her shoulder, as if she were going on a trip. They sat at the counter and squeezed their tea bags. "Calvin," Kate said, and waited, perfectly still, her head tilted, as though she were listening for distant hoofbeats, feeling for tremors. "Now that," she said, "was definitely a contraction, I think."

Calvin rinsed the dishes and they put on their coats. "Wait a minute," Kate said. "The painters." What had started as a small project—covering some water stains on the dining room ceiling—had grown since September, wall by wall and room by room, into a full-scale painting of the downstairs. "While they're at it," Kate kept saying. Calvin wasn't thrilled by the prospects, the disruption and the expense, but neither was he handy and willing to do it himself. "Come on, humor me," she had told him. "It's my nesting instinct." Last month, the two painters recommended by one of Kate's well-to-do colleagues had arrived to give an estimate, wearing paper caps and dressed in white, creased and crisp as naval officers, and now, finally, they were scheduled to start the job this morning.

"Okay," Calvin said. "Just a minute." He taped a note to the door and left the spare key in the mailbox. Calvin opened the car door for Kate, and she settled in, the bucket seat pushed back all the way, and they were off.

It was a twenty-minute drive to the hospital—Calvin had timed it, just for fun—but they stopped once at a mailbox so Kate could throw in the last of her shower thank-yous and then again at a convenience store because Kate insisted she wanted something to read. She ran in and emerged with *Time, Redbook,* two daily newspapers, and a bag of fun-sized Snickers. "Don't laugh," she said. "It could be a long day."

By the time they were back on the road, traffic had picked up—it was seven fifty-five now according to the digital dashboard clock—and Calvin changed lanes back and forth in a futile attempt to make better time. He took a shortcut and got stuck behind the flashing red lights of a school bus stopped in the middle of the street while a boy they saw on a porch was wrapped and mittened by his mother, like a hero arming for battle. Kate held the newspapers flat on her lap, but she wasn't looking at them anymore. She was having contractions now, no doubt about it. She grabbed the door handle with both hands and her legs stiffened and she moaned, low and long syllables of misery and disbelief. Then it passed. "I'm okay," she said weakly, but her face was paper white and there were little beads of sweat on her upper lip. Calvin fiddled with the heater vents, sprayed the windshield with bubbling blue cleaner, and prayed they'd make it.

At the hospital at last, he stopped the car in a loading zone, turned the flashers on, and helped Kate out of the car. They rode the freight elevator with a woman in a bathrobe hooked to an IV on wheels. She breathed through her nose in irregular exasperated bursts and stared into the cellophane-wrapped sweet roll she held in her hand. It had white icing and yellow filling, like an egg yolk, and there was a plastic fork jammed into the center. She got off on two, and finally, the doors opened on three, the maternity floor. While they waited at the desk, Kate was stricken with another long contraction. She dropped her newspapers with a thud. ''It's coming,'' she said quietly. ''Right now.''

Calvin felt a strong hand on his elbow. It was a nurse. ''Right this way,'' she said, and led them past a white board with names and times and dilations recorded in red grease pencil like stock market quotes. Olson-Weir had been there for almost twenty-four hours and was only at four. Fernandez was at six and a half. The nurse put them in an examining room and took Kate's blood pressure. She told them there was a birthing room free but it was being cleaned.

The rest was a blur. Waves of amniotic fluid puddling on the floor and Kate, her voice dopey with pain, apologizing for the mess. The paper scrubs someone told him to put on over his clothes, a green hat, like a shower cap, and the delivery room, blinding chrome and bright lights, the doctor's tense eyes above her mask, a team of nurses materializing out of nowhere, their shoes squeaking across the floor. Calvin stood at Kate's head while she pushed and pushed, her fingers digging into his forearm, eyes open but somewhere else, cheering into her ear, chattering like an infielder, talking urgent, loving nonsense.

The doctor said, ''One more strong one,'' and then, there

was a cry. "It's a girl," she said, and held her up, a slippery, bawling bundle. Kate smiled weakly, her lip quivering and tears pooling in her eyes.

Calvin watched the baby's tiny arms and legs twitching and thrashing, full of nervous life, her blue skin, covered with a fine film, turning slowly, miraculously, pink before his eyes as she swallowed her first great gulps of oxygen.

"Have you got a name for your daughter?" the nurse said.

His daughter. It took a moment for it to register, who that was, his daughter. "Yes," Calvin said. He put his finger into the palm of her little red hand. "Grace," he said.

In the recovery room afterward, Kate sat propped with pillows, exhausted and sore, comforted somewhat by the latex glove filled with ice a nurse brought her wrapped in a towel, like an obscene secret, while she talked to her mother on the telephone. Kate held the receiver toward Calvin so he could hear her happy clamor, too, all the way from Duluth. The name was a surprise, for her mother's mother, Kate's favorite grandmother, who'd spoiled her rotten until the day she died, let her drive her Dodge around an empty parking lot on Sunday mornings when she was twelve, baked her Christmas cookies in July.

Then it was Calvin's turn. He turned the big black rotary phone toward him and dialed his parents' number. It was Friday morning, no telling where his father was. He listened to the phone ring once, twice, three times, his finger on the little button, just in case. There was a click and then his voice on tape, tinny and vacant. Calvin waited for the beep. "We have a new baby girl," he said. "Grace. She weighs seven pounds exactly. Kate is fine."

Calvin hung up the phone. He felt a dark gnawing fear, something rabid lurking in the shadows.

"Hey," Kate said. She reached out toward him, her wrist beautiful and frail beneath the plastic hospital bracelet, and touched his chin with a cold finger. "You missed a spot," she said. "A big spot."

Later in the day, after Kate had been moved to a private room, Calvin stood at the plate-glass nursery window while a smiling nurse in a pink cardigan jostled bassinets like bumper cars. She maneuvered little Grace into the front and parked her at the window. She was swaddled tight in a white blanket, a tiny white cap with a pink ribbon pulled low on her head.

Then she opened her eyes. Bottomless, unblinking blue pools. She looked up at him, wrinkled and still and magnificently serene, like some ancient holy sage. On the last day of Lamaze, their instructor had described what newborns really looked like, and projected on the overhead a long gruesome inventory of potential but only temporary irregularities—stork bites, bruises, cone-shaped heads, enlarged genitals—that he and Kate had laughed nervously over on the way home. Nobody told him that she would be beautiful. Something was happening in his chest, a slow subterranean shifting, his heart's own earthquake. Used to be, he wondered about the unfathomable chemistry of parental love, never quite sure what all the fuss was about. So now he knew.

Calvin washed his hands with scented liquid soap, tied on a yellow gown, and asked for Grace at the desk. A nurse disappeared for a moment and then returned, beaming with vicarious pleasure, like a librarian with a rare book or a maître d' with a fine wine, and presented her to him, a neat, sweet-smelling package. There was an oak rocker in the room, and while Kate dozed, Calvin sat with Grace cradled in his arms, studying her face. She had elegant black lashes and the faintest golden suggestions of eyebrows. When she started to fidget in her sleep, her mouth working in little spasms, he talked to her. He explained who he was, where they were, what a hospital was all about.

Later, when Grace had to be returned to the nursery—it was dark already, who knows what time—a fellow brought in a tray of food, mashed potatoes and peas and breaded pork chops, which Kate picked at and Calvin, suddenly ravenous, cleaned down to the bone. He had just broken open the bag of candy bars when his mother and sister Maureen walked into the room, carrying orange visitors' passes, big as license plates.

"Welcome wagon," Phyllis said. She was carrying a bouquet of flowers in a white coffee mug full of sunshine and rainbows. "Another beautiful little Lamm."

"She's gorgeous," Maureen said, and they kissed Kate's cheek ever so gently and patted her shoulder. They pulled up chairs and Calvin told them about their morning—the Lamaze bag they never got around to opening, the newspapers and magazines, Kate's matter-of-fact announcement at the nurse's desk. It made a good story.

Maureen brought out a shopping bag full of pink baby things and held them up while Kate and Phyllis made appreciative noises. They were adorable.

Calvin helped himself to a candy bar and rolled the bedside tray over to Maureen. "Oh, man, Snickers," she said. "No," she said. "Absolutely not."

"Okay," Calvin said.

"Just one," she said, and scooped up a handful.

The phone rang. It was Kate's friends from the office, P.J. and Monica, down in the lobby, waiting for a pass. "We're leaving right now," Phyllis said. "Come on, Maureen." She kissed Kate and hugged Calvin, and held him hard, her arm locked around his neck like a muscular vise.

"Take care of her," she said in his ear. "Do you understand?"

P.J. and Monica came in a few minutes later, with cards and balloons and a computer-generated banner—IT'S A GIRL! it said, in jagged black letters—that they taped across the window. What was it like? they wanted to know. "Not that bad," Kate said. "A piece of cake." Even her laugh was exhausted now, like a recording played at a slower speed. While they chatted, Kate's eyes got heavier and heavier, and by the time they announced on the loudspeaker that visiting hours were over, she was fast asleep, her Styrofoam cup of water still clasped in her hand. Calvin thanked P.J. and Monica for coming, gave them each a candy bar for the road, and they tiptoed out. He pried the cup out of Kate's hand, sat in the rocker and closed his eyes, and must have drifted off himself for just a minute. A nurse touched his arm. "You can come back at seven tomorrow."

"Okay," he said. "Okay." He took his coat from the closet and straightened the banner and filled Kate's pitcher. He left her door open a crack.

It was quiet on the floor, a couple of rooms flickering silently with the light of a television, the nurse at the station bent over her paperwork. Calvin walked past a long line of wheelchairs, collapsed and jammed together like shopping carts at the grocery, and turned the corner. The hall lights had been dimmed, but back-lit by the red elevator light, he could see a blocky figure in an overcoat, standing at the nursery window, the flesh of a face reflected in the glass. Calvin stopped, and the man turned away, executed two quick steps, like a military maneuver, and disappeared inside a door under the exit sign.

Calvin ran to the window, cupped his hands around his face, and squinted into the nursery. There was Grace, angled right in front, her little chest rising and falling peacefully.

He turned and, across the hall, opened the door and stepped inside the stairwell. There was an orange metal railing and a big red 3 painted on the wall. He leaned his head over the rail, and peered into the shadows below, hearing the sound of leather soles clattering down the concrete steps, turning and turning into the darkness.

Calvin drove home in a sort of altered state, jumpy and raw. The world looked different to him, more vivid, full of mysterious purpose and unlikely beauty. A woman in earmuffs was pumping her own gas under the bright lights at SuperAmerica, her breath appearing in little steamy clouds, like smoke signals. A black-and-red-checked arm at the McDonald's drive-through was reaching from a VW beetle up to the window, straining, like Michelangelo's Adam, for a white bag of food. Even Kate's *Redbook* on the dashboard struck him as poignant and precious, like something you should put in a scrapbook.

There was an ad on the radio for *Loving Me, Loving You,* a videotape featuring Dr. Jerry Murray. "I will show you how to develop mature love," Dr. Murray said. "If you already have love in your intimate relationships, that's terrific. I'll show you how to intensify it.'' Calvin pushed in a tape—The Pretenders—and turned it up until the speakers shook.

He couldn't say for sure that it had been his father at the window. A dark overcoat, a pale forehead, black leather shoes. It could have been anybody. Why would he have come? It didn't make any sense. But he couldn't forget it. A man standing over his baby, breathing on the glass.

At home, when Calvin pushed the front door open, he knew right away that something was wrong. Thought for an instant not just that they'd been robbed, but that there was a robbery in progress. The living room, illuminated by their neighbor's floodlight seeping eerily through a side window, was empty, the rug removed and the bare wood floor shimmering silver, like a ghostly stage. There was a tall shadow looming near the stairs, a glowing red light, some murmuring. It smelled like chemicals. Then Calvin remembered: the painters.

He found the front hall light. There were two big white buckets just inside the door and a tray of brushes. The shadow was a stepladder: on the top step, there was a trouble light wrapped in its cord and a paint-flecked boom box playing softly, a talk show.

Calvin turned the radio off and walked slowly from room to room. The living room furniture had been pushed into the kitchen and covered with a canvas drop cloth, a single lumpy shape, like some curious contraption about to be unveiled. There was a pizza box balanced on the garbage pail and two empty Coke bottles on the counter.

The dining room floor was flecked with dust and paint chips, and the long crack snaking across the ceiling was filled with gray spackle. The window frames had been painted glossy white—eggshell, it was called on the chart. He found the telephone and answering machine, both plugged in, stacked together on the floor. He sat down beside them, cross-legged, and replayed the messages: three hang-ups, a screaming prerecorded sales pitch for siding, and another hang-up, this one with faint jangling music in the background.

Calvin hadn't seen his father since that day in September, laid out in his chair, puffy and bloated, a horrible grinning corpse. At that moment, he knew what he knew, and it made him sick. He had walked out and got some fresh air and tried his best not to think about it. Gone home and pulled Kate to him and held her as tight as he dared. But now, on the happiest day of his life, his father was back, a menacing reflection looming in the dark.

When the phone rang, shrill and echoing in the empty room, Calvin started. He grabbed it before it rang again. It was Kate. "Guess who's here?" she said.

"Who?" he said. "Who is it?"

"Our little angel, who do you think? All dressed up for her midnight feeding. We're figuring it out together, and she's being very patient. I wish you could see her right now."

"Me too," Calvin said.

Calvin parked in front of the house and killed the engine. It was after midnight now, the streets deserted, an old-fashioned green street lamp flickering yellow on the boulevard. The curtains were drawn, but there was a light burning in the living room. Calvin sat behind the wheel, watching the house, like a cop on surveillance, imagining the life inside, his father planted in the living room, his mother in her bedroom with her ladies' magazines, diets and recipes, and her lists, birthdays and anniversaries, things to do. He imagined years ago, what it looked like, the same clapboard and black front door, flower boxes and shutters, and inside, he would be in his makeshift bedroom on the third floor, his own little world, football posters tacked onto the slanted eaves, tucked into his road rally bedclothes, and beneath him, somewhere in the house, his father, moving through the dark, prowling.

Calvin got out of the car and walked slowly toward the house. It was crazy, he knew, but couldn't stop. He stood in a frozen flower bed and peered through a crack in the curtains into the living room. His father was in his chair in front of the television, his bare feet, veiny and pink, elevated on a hassock, his toes long and elegant as fingers. A newspaper and a glass of milk were sitting on the carpet at the side of his chair, and the remote control was tucked into the breast pocket of his white shirt. He had a pen in hand and a pad or little book in his lap, which he was studying thoughtfully, glancing from it to the television. Keeping score? Working a puzzle? Alone, after midnight, absorbed by his game and bathed in the light of the television, he looked as Calvin had never seen him before, content, at ease, pleased with himself, quietly amused.

Calvin stepped through a tangle of shrubs and up the porch steps. He knocked hard on the storm door and just kept knocking, beating out a slow, insistent, punishing rhythm, like a battering ram. The porch light went on overhead, and his father opened the door a crack and peered out, squinting.

''Dad,'' Calvin said.

''Who's there?'' his father said. ''Calvin? Is that you?''

''It's me,'' Calvin said.

"Well," he said. "The proud papa." He undid the latch and opened the door.

Calvin grabbed him by the shoulders and shook him. His father felt flimsy, hollow bones and papier-mâché. "Stay away from her or I'll kill you," Calvin said. "Do you understand? Do you understand?" His father's face was white and soft, his eyes wide and vacant. His glasses flew off, and he started to stutter. He was a scared old man.

His father wrapped his arms around Calvin, like a fighter in a clinch, grabbed Calvin's jacket with desperate fists and hung on, and for a moment, they were dancing, a jerky, violent two-step, and then Calvin shed him, pushed him off, away, threw him in an ecstasy of muscular release over the precipice of the steps, and turned and left him there, writhing and thrashing in the bushes like a gut-shot deer.

8

THE STORM OF
THE CENTURY

On the Monday after Christmas, when the local weathermen were predicting what might be the storm of the century, Phyllis arrived at the Greater Buffalo International Airport—two dingy terminals smelling of popcorn and sawdust—with a big plaid suitcase on wheels, a shopping bag full of wrapped gifts for Lucy, and two Sunday newspapers, both the *Minneapolis Tribune* and the *St. Paul Dispatch,* for Ellie, who, she always seemed to believe, was starved for news about her hometown. To Walter, she looked different, older, of course—it had been years since he'd seen her last—but also smaller, shorter and more stooped, not just the slow shrinking of age, but heavy with misery, as if buried in her suitcase or hidden at the bottom of her shopping bag were dense lead weights of sorrow. She kissed Walter's cheek and hugged Ellie cautiously

and softly patted her back. Lucy, who had been prepped with
photographs and stories and had bubbled with talk of Grandma
for the past week, turned shy at the last minute and clung to
Ellie's leg, intimidated apparently by the real thing, Grandma-
in-the-flesh.

Walter drove the wagon home, and watched Phyllis in the
rearview mirror next to Lucy in her car seat. Phyllis asked
questions, until Lucy finally announced, ''I'm a little bashful,
please.'' A minute or two passed in silence and then Phyllis
fished a book from the floor and asked Lucy if she wanted to
read. It was *Cinderella,* the colorful Disney version, which Ellie
despised. Lucy couldn't get enough of it. ''Yes, please,'' Lucy
said, and that seemed to break the ice. When they pulled into
the driveway, Cinderella had just placed her foot in the glass
slipper and Lucy was clapping her hands in delight. ''This is
it,'' Walter said.

He carried the bags in while Phyllis looked around the
house. She admired everything, the woodwork, the rugs,
Lucy's drawings on the refrigerator. Phyllis had never been to
Buffalo before. Too busy right now, she would write. When
the fares drop. After the holidays. As soon as Maureen finds a
regular sitter. The real reason, of course, was Hal. He wasn't
welcome, they all knew it, and for better or worse, it seemed,
they were a couple, joined together by unfathomable iron
bonds of dependence or shared history or maybe just a need to
keep up appearances. They sent out a Christmas card with a
photograph every year, the two of them all smiles, like a pub-
licity photo, as if he were running for office. Now Phyllis was
traveling alone and it wasn't clear whether this was a vacation
or some sort of transition.

Lucy opened her gifts—a blue denim purse, a book about
whales, a ballerina's tiara, a raccoon hand puppet that looked

almost real—while Ellie busied herself in the kitchen with coffee and crackers. Walter knew that she'd had her doubts about the visit. She was suspicious. ''Why?'' she had asked him. ''Why *now?*'' Phyllis had called and talked it over with her two or three more times, and assured her that it was just to catch up. She wanted to take it easy—no guided tours, nothing fancy. She wanted to see their house, play with Lucy, cook them a dinner. That was all. Finally Ellie agreed. She really liked the idea of her mother making dinner. ''I'm going to hold her to that,'' she told Walter.

Ellie brought a tray into the living room. Walter turned on the radio, and they listened to the weather. A lake-snow advisory, the announcer was saying. Up to twenty inches in the snow belt, blowing and drifting. Poor visibility. ''My goodness,'' Phyllis said. Snow squalls and possible whiteouts. Walter explained that no matter what Jay Leno might say, it really didn't snow that much in Buffalo. Ellie suggested that, given the weather, Walter and Lucy should take Phyllis to the grocery now to get what she needed for her dinner, while she finished up a little bit of work she had left to do. ''Yes,'' Phyllis said quickly, ''of course.'' She seemed nervous, if not exactly frightened by Ellie, then at least a little timid, deferential. If Ellie wanted her to go shopping, she was going to go shopping.

Just a few wet flakes of snow were falling, but the grocery store was packed, the aisles jammed with people filling their carts—canned goods, milk, eggs—with a kind of controlled urgency. Walter, who did most of the shopping, liked to go alone, at odd hours. It felt strange to be there with Phyllis. He worked from a list and used coupons. Phyllis seemed a bit overwhelmed. She wandered ahead of the cart, like someone in a museum, studying the lobsters in the seafood section, the array of gourmet cheeses, the roasted chickens in the deli. She took a sample of something on a toothpick from a woman with a frying pan and a spray can of cooking oil. "Only thirty-five calories," the woman said, but Walter said no thanks. Lucy perched happily in the cart, her new tiara glittering on her head, and nibbled a cinnamon-raisin bagel Walter had snatched for her from an almost empty bin.

Phyllis finally found her way to the meat counter, where she stood, a little perplexed, squinting at the steaks and chops. She rang the bell and asked the butcher a question, and then she pointed at a big hunk of red meat, which he wrapped and taped and marked with a red pencil. She grabbed a bag of potatoes, carrots and onions, some spices. While Walter and Lucy waited in line to check out, she circled back to the bakery and returned with a cherry pie.

On the way home Walter pointed out what might be of interest, but there wasn't much—the park, some fancy houses. Phyllis talked about the grocery store. Walter didn't know her very well. She seemed nice enough.

Back home, Walter put the groceries on the counter, and Phyllis found an apron and tied it on. Walter showed her how to light the burners, where the pots and pans were, how to work the microwave.

Ellie was in the living room reading a book. "What did she get?" she asked Walter, and he told her, a roast, potatoes, vegetables. "Grandma's Sunday dinner," she said. "She used to make it for us, too, I think, back before she discovered KFC. Well," she said. "That's something. I'm starved."

Ellie got up and headed into the kitchen. She left her book cracked open on the table, another mystery from the library. Lately she brought them home by the armload. Walter, who liked history and biography, books about the Civil War and

Lincoln, didn't get it. In real life, people dropped dead from heart attacks or wasted away with cancer and AIDS and cirrhosis. Sometimes they got shot in drug deals or got hit by drunk drivers. In mysteries, everybody got murdered, one after another, by the most bizarre means imaginable—poisoned ink, ice picks, silk cords, deadly scorpions. On the cover of Ellie's book was an ivory-handled dagger, red with blood. Walter had always assumed that what Ellie liked was that if you read carefully and paid attention to every detail, you could figure it out yourself. He picked up the book, marked Ellie's place with the library card, and turned to the first chapter.

Walter read a few pages and looked up. He could see Ellie in the kitchen. She was leaning on the counter with her arms folded, watching her mother, who was working at the cutting board with a big knife. She was chopping carrots, very deliberately, and Walter could hear the slow whack-whack-whack of the blade on the board. Ellie wasn't saying anything. She looked stern, as if she were supervising something.

Walter lifted his legs onto the couch, set the book on his chest, and closed his eyes. When he woke up, he could smell something cooking and hear voices. He sat up and peered into the kitchen. Phyllis was at the table, holding a coffee cup, talking to a raccoon. She was asking questions—"Are you getting hungry? What would you like for dinner?"—and the raccoon rubbed its chin with little brown paws and answered in a squeaky falsetto, "Yes. Grass and leaves, please." Lucy was working the puppet from under the table, where she was squatting, grinning like a gargoyle, peeking around the ledge of the table up at her grandmother's face. Ellie was nowhere in sight.

Walter stood up and stretched. He walked to the front window and pulled back the curtain. It was dark now, and the street lamp on the boulevard was shining. Electric candles burned in every window of the Hassenfratzes' house across the street, and next to them, the Kormans had a spotlight planted in their front yard shining on their extravagant Christmas decorations: blinking lights in the bushes, giant candy canes lining the walk, Santa landing on the roof in a red sleigh, a mechanical Mrs. Claus rocking on the porch with a handful of knitting. There had been a light dusting of snow only, no more than an inch or two, and it was blowing now in little swirls, like miniature white dust storms. Next door, old Mr. Mitchell, wearing a black fur cap big as a wild animal, was clearing his front steps with a push-broom. The storm of the century had never materialized. It must have passed over or veered off at the last minute. Walter decided to let the snow go for now; he could shovel in the morning.

Phyllis called him to dinner. In the dining room the overhead light was dimmed, and the table was set with cloth napkins and their good stoneware and two tall candles. Lucy ran in from the kitchen with the red plate—"YOU ARE SPECIAL TO-DAY," it said in white lettering—and switched it with the one at Phyllis's place. Ellie came in, kissed Lucy, and sat down. They held hands and Lucy recited her nursery school's grace.

"Amen," Phyllis said.

They filled their plates, but there was something wrong with the food. The meat was overdone and stringy, the carrots were rubbery, and the potatoes weirdly blackened, as if they had been dyed. There were big floury lumps in the gravy. Everything smelled like smoke.

Nobody said anything. Lucy held the raccoon in one hand, her fork in the other. She pushed things around on her plate, but she wasn't eating. The raccoon dipped its face into her glass of milk and emerged with a white spot on its snout.

Phyllis sat with her hands on her lap, staring down at her plate. She looked as if she might cry. But Ellie, who never cared much for meat, was forking up big pieces of black beef. She looked stiff as a West Point cadet eating by the numbers. Walter broke open a potato. It looked normal inside. He took a small bite and chewed it slowly. They sat there in silence. A wind rattled the storm windows, and Lucy hummed quietly to herself. Ellie's knife and fork clicked.

"I'm sorry," Phyllis said. "This is a disaster. I forgot to set the timer. I used too much liquid smoke."

"That's okay," Walter said. "Don't worry about it." Ellie kept putting it away, bite after bite.

"I'm sorry," Phyllis said again. "I'm sorry for everything," she said, and made a big sweeping gesture, across the entire table and beyond. She stood and took her plate into the kitchen.

She was scraping her plate into the garbage when Walter came in. She looked up at him. "Ellie thinks I know how to cook," she said. Her eyes were wet. "I never did. I never knew what I was doing. I still don't." Walter took the plate from her and put it in the dishwasher.

"What about that pie?" he said.

Phyllis cut four big slabs and Walter scooped ice cream. When they brought it into the dining room, Ellie's plate was clean, and she was talking quietly to Lucy. Lucy smiled. "Grandma was sad," Lucy said. "But now she's happy again. Okay?"

Once Lucy was in bed, they settled on the couch in the living room to watch the family movies Phyllis had brought along with her from Minneapolis. Maureen recently had had them

transferred to videotape and given them to Phyllis as a Christmas present. For some reason, Ellie could not recall ever having seen them before. Years ago, Phyllis explained, Uncle
Charlie borrowed the projector, and then he moved to Chi-
cago, and they never saw it again. Eventually Hal lost interest
in home movies.

Walter put the tape in and adjusted the tracking. The film
began with several short and shaky glimpses of billowy white
clouds in a blue sky and the branches of a birch tree. "That's
our front yard," Phyllis said.

"I climbed that tree," Ellie said. "I carved my initials on
it."

There is the house, white clapboard with black shutters,
some nondescript shrubs in the front bed and a window box
full of red flowers. There is too much sunlight and everything—the house, the lawn, the sidewalk—seems to be tinted
yellow. The camera slowly circles a car parked at the curb, a
Buick Roadmaster with big fins and whitewall tires. "Hal
loved that car," Phyllis said. "We drove it until there were
holes in the floorboards."

A little girl and boy are coming down the front walk together, all dressed up, a well-groomed little couple. Maureen
and Geoff. She is eight, maybe nine years old, wearing a yellow dress and white gloves. He is wearing a white shirt and a
narrow black tie. He has a sport coat folded over his arm and
his hair is combed wet with a little bump in front. Maureen
sticks her tongue out at the camera as she goes by.

Little Ellie appears in the front door with something on her
head, a round white hat with a ribbon, and she steps outside
and stands on the porch, dressed in a blue sailor dress, squinting, her thick black hair cut short and curling around her ears,

her little hand raised to the camera, waving, waving. She looks down, toward her feet, and tugs nervously at her skirts—just like Lucy when she is shy—and waves some more.

"Bye bye," Phyllis said to Ellie's image on the screen, her voice soft and sad. Walter turned to her on the couch. Her hand was raised, waving. "Bye bye," she said.

Then everything is black. A red light appears, bobbing faintly in the foreground. There is some shadowy movement, more red lights, what looks like smoke. Then white letters: GREAT NORTHERN.

"The train wreck in Wisconsin," Phyllis said. "Remember? We were at the Howard Johnson's and we heard that horrible noise right out back? Hal spent practically the whole night out there. I didn't know he had his camera."

Walter leaned forward, but he couldn't make out very much. The shape of a man dragging something. A splintered crossing arm, bent rails. It went on and on. The reel dissolved finally into bright white circles and ended, but on the next one, there was more of the same. Ellie got up and held the fast forward button, and the machine whirred and the scene jumped, an emergency vehicle, a man directing a crane with frantic, crazily speeded-up gestures.

Watching this, seeing the world through his father-in-law's camera, this furious chaos of disaster, Walter wondered whether this was what it felt like to be him. It gave him the creeps. What kind of man took so much footage of a train wreck? Walter knew the type, saw them all the time on the job. They listened to police-band radios and followed sirens and arrived at accidents not just to gawk—Walter could understand that, it was human nature, he supposed—but to record it all on their video cameras. They were news hounds, they would say, looking to sell something to the networks. But Walter knew they loved the spectacle, the blood sport, the broken glass and twisted limbs.

The whole next roll had been double-exposed. There is a shot of Phyllis framed in the window of a car. She is wearing dark glasses and a beret with a feather dangling from it. "Look at that hat," Phyllis said. "My God."

"You had style, Mom," Ellie said. "You really did." Phyllis looks glamorous but gaunt, and Walter imagined he could feel some invisible aura of unhappiness clinging to her, even then, like the smell of smoke on your clothes.

Superimposed over Phyllis is a scene of the children welcoming a new baby. They are sitting on the couch, lined up oldest to youngest, right to left, Maureen, Geoff, and Ellie, all waiting their turn to hold baby Calvin. Maureen, with heavy black glasses now, is wearing a surgical mask—"She had a cold," Phyllis explained to Walter. Maureen gently and expertly supports the head and passes Calvin, a blue bundle, on to Geoff. Ellie leans over and peeks, her legs quivering with excitement, but Geoff is possessive and half-turns away, like someone who doesn't like his newspaper read over his shoulder. He strokes the baby's cheek, a little roughly, and then looks up, as if reprimanded. All the while, the image of Phyllis remains on the screen, still staring eerily straight ahead, the green scenery whizzing by behind her.

One scene follows the next, birthdays and holidays mostly, a frenzy of unwrapping and a tangle of torn paper, circles of candles burning in one cake after another. The films are not quite in order, so that sometimes the children grow older, sometimes younger from reel to reel: suddenly, after attending a school dance in a fancy gown, Maureen's front teeth are missing again. Then the Buick is back and the siding is off the house, and Phyllis—who is glimpsed only rarely and then mostly in part, her hands cutting a cake or unzipping a snowsuit—seems almost girlish again.

Nothing lasts very long. There is a little bit of some sort of Halloween parade—a stream of costumed kids marching down the street in broad daylight, a soldier in green fatigues, a pirate holding a stuffed parrot in place on his shoulder, an Indian chief with an elaborate headdress, a red Crayola crayon—but before Walter could begin to guess who's who, it's over.

Then in a picnic area at twilight, surrounded by redwood tables and coolers, a broad-shouldered man in a V-neck sweater with black hair and glasses is lighting sparklers and handing them out to a line of kids. Maureen and Geoff tear off with theirs but Ellie lingers by his side, too frightened to move. The man leans down and speaks to her. She hands her sparkler to him, a sizzling baton, and with great flair, he executes a precise orange pattern of lines and loops in the night air, almost certainly writing her name in grand fiery letters. Ellie claps her hands in delight, and the man smiles down at her, a slow, slightly crooked grin full of affection. Phyllis appears suddenly from the shadows behind the man, touches him on the arm, and points into the distance. They stand together side by side, Ellie curled around their legs, staring off into the darkness.

Then it's bright sunshine again, and an old man in rimless glasses and denim overalls pushes a wheelbarrow full of dirt across a lawn and pauses to wipe his forehead with a white handkerchief. In a dimly lit kitchen, a baby gets a bath in the sink. After that, Ellie, maybe eight years old, wearing a pointed party hat, cautiously opens a wooden crate, lifts out a grotesquely long white rabbit, and drapes it over her shoulder. "Flopsy," Ellie said. There are a few seconds of a motorcade—helmeted cops on cycles, a downtown street lined with spectators—and then Flopsy is back again, hopping a zigzag path through the living room, sitting in a box of shredded paper, nibbling a lettuce leaf.

Next is a crowded public beach: white sand and blankets and plastic chairs, women in straw hats and sunglasses, men with hairy chests and beer guts, the long legs of a lifeguard's chair, a boy in a crewcut—Calvin?—with an inflatable dragon locked around his waist. Ellie, in a dark one-piece with a ruffle skirt, wearing a rubber bathing cap, her nose covered with white lotion, her eyes closed tight, one of a row of bodies lying on towels, shoulder-to-shoulder sunbathers. There is a look of grim determination on her face. The camera, hovering almost immediately above her now, moves over her slowly, from head to foot, shoulders and chest and legs, lingering and lingering, too long. Suddenly the screen explodes with snow and crackling static. Ellie was standing over the television. "Enough of that," she said.

Walter sat on the edge of their bed, paging through the sports section of the Minneapolis paper, while Ellie stood looking into the oval mirror of her antique dresser, getting ready for bed. She was wearing red thermal long johns, a matching long-sleeved top, and a pair of gray wool skating socks. (She was always cold in the winter and used to express amazement and gratitude that in bed Walter seemed to throw heat, like an electric appliance.) They could hear Phyllis running water in the bathroom.

The newspaper was just a prop. Walter enjoyed her evening

ritual, the applying of lotion, the brushing of her hair, and even though he never fully understood its purpose—why primp to go to bed?—he loved to watch. But he pretended not to, and she pretended there was nothing of a performance about it, though Walter was sure there was, sometimes.

But not tonight. She was completely absorbed, working furiously, brushing her hair so savagely it must have hurt, her lips moving silently, talking to herself. While they had sipped their coffee in the kitchen, she had looked stunned, like someone who had just witnessed a horrible accident. Walter wanted to reach her. He wanted to throw her a rope. But he never knew the right thing to say. So he made small talk. At least it was a human noise.

"You were a cute kid, Ellie," he said.

Walter heard footsteps in the hall, the slow scuffing of bedroom slippers, and then the door to Lucy's room creaked open. Phyllis was looking in on her.

"That little blue suit," he said. "We should get one for Lucy."

She nodded and kept brushing.

"Who was that guy with the sparklers?" Walter said. "Your uncle?"

"What?" Ellie said. She looked at him in the smoky bureau mirror.

"The guy with the sparklers," Walter said. "He had those glasses, he looked like Clark Kent. Is that your uncle?"

"Why would you ask about him?" She pointed the hairbrush at him in the mirror like a weapon.

"I don't know." Walter put the paper down. He was somebody special, it was obvious. The way he looked at Ellie. "Was that Uncle Charlie?"

"No," she said sadly. "That wasn't Uncle Charlie."

"Who then? Who was it?" Walter said. "What's the mystery?"

She turned around to face him. "His name was Jack Brady. He lived across the street from us. I think my mother had an affair with him."

They lay in bed, the digital alarm clock glowing red, the steam radiators sputtering, and whispered late into the night. Walter listened while Ellie spun out her theory. Her mother must have been overwhelmed with the babies, her husband was always on the road, fooling around even then, no doubt; she was lonely, and Jack Brady was a nice man. It made sense, Ellie told Walter. His wife Maggie was manic-depressive, everybody knew it. She was a pale woman with big watery eyes. She spent most of her time indoors, and when she did venture out, she wore a big coat and dark glasses and a scarf on her head, like a celebrity in disguise. At home she listened to screechy opera recordings which, in the summer, you could hear a half a block away. Jack loved children, but they didn't have any of their own. Everybody used to feel a little sorry for him. More than once they saw him at night, in the driveway across the street, sitting in his car with the overhead light on, reading a book. He must have been desperate to get away, but too loyal to really leave.

Ellie could remember that he spent a lot of time at their house. When her father was out of town, he would come over with a cold bottle of Budweiser shoved in his pants pocket— Maggie didn't like drinking—and would sip it at the kitchen table and chat. He sang nonsense songs in a deep baritone and laughed at Ellie's riddles and never once raised his voice. He taught her to play poker, and they used to play acey-deucey, betting with whatever was on hand, pretzels, toothpicks, and M&M's, which Jack used to bring over by the pound. He was an engineer and knew how to fix things. When their water heater broke one day, and her mother stood sobbing in a puddle of water down the basement, Ellie ran to get him, and he came over with his red toolbox, and everything was okay. "I loved him too," Ellie said. "He was a good man. He always smiled at me. I used to pretend he was my father."

When she was in fourth grade, Ellie said, Jack Brady was killed in a car accident. He was up north, and late one night, his car went off the road and hit a tree. Her mother went to pieces. She couldn't get out of bed the day of the funeral. "That's when she started her serious drinking in the basement," Ellie said. "That's exactly when it was."

When it was time to leave, she said, Jack Brady would never say good-bye. He would say, "See you all of a sudden," which they all thought was funny. Ellie said it again, aloud, "See you all of a sudden."

There was a noise outside, and Walter got up and went to the window. A yellow city truck was coming down the street, its blue light flashing, a thin trail of sand spreading from the tailgate. He watched it rumble out of sight. Across the street, Mrs. Claus had fallen out of her chair on the Kormans' porch: in the white beam of the floodlight, he could see that the rocker was tipped on its side, and she was lying next to it, wiggling rhythmically back and forth across the steps in quick convulsive starts, as if she were having a seizure. Walter didn't know what to think. Could it be true? He was not naive nor had his life been particularly sheltered, but Ellie's family had taught him some things. That adults could do the unspeakable to children. That his wife could be unhinged by their invisible demons. That he had it in him to wish another man dead, dead, dead, and burned in the darkest corner of hell. So grandmothers had their secrets, too. Maybe it all boiled down to this: anything was possible.

9

THE OLD

FAMILIAR PLACES

It was a soft tissue injury, so nothing showed up on the X ray, but it still hurt like hell. Back in December, Doc Kessler had clipped up the picture so they could study it together, Hal's backbone, notched and segmented, in ghostly outline. Kessler had used a pointer and recited the names, cervical vertebrae, thoracic, lumbar, everything normal. He was a small, scholarly, silver-haired man with a neatly trimmed mustache and a kind of Old World dignity. He had treated Hal for years, administered his flu shots, monitored his blood pressure, persuaded him years ago to quit cigarettes.

Kessler shrugged. There was nothing he could do for him. He gave him a brace and the name of a chiropractor and wrote him a script for a muscle relaxant.

"How did it happen?" Kessler wanted to know.

Hal didn't have an answer ready. "I was mugged," he said at last.

"Mugged?" Kessler looked at him, surprised, genuinely pained. He shook his head sadly. "What a world," he said. "What a world."

Hal felt best when he was behind the wheel, snug and secure, his neck and spine pressed firmly against the back of the driver's seat, Sinatra on the speakers. He'd seen him at Caesar's in the early sixties, in his prime, before he'd thickened up and grown jowly. He was smooth as silk back then, the chairman of the board. He sang all the old songs, "I'll Be Seeing You," "Night and Day," "Come Fly with Me," "I've Got You Under My Skin."

At these times, it seemed to Hal that it was the world, and not him, that was behind glass, enclosed and encapsulated, the houses with their smoking chimneys, children in stocking caps and scarves, snowflakes flying, just like a domed paperweight, a snow globe.

"No fault," Phyllis told him. "Like a car accident. That's the way it's done nowadays." She had talked to a lawyer already and filed the papers. Now, after almost forty years. They were in the kitchen. It was a late morning in the middle of January, Martin Luther King Day, the holiday no one knew how to observe. Outside, it was twenty degrees below zero. The window above the sink was etched with frost in complex swirls, like an elegant work of ice-cold art.

Hal tried to concentrate on what Phyllis was saying, but his neck was killing him. She sounded rehearsed, oddly formal, as if she were speaking someone else's lines. She kept moving around—at the sink, fiddling with the disposal switch. Working her way down the counters with a sponge. Peering into the refrigerator. She wouldn't hold still. Jammed into his brace, Hal could move only slowly and awkwardly, turretlike, head, neck, and shoulders all together. He couldn't get a bead on her.

Hal packed up the next day, a couple of suitcases and some boxes. He resolved to travel light. He was downsizing, Hal told himself. He read the business page. It was a normal, even desirable, part of the business cycle. But after slamming the trunk and sliding behind the wheel, he looked to the house and saw Phyllis standing in the window, still and stately, watching him, and he knew that this was it, something horrible and final. He drove off, having glimpsed it, what had become of his life, his throat constricting, nearly choking on it.

He took a room at the Midway Motor Inn on University Avenue in St. Paul. The room was decent, and it was cheap. There were coffee and pastries in the lobby every morning, and he was only a couple of blocks from I-94. But he didn't have a garage, so when another cold snap hit—below zero for six days straight, windchills like Siberia—he had to go out a couple of times a night and start the car. He bundled himself in his overcoat, scarf, gloves, fur hat, but still it was frightening. His eyebrows stiffened with frost. A layer of snow on the pavement squeaked beneath his shoes, like Styrofoam. The stillness was eerie, unearthly. The parking lot was a desolate planet.

During the day, he made a few calls. He went to his court-
ordered sessions and told the social worker what she wanted
to hear. At night he watched television in his room. He took
his pills and propped himself up with pillows. One night he
called for a girl. An hour and a half later, one showed up,
wearing jeans and a lacy blouse tied above her waist, no coat.
Angel, she said her name was. She was blond, bleary and
washed out, on drugs maybe, jangly and distracted, as if she
were hearing voices, or tuned into something on invisible
headphones.

Hal tried to talk to her, but she wasn't interested. She did
what she did and jammed the money in her jeans. Hal thanked
her and said good-bye, but she didn't respond. She closed her
eyes and coughed, a deep miserable rattle. And then stepped
out the door, into the deadly cold darkness.

Behind the wheel at four in the morning, running the car in
the parking lot, going nowhere, Hal imagined what it would
be like. Carbon monoxide was a colorless, odorless gas, but it
was lethal. Some people listened to music while they waited.

St. Joseph stared at him blankly, brown and bearded, a
chipped hand raised in awkward benediction, votive candles
flickering at his feet. Hal realized too late, after slipping into
his customary pew at St. Mark's, right side, near the front,
that in his condition, it was a mistake. To see Monsignor
Mulville, at the lectern now, delivering his homily, he had to
shift his whole torso in the cramped pew, and his feet got

tangled in the kneelers. Finally he gave up, sat still and straight, and studied the shrine in front of him and listened.

Hal wasn't sure why he had come to Sunday mass, *his* mass. He was in pain. He was afraid that he was disappearing, ceasing slowly to exist, fading gradually away. He wanted to see some friendly faces; he wanted to be where he belonged. He wanted to hear something about redemption. Maybe, after mass, Hal thought, he could ask Mulville to hear his confession.

Now Mulville was preaching about duty, rightful obligation. He was a small man who spoke in a nasal whine. His favorite words were of the weakest sort: "suggest," "invite," "attempt." This was the traditional mass, no guitars, and nobody wanted fire and brimstone. Mulville loved good wine and classic cars, had a vintage VW convertible in the rectory garage that he drove only in summer. Hal had never been quite clear on what vows were required, whether poverty was among them or not. Mulville finished, gathered his robes, and sat down. From the back of the church, there was a sneeze and the sound of a woman's irritated voice. "How should I know?" she was saying. "Look in my purse."

At the offertory, Joe Thornton came around to take up the collection. Hal had passed him on the way in, whispering with Tony Ramos and a new guy, the three of them huddled in the ushers' back pew, like the bullpen. Joe worked for the state and had a couple of kids in college. He used to be president of the church council and became one of the first eucharistic ministers back in the seventies, when things opened up. Joe stared at him. Hal had left his neck brace at the motel, but he still must have looked odd, bent unnaturally, as he reached stiffly for his wallet. Joe raised an eyebrow, maybe surprised, maybe something else. Impossible to read. Hal couldn't say what the man was thinking. How much did he know? What were they saying about him in the back pew? Hal laid a five on the plate and handed it on.

When it was time for communion, Hal stood and made his way down his pew. He glanced at Joe, standing in the center aisle, his usher's pin in the lapel of his blue blazer, God's sworn sheriff. Hal folded his hands and shuffled toward Monsignor Mulville and his golden chalice.

Bless me, Father, he would say, for I have sinned. Hal hadn't gone for years. By the time the children were old enough, confession had become penance and then something else, even less intimidating, reconciliation. What he remembered best was the smell, furniture polish and nervous sweat, his own and the priest's too. When he got to the end of his list, modest amounts of impatience and anger, sloth and greed, the priests always sounded relieved, Mulville or one of his young associates, whoever it was hunched there in the darkness on the other side of the screen, glad that it was just that and no more, as if they were not quite up to absolving transgressions of the darkest sort. There were things that even they didn't want to hear about, not really. Sometimes he said his prayers afterward, sometimes not. It didn't seem to make any difference.

Hal approached the altar, like the rest of them, hands clasped, the whole congregation, all looking grim and beaten down, like prisoners of war on some sort of death march. Finally, they were face to face. Monsignor Mulville, burst blood vessels mapping his face, who even at the monthly meetings of the Holy Name Society used to arrive smelling suspiciously of what he liked to call liquid refreshment.

"Body of Christ."

Hal didn't believe any of it, really, maybe he never had, not the body and blood, not the resurrection of the dead, not Lazarus, not the forgiveness of sins, not the life and the world to come. Nothing. And Mulville didn't believe it, either. He was going through the motions, Hal suspected, suffering with his own imploded, ingrown desires. He should absolve Hal?

"Amen," Hal said, and took the host in his cupped hand. Maybe all of them were right, maybe he was sick, but there was no cure for him, not here.

Hal placed the wafer on his tongue and made the sign of the cross. He circled down the outside aisle, past his pew, past the heavy oak confessionals and the stations of the cross, Jesus falling a third time, toward the ushers in the back of the church. Joe Thornton held out a bulletin to Hal, insistent as some political crazy on a street corner, but Hal brushed by him, out the door and into his car, the taste of the host lingering in his mouth, brittle and bland, like starched paper.

Hal drove down Dillard out of habit, and before he knew it, he was there. Gibbon was lined with cars on both sides, the overflow from the Lutheran church down the street. Their minister was a local celebrity, an annoying, coifed presence on the ABC affiliate, offering a thought for the day between weather and sports at six and ten, a preacher who really knew how to pack them in. It still bugged Hal. Families flowed down the sidewalk in their Sunday best. Why do they have to clog up our street? he used to ask Phyllis. Why couldn't they just build a bigger lot?

The curtains were drawn. Phyllis would never believe it,

but Hal missed her sorely. When he used to come home, the lights would be on, and she would always be there, something warming in the oven, willing to talk. He missed his children, too. Calvin used to come for Sunday dinner. Geoff talked football with him, and Maureen cut his hair. Ellie always remembered his birthday. It was as if he had been severed from all of them at once, in one horrible catastrophe. If he were a child, you would say that he had been orphaned. But when it happened to a grown-up man, there wasn't even a name for it.

Hal circled around and made his way slowly down the frozen, rutted alley. The garage door was open, and Phyllis's car was gone. He pulled onto the concrete apron. He killed the engine, got out slowly, and looked around. Through the windows of the yellow house across the alley, Hal could see a big-screen television flickering, basketball highlights. When the Rileys still lived there, the two older boys used to pee out their second-story bedroom window and shoot BB's at the neighbors' cat. Now one was a schoolteacher and the other did taxes. It wasn't clear anymore who lived there now. People and cars came and went so quickly you couldn't keep track, all of them loud and a little ragged. It was like a halfway house.

Inside the garage, Hal could see that things had been moved around. His workbench was littered with tools same as always, and there was the usual tangle of old bicycles and his mower and snow blower and a pile of lawn furniture, but the covered cardboard boxes he had carefully stored years ago on the back shelves were now scattered chaotically across the floor. Some of the boxes had been opened, rifled through, the lids tossed aside.

Hal took a closer look. They were his magazines, some *Time* and *Look,* a few *Saturday Evening Post*s, but mostly *Life,* vintage volumes from the golden years, the late forties and fifties, the sixties, before Dallas and Watergate. He squatted beside the boxes and shuffled through them, a black-and-white world of heroic men and beautiful women, Patton and Bogart, Marilyn and Sophia Loren. They were classics. Every page—even the ads, Ivory Soap and Jergens lotion, Lucky Strikes and Chesterfields—was heartening, comforting and familiar, a part of America's family scrapbook.

Phyllis was going to throw them out, Hal just knew it. He didn't want to haggle with lawyers. They were his. He opened the trunk and pushed some samples to the back. He secured the top of a box and laid it in above the spare. Then he went to work. The boxes were densely filled, heavier than he expected. When one almost slipped from his grasp, Hal took off his gloves to get a better grip. He packed them in, pushed and rearranged and jammed and finally made them fit, every single one. By the time he was done, his hands were red and raw, burning with cold. His breath was coming in rapid, noisy gasps as he got back in the car and pulled away, and he was sweating under his overcoat, a cold sickly film of perspiration coating his skin.

Hal sat on his bed that night, contorted with pain. He couldn't hold his head upright. His neck and shoulders were throbbing. To raise his arms was agony. He had saved some things, but he had stupidly aggravated his injury. He shouldn't have lifted those boxes. He inched his way to the bathroom and took a long, hot shower and then rubbed himself slowly with Ben-Gay. He swallowed his pills, a double dose.

After an hour or so, he was starting to feel better. If he lay absolutely still, the pain almost disappeared entirely. Tomorrow he would take it easy, no heavy lifting. There was nothing that he had to do. This was an inconvenience, but it was nothing really, Hal decided, just before he drifted off to sleep, nothing that he couldn't live with.

10

LITTLE CREATURES

Late in January, Dylan started reading his sister's little green diary again. He knew right where she kept it, top left dresser drawer, underneath a pile of woolly pastel socks. He'd been looking into it from time to time since back in November when she'd gotten it for her birthday, but there wasn't much—what she got on a quiz, how ugly she felt, who liked who, what she ate for lunch. He would scan the pages in search of his own name, which appeared only rarely, the subject of bland factual statements. *Dylan has the flu. It snowed six inches and Dylan shoveled.* But now, since their father had moved out—packed and said good-bye to them in the vestibule on New Year's Day, his big leather suitcase streaming colored airport tags like confetti, their mother in the kitchen angrily banging pots and pans—she was writing again, about him, in half-crazed undated entries, using language he'd never heard from her, even her handwriting nearly hysterical, tremulous words run together in passionate red ink: *scumfacefuck pigstinkpervertbastard.* On and on. Sweet little Becky, who wore fuzzy pink bedroom slippers, whose favorite movie was *Beauty and the Beast. I hate you,* she wrote again and again, *slimesickprick.* Dylan sat on the floor, his foot tucked under him and falling asleep, and stared at the page, his heart racing.

Cut it out, he printed finally in neat letters in the middle of an empty page, and buried the book in the drawer. The next time he looked, the diary was gone. He couldn't find it anywhere.

At breakfast, Becky asked him for the milk and read the cereal boxes, same as always.

"I miss him," Dylan said to his mother. She was standing at the counter laying down slices of whole-wheat bread for their lunches like a blackjack dealer.

"I know you do," she said. That's all. She wouldn't say it, that she did too.

"I really miss him," he said.

"Mom," Becky said, from behind her cardboard wall, Cheerios, Chex, Life. "Could you please ask Dylan not to talk with his mouth full?"

"Dylan," his mother said. "Don't talk with your mouth full." She was carefully placing sliced green olives into Becky's cream cheese sandwich as if it were some kind of work of aₗt. It was sickening.

Dylan got up from the table. Becky pulled her chair forward, still reading, and he edged behind her. He pinched her on the upper arm as he went by, hard. She jerked and looked up at him, her mouth open but not making any noise, shocked and sad, as if she'd been shot. There were tears welling in her eyes, and he was glad.

He called from time to time, mostly at night, when Dylan was in his room. His mother would buzz him on the intercom and hang up the phone downstairs when he picked up the extension in his parents' bedroom. He'd sit on his father's side of the bed and talk, the bedside table still crowded with a pile of his paperbacks and magazines.

"What's up?" his father would say, first thing, not even hello, and suddenly the ball was over the net and in Dylan's court, and then he'd search for something to say, something innocuous, something he might find interesting—a television program, a ball game, a good grade—and before he knew it, they would be talking about nothing. His father would sound relieved, and they could talk long enough that it wasn't embarrassing. "What's up with *you?*" Dylan wanted to ask, but he was too timid or too slow, or maybe, deep down, he really didn't want to know.

During the day, Dylan knew, his mother had been talking to a lawyer. He came home and found her bean bag ashtray next to the telephone, full of butts, and a yellow pad covered with notes and doodles. *Visitation?* she'd written in shaded block letters. *Irreconcilable Differences,* it said across the top of a fresh page, and beneath it were three long columns of words she'd made using the letters of those words, an old car-trip game: *can, cad, cab, cable, con.* There were rows and rows of identical three-dimensional boxes—the same kind he filled the margins of his school notes with—and inside several were drawings of little creatures with big ears and long tails, like mice or raccoons, sullen and cramped in their Magic Marker cages.

"When's Dad coming over?" Dylan asked his mother. "When do I get to see him?"

"Soon," she said. It was what she would tell him when he used to pester her for a collie.

"He's still my dad," Dylan said.

Finally, arrangements were made. He called on Valentine's Day, and told Dylan that he'd pick him up at two o'clock on Saturday. "Just the two of us," he said.

His father's little black Miata pulled into the driveway right on time, and his mother gave Dylan the once-over, smoothed his hair, picked invisible lint from his shoulder, protective and sad, resigned and a little angry, too, though not at him exactly, as if he were going off to war. Becky stayed in her room, studying.

His mother tugged at his collar, and Dylan leaned away. "Mom," he said.

"Take care," she said. "Be good. And don't forget to wear your gloves."

"Okay, okay," Dylan said, and headed out the door into the bright afternoon, zipping his jacket as he cut carefully across the lawn, slick now with a thin layer of melting snow.

His father reached over and pulled up the lock and pushed open the passenger door, and Dylan eased himself in. He was almost six feet tall, and there wasn't much leg room. "Hi, Dad," Dylan said. The stereo was turned up, Paul Simon singing "Graceland," the bass and drum hammering mind-lessly from a speaker in the door like the rhythm-master on his grandmother's organ.

"Hey, kiddo," his father said. He was wearing dark glasses and a blue-and-white ski sweater decorated with dancing rein-deer. Dylan could see his mother in the front window, watch-ing from behind the drapes while they backed out of the drive, her face grimly frozen, a dark mask of disapproval.

"I've got something for you," his father said. He reached back and pulled a big red box through the bucket seats and put it on Dylan's lap. Dylan lifted the top and dug through the layers of tissue.

"Rollerblades," his father said. Dylan lifted them out, heavy black boots with four neon green wheels.

"Cool," Dylan said.

"Nine and a half, right?"

"Same as you."

"I thought we could go to Harriet and try them out."

"Dad," Dylan said. "It's the middle of February."

"The paths are clear. I was out yesterday, and it was great. You'll love it," he said. "I promise."

They drove over the Mendota Bridge into Minneapolis, Dylan lacing his blades, and his father zipping in and out of lanes, puffing a cigarette, shifting and down-shifting, talking to the traffic the whole time.

On the way to the lake, they drove down Grandpa Hal's street. It wasn't necessarily the best way to get there, but it wasn't out of the way, either. It was just where they cut over. They hadn't been to visit since the thing with Becky began, not even over the holidays, when instead of eggnog and presents on Christmas Eve, they got money orders in the mail, fifty dollars each. All of a sudden, Becky became a celebrity witness and their grandparents were off-limits.

Last summer, his father had sat down with Dylan in front of a ball game on TV and tried to explain what was going on. That's when things started to fall apart, Dylan thought, when things got weird—the neighbors' gawking at a cop car in their driveway, Becky's changing schools and seeing a psychiatrist, her goofy diet and psycho diary, too, and his mother, her slow, smoldering anger, a ticking time bomb, quiet but ominous, staring at him over dinner, silent and suspicious, as if he'd done something wrong. His father had said the words, and Dylan had nodded, but it didn't register—abuse? Grandpa Hal?—and then there had been a pitching change and a commercial, and that was the end of it.

In December, driving down the same street on the way to pick up a pizza, Dylan and his father had seen him, Grandpa Hal. He had been coming out the front door and down the walk, chin up like a soldier, his stride weirdly slow and out of synch, stiff and cautious, a man walking across ice. He was wearing a shiny black windbreaker and had something strapped around his neck, some kind of flesh-colored brace, fastened under his chin like a sturdy turtleneck. Dylan didn't say anything, and neither did his father, but they both saw him, plain as day. Dylan leaned forward and watched in the side mirror after they passed, and saw him stop and turn after them, slow and mechanical, like a robot, his grandfather's image shrinking as his father accelerated down the street, his hands tight on the wheel.

At Lake Harriet, they parked in the outer circle, and sat in the car with the doors open, Dylan in back, his father in front, putting their blades on. The lake was frozen, white with snow, so vast and desolate that, except for the band shell across the lake, it might have been the North Pole. His father tied double knots, stood, and rolled to the back of the car. He took a helmet from the trunk and strapped it on. It was a big white bubble, and it made him look geeky, like one of those hairless extraterrestrials on *Star Trek* with too much brain, but his father had always liked sports that required special equipment, costumes. He golfed with two-tone cleats and plaid slacks and his gigantic leather bag with an umbrella and plastic tubes for the irons and numbered mittens for the woods. When he used to play tennis, he wore designer shorts and brought a spray bottle of water with him.

"Let's go," his father said. Dylan stood up slowly. He hung onto the car door. He used to go to the roller rink with Becky, but that had been years ago. While his father stretched, he crossed the street with wobbly baby steps and stepped over the curb and onto the blacktopped bike path. He pushed off and nearly toppled forward but steadied himself at the last minute, flailing his arms like a clown. He rolled slowly down the path with short cautious strides, his wheels clacking, feeling stupidly awkward and self-conscious, a big clumsy retard on skates.

His father rolled up beside him, grinning. "Didn't I tell you?" he said. "It's great, isn't it great?" They skated together for a while, his father smooth and effortless, looking up into trees at birds, as if he were taking a Sunday stroll, and Dylan, working hard, still unsteady, always just almost off-balance. Little clouds of steam were coming from his mouth, and a raw wind blowing across the lake was stinging his ears. He wished he'd brought a hat.

"Dad," Dylan said. "What's wrong with Grandpa Hal?"

"What are you talking about?" His father looked at him, his face suddenly gone mean somehow, his lips tight and eyes hard, the way he glared when Dylan and Becky acted up in public.

"That thing on his neck? What was that about?"

"Nothing," he said. "I don't know. Nothing to worry about." Dylan looked up and saw that there was someone coming at them on long, wheeled skis, pushing himself along with regular ski poles. "Now watch it," his father said. "Watch where you're going."

The skier drove past them puffing rhythmically, a wiry guy in gray sweats stained with perspiration. Dylan's father put his head down and pulled ahead, a few strides at first, then more and more.

"Dad?" Dylan shouted into the wind, but he was already out of earshot, ten, twenty yards ahead, his arms swinging and legs driving, leaning into a turn and disappearing around the bend.

Afterward they stopped at his father's new place in St. Paul, supposedly to pick something up, but really, Dylan realized, because his father wanted to show it off. He had rented an apartment on the third floor of what once had been a riverside mansion. "A railroad baron built it in the nineteenth century," his father said as he led Dylan up the steep back stairs, which smelled like food, something spicy and foreign.

Inside it wasn't much. The living room was a dingy square, scarred hardwood floors and pale tobacco-stained wallpaper, empty except for a shiny gold exercise bike with a tremendous caged fan in front. It reminded Dylan of the bicycle Miss

Gulch pedals through Dorothy's nightmare. The kitchen was a strip of Formica counter and a couple of miniature appliances: a two-burner stove and a squat little refrigerator, like a safe, the kind college students put in their dorm rooms.

While his father used the bathroom, Dylan looked around. There was a futon mattress lying right on the bedroom floor, and next to it, his clock radio and brass change tray from home alongside a little television set, hardly bigger than a toaster. The closet was full of shirts and suits in plastic from the cleaners, and his suitcase was open on the floor, stuffed with dirty clothes.

Dylan wandered into the living room and climbed onto the bike. It had a good comfortable seat, soft leather. It was brand new: the odometer read 3.2. He slipped his feet into the toe clips on the pedals and reached for the handlebars. They moved back and forth in tandem as you pedaled, so it was complicated and a little awkward at first, like riding a bike and doing sit-ups at the same time. After a while, though, he got the hang of it and started to pick up speed, and the fan in front began to purr and throw back a nice breeze. He got the red needle on the speedometer up to twenty-five and held it there, riding the bike like a rodeo bronco, jerky and exhilarated.

When he looked up, his father was in the kitchen, pacing in front of the sink and talking into a flat cordless phone. They used to laugh together at their old neighbor Mr. Capistrant, a real estate salesman with a company blazer and a trunkful of matching for-sale signs, who would sit on his deck with his cellular phone, sunning his psoriasis and shouting about counter offers and inspections, siding and asbestos. Now his father had one. It seemed so fake, the phone unconnected to anything, his father looking like a kid with a toy, pretending. It wasn't real.

Dylan lifted his legs from the pedals and let the bike run down. "Uh-huh," his father was saying as he rifled through a stack of mail. "Uh-huh," he said, wiping off the counter with a wet rag, "uh-huh, uh-huh," the same little hiccups of attentiveness he made to Dylan over the phone. And then he understood. His father was already gone and he was never coming back. Weeks would pass and years, and his father would stand in the kitchen talking to him on the phone while he read his mail, and then he would hang up and cross him off his list of things to do.

His father put the phone down, and Dylan told him that he had to use the bathroom.

"The water pressure is lousy," his father said. "The woman who lives downstairs is Pentecostal or charismatic or some damn thing. When the spirit moves her, she turns the water on full blast, kitchen and bathroom, and prays. Just so you know." Dylan didn't say anything.

"Really," his father said. "I'm serious."

"How does water help you pray?"

"How would I know?"

In the bathroom, Dylan pulled the light chain and looked at himself in the mirror. His eyes were glassy. He opened both taps, hot and cold. The water ran in two faint streams. He splashed his face and thought about the woman below him, praying over her sink, like an altar, feeling something flowing, hearing the spirit moving through rusty pipes, gallons and gallons of water wearing away the porcelain, like Niagara pounding on the rocks. He thought about saying a prayer. *What for?* He took the rubber stopper and pressed it into the drain. He watched the water gather in the bowl, rising slowly as a flood.

When he stepped into the hall and closed the door behind him, he could still hear a gentle splashing. His father was standing at the front door jingling keys and coins. "Okay," Dylan said. "I'm ready."

They ate dinner at a restaurant on the 494 strip, where the parking lot was full of BMW's, one next to another, different colors and models, like a showroom. It was dark inside. Their waitress, a tall girl with a short skirt and a Florida tan, brought them a pitcher of water with lemon and told them about the specials. Dylan ordered the most expensive steak on the menu, and like his father, asked for it rare. It arrived with a little flag stuck in it, blue and gelatinous, barely warm inside, but he wouldn't send it back. "Are you sure?" his father asked, but Dylan wouldn't do it. He doused his potato with sour cream and ate it, skin and all. He took little bites of the steak, kept it from touching his tongue, and swallowed fast. It wasn't pleasant, but he could do it. He felt as if he were proving something, though he wasn't sure what exactly. Without being asked, the waitress wrapped up what was left in aluminum foil and presented it to him, a shiny long-necked swan.

On the way home, driving down a dark, empty stretch of county road, they got pulled over by one of the local cops. His father saw the squad car parked on the median with his lights off as they shot by it and he covered the brake, but it was too late. "Goddamn it," he said when the flashing red light went on. "Goddamn it." The cop put his hat on and sauntered up to the car with a flashlight in his hand. He asked for a license and registration.

"I've got you clocked at sixty-three in a forty," the cop

said. He sounded practiced and completely dispassionate, with just the hint of a Southern accent, like the voice of Mission Control at a space launch. His father couldn't have been more polite. Dylan stared through the window at the patrolman's imposing torso, fascinated by his revolver and handcuffs, by the bullets on his belt, part of him frightened by the cop's brute leather-and-lead authority, part of him enjoying the spectacle of his father squirming, the light in his eyes this time, thanking the man for his ticket.

At home, Dylan waved to his father as he backed out of the drive, a dim silhouette behind the wheel, his car buzzing in reverse like a big toy. He stood for a moment on the front steps, his rollerblades tied around his neck, his aluminum foil swan in one hand, his house key in the other. Then he got an idea. He stepped out of his sneakers and into his rollerblades, knelt and tied them up, and pushed the door open.

He stepped over the threshold and glided smoothly across the hardwood living room floor. He rolled into the dining room, got caught on the corner of the rug, and righted himself with his hand on the back of a chair. He could see his mother and Becky on the sofa in the family room. They were huddled together beneath an afghan, a bowl of popcorn between them, their faces illuminated by the flickering light of the television screen, the two of them looking identically dopey, moist-eyed and soggy with movie romance.

"Hey," Dylan said, "I'm home," and they looked up, his mother stubbornly unamused, almost indifferent, and Becky, exasperated and superior, rolling her eyes, *how stupid*. He turned into the kitchen. Glided past the refrigerator and dish-washer, grabbed a half-empty Diet Coke from the center island, and took a big swig. He made another turn through the house, picking up speed in the living room's long straight-away.

In the dining room his elbow bumped a vase on the hutch and it crashed to the floor, an explosion of broken glass and water, satisfyingly loud and wet, like the bursting of a jagged water balloon. "Goddamn you, Dylan," his mother screamed, standing, the afghan wrapped around her like a shawl, suddenly livid, "What's the matter with you?" and Dylan accelerated through the dining room, his wheels crunching through the shards of broken glass. In the kitchen he caught a glimpse of himself reflected in the black microwave door, freakishly tall, sweaty and wild-eyed, and he pushed on, back into the living room, studying the formal family portraits on the mantelpiece, the four of them in red Christmas sweaters, slick hair, and big smiles, fixed in wood frames and sparkling glass, eyeing the cut-glass bowl of fruit on the dining room table. Everything was breakable.

Becky was crying now. "For chrissake, Dylan, stop it," his mother said. "Stop it," she said, "stop it," but he just kept going, around and around, faster and faster, full of desperate strength, no idea what was going to happen next.

11

CONFERENCE

CAPABILITY

"You're it," Maureen told her father's recorded voice. It was a dark morning in late February, some President's birthday. She'd been exchanging messages with him—playing telephone tag—for almost a week now, trying to schedule a haircut ever since she got his new number. "Give me a call," she said. "We'll set something up."

She knew he'd want to be seen, sooner rather than later. He was overdue. Call it vanity, but her father had always understood the importance of hair, of looks. When she'd dropped out after one semester at St. Thomas and enrolled in beauty school, he was the only one in the family who didn't seem disappointed or embarrassed. His whole life, he'd needed to make an impression, it was part of his work. It *was* his work. He was a handsome man still, always had been, like an old movie star. No wonder women found him attractive. He'd gone not so much gray as silver at the temples, and looked almost dignified now, like Gregory Peck. His hair was fine, though, starting to thin, and needed to be layered. If he let it go, it would get wild and fly away like a mad scientist's.

She'd been cutting him for years. When she was a little girl, she sometimes went with him to Gabe's, an old-fashioned barbershop, *Field and Stream* on the table and Paul Harvey on the radio, the stink of Vitalis in the air. She could tell he hated it. She understood that there was a kind of delicacy about him, a shyness. Back home, she used to stand behind his chair with a comb and glass of water and play barber while he read the newspaper. She held his head steady, big as a St. Bernard's, and parted his hair this way and that. And when she was done, he would always make a show of admiring himself in the mirror and tip her with all the loose silver in his pockets. No matter what anybody said, no matter what he'd done, he was no monster.

Maureen's telephone had all the features—speed dial, conference capability, call-waiting. That's how she found herself later that morning in the kitchen taking a call from her father on one line, with her mother holding on the other, Joan sitting in the chair all the while getting a facial and perm. It was weird, but Maureen pulled it off.

"Oh, hi," she said to her father. She kept her voice neutral. If she let on, Joan would freak. "Come anytime today after four," she told him and then clicked off. "Mom?" she said. "One o'clock at the Whitney, okay? Semi-dressy. Meet me in the lobby."

"Sorry," she told Joan, and slipped the phone back into the pocket of her smock. "You were saying?"

She was telling her about Geoff. Except that Becky was sitting in the next room and Joan was wearing an oatmeal mask, her face caked with stiff khaki-colored cream, so she spoke in a hoarse whisper, her lips barely moving, like an angry ventriloquist. Maureen could only catch bits and pieces. He'd picked a fight and walked out on the first of the year, as if leaving the family were on his list of resolutions. Joan said something about counseling, he was or wasn't interested, it wasn't clear. Her jaw was set, her lips twitching furiously. A lawyer was involved, child support and visitation. There was more, which she couldn't get into.

"I get the picture," Maureen said. She wasn't surprised. They had never really been happy together. They'd fought at their own groom's dinner. Once she'd seen Geoff in a dark corner of a downtown bar with a woman, their knees touching under the table. What Maureen wondered was how he and Joan had stayed together this long.

"All right," she told Joan. "Lean back." Joan closed her eyes while Maureen rinsed her. Joan's face, still covered with mud, was impassive and waxen, unreal, yet eerily familiar somehow.

Maureen rolled Joan away from the sink and toweled her off. "My dad is gone, too, you know," she said. "Mom gave him the old heave-ho."

Joan rolled her eyes. She'd always disliked him, even before.

"All of a sudden, everybody's busy leaving."

"Speaking of which," Joan hissed, "how's Ritchie?"

"Same old same old," Maureen said. This was how Joan tried to score points. "Charming. Broke." She took a pick to

Joan's hair a little more briskly than, strictly speaking, was necessary. "Now he's asking *me* for money." She laughed and turned on the dryer. He'd called the night before. He needed bass strings and a new clutch. The band was making a new demo, he said; they were really on the verge of something, he was sure this time, something big. Any day now. She'd sent him fifty, which was more than she could afford.

When Maureen was finished with the dryer, Joan pulled a long strand of hair under her nose and sniffed. "I know it stinks," Maureen said. She had long ago gotten used to it, overpowering but not entirely unpleasant, the fragrant chemical smell, grown to like it really. "But remember, you can't wash your hair for at least a day. Otherwise it won't take."

Maureen looked at her watch. "Okay," she said. "You can wash the gunk off now." She watched her scrub and dry off. When she was done, Joan made her mirror face—pursed her lips, angled her head a little—pouty and practically playful, a pose like nothing she ever showed the world.

"My face is tingling," Joan said. Her skin was pink now, but there were still signs of wear, crows' feet and the beginnings of bags, angry wrinkles starting to carve up her forehead.

"That's good," Maureen said. "It's supposed to tingle."

Becky came into the kitchen then, stretching and yawning. The nuns at her school were on retreat, so she'd had the day off. She'd been curled up on the couch with headphones, checking out Ritchie's vinyl. Her hair was mousy, straight, tied back into a drab ponytail. She was wearing Levi's and an oversized U of M sweatshirt.

"Honey," Joan said, still watching herself in the mirror, fluffing her hair.

Becky reminded Maureen a little of Kate Moss working her

neo-Twiggy look. She was waifish. *Really* waifish—she didn't seem to be trying. Her eyes looked sunken and her collarbone was jutting sharply from beneath the sweatshirt. Maureen knew that she was seeing a shrink. Even her hands were pale and bony. Maybe she was purging.

"What do you think?" Joan asked.

"Good, Mom," Becky said, bored. "I like it."

She definitely needed something, highlights, a little color, some depth, something. Her skin was breaking out, bad. There were blackheads on her forehead, an angry patch of pimples on her cheek. A little foundation maybe, the right tint, could work wonders.

"Hey, Becky," Maureen said. "Take a look at this." She handed her the latest *Elle* opened to a Revlon ad. "How about a shag? It would give you some height." Maureen framed her with her hands. "Or a blunt cut? Something chin-length, maybe, some bangs."

Becky looked at her mother. "It's okay, hon," Joan said. "We have time."

Maureen put her hand under Becky's chin. "We could clean up those eyebrows, too."

"No thank you," Becky said.

"Tell you what," Maureen said. "I can do your eyes, some lip liner—the whole nine yards. I'll even wax your legs."

"Go ahead, Beck," Joan said. "It'll be fun. Like one of those glamour things at the mall."

"A makeover," Maureen said.

"No thank you," Becky said. She was turning red.

"It's all hypoallergenic."

"She's shy," Joan said.

"Mom," Becky said.

"You'll be beautiful," Maureen said. "I promise."

"Your friends won't recognize you," Joan said. Becky seemed to shiver then, something involuntary, as if she'd been hit with some kind of electric charge. Maureen could feel it coming, the explosion.

"Leave me alone," Becky said. "Just leave me alone." Her voice was barely audible, ferociously understated. "Please."

"The girl has problems," Maureen told her mother. They were at the Whitney, surrounded by beautiful people sipping sparkling water and forking up tiny salads, all of them tanned and trim. Everyone looked famous.

Phyllis looked warily down at her gazpacho, as if she were scared of it. "Becky?" she said.

"Big problems," Maureen said. "Let's just leave it at that." A fancy lunch had been her idea, a way to launch her mother's new life as an independent woman. She needed to get out more.

"Everybody's got problems," her mother said. She was wearing an elastic-waist skirt and a pale poly blouse. She looked tired. "I remember you at that age. I seem to recall that you used to breathe fire from time to time."

"Not like that," Maureen said.

At the next table, two women were exchanging gifts. They were identically petite, blue-eyed blondes, a perfectly matched set of Scandinavian dolls. "Lovely," one of them was saying, "just lovely," and held up something silver and sharp. A letter opener.

"You could be a hellcat and you know it."

"If you say so." What Maureen remembered was her mother raising hell, talking to herself in the kitchen, pissed off. She remembered the other kids scattering, her father slipping silently in and out. She remembered spending as much time as she could at Lisa Hatcher's, coming home late, creeping up to her room and closing the door. Wishing for a padlock.

"Anyway," Maureen said. She raised her water glass. "Here's to—" She was stuck. She couldn't think of how to say it. Her mother was looking at her, glass in hand, waiting. "Here's to you, Mom."

"To me," she said, and they drank.

"So what was it?" Maureen asked. "The moment of truth, I mean?"

"The moment of truth?" her mother said. "Do you mean when the lightning struck? When I saw the light?"

"Come on, Mom. You know what I mean."

"It's not like that, not in real life." Their waiter brought their salads, offered them grated cheese and fresh ground pepper. Her mother leaned back and admired her plate.

"Dig in," Maureen said.

Her mother took a cautious bite. "What was wrong was always wrong," she said. "We just finally admitted it."

"You, Mom. *You* admitted it. That's what I heard. It was your idea."

"It was very amicable. Isn't that the word? No shouting, nothing unseemly. I made the motion, and your father seconded it."

"It was the other woman, wasn't it? What's-her-name, the red-haired floozy. You couldn't stand it."

Her mother shook her head.

"Then why? Why now, after all these years?"

"Do you remember how the nuns used to answer the really hard questions? What they used to say? 'It's a mystery.' "

"I hate that."

"Me too."

Her mother picked around the grilled chicken in her salad and asked Maureen what was in it—pine nuts, goat cheese, arugula. Maureen wondered how her father was holding up. On the phone, he sounded depressed, beleaguered. His neck was killing him. "Fantastic," her mother said, and shook her head in happy disbelief. She wasn't taking it too hard.

"What's with Calvin?" Maureen said. "He never calls anymore. Not since he beat up Dad. Can you imagine? Pummeling his own father like that?"

"He's busy, that's all," her mother said.

"Dad told me that he just snapped. He went berserk. Calvin, of all people."

"He brought Gracie over last Saturday. He was not in the least bit berserk."

"Not now, not anymore. He must be full of guilt. Wracked."

Her mother sipped her water, daintily patted her mouth. In her eyes, Calvin could do no wrong.

"Now what?" Maureen asked.

"Coffee?" Phyllis said timidly, as if she were venturing a guess in response to some Miss Manners quiz on luncheon etiquette. "Dessert?"

"I mean, you," Maureen said. "After the divorce. What are you going to do?"

"That's what I've been asking myself. What should I be when I grow up?"

"You should take a class, something practical. Marketable skills—that's what you need now."

"Maybe I will," she said. "One way or the other, I'm

going to get on with my life. Ellie says it's about time. 'Don't look back,' she says.''

''Ellie,'' Maureen said. All of a sudden Ellie was an expert, a regular long-distance Dear Abby. ''Ellie's got an edge. Have you noticed? Some New York thing. This attitude. This pissed-off—pardon my French—for-no-particular-reason attitude. Get over it, I want to tell her. Life goes on.''

The back of his neck was red and lined with wrinkles, crosshatched, scored like an Easter ham. She tied the smock and gently lowered him to the sink. He groaned.

''Sorry,'' Maureen said. It was late afternoon now, the sky just beginning to darken. Terri was at choir practice, and Rick was across the street playing Nintendo with his pal A.J.

Her father had appeared at the door nervous and apologetic. ''If you're too busy,'' he'd said, ''I understand.''

''I'm not too busy,'' she'd told him. ''I just happen to have an opening. Take a seat.''

She ran the water until it was warm and sprayed him down. He closed his eyes and sighed. Wet, he looked vulnerable, all skull and scalp and weathered flesh, a little defeated. Maureen knew he was hurting. She took a big drop of shampoo in her hand and lathered him.

She silently massaged his scalp. Some customers liked to talk, to blow off steam about their kids and jobs or go on about diets and makeup, plans for their holidays; some, the men usually, liked for her to keep up a line of patter. Her father, she knew, preferred silence. He lay back in the chair completely at ease, his eyes closed, his face slack, relaxed.

The phone rang just as she was rinsing him. She held

the water nozzle with one hand and took up the phone with the other. It was Heidi K., one of her regulars, who needed an appointment for color before the weekend. She sounded desperate. "How about tomorrow?" she wanted to know.

"Can do," Maureen told Heidi. "See you at ten." She wrapped her father's head in one towel and draped another around his shoulders. "It never ends, Dad," she said. "What would they do without me?"

She positioned him in front of the mirror, picked up a comb and scissors and went to work. She drew a line with her comb, lifted the top layer, held the hair between her fingers, and clipped it evenly, working her way layer by layer across the top of her father's head, her hands moving surely and automatically, lifting and clipping, lifting and clipping. She loved the clickety-clack racket of her work, the sculptor's satisfaction of watching a good cut slowly take shape. She did the sides next, which she liked to keep short in order to minimize the gray.

She could smell his aftershave. It used to rub off on her, cling stubbornly to her no matter how much she scrubbed or doused herself with her mother's powder and cologne. She would wear him like a stain, breathe his essence for hours.

The phone rang again. "The joint is jumpin'," Maureen said.

There was silence on the other end at first, just the faint hum of a long-distance connection. "Mo?" a woman's voice said. Nobody called her that, not anymore. It was as if she were riding a fast-dropping elevator—she could feel her insides wobble. "Is that you?"

"Yes?"

"It's me," the voice said. "Ellie."

"Oh," she said. "Hi."

"Ellie, your sister."

"Sure," Maureen said, and took a step back from the chair. Her father was watching her in the mirror. "So what's up? What can I do for you?"

"It's been a while," Ellie said.

"Yes," Maureen said.

"Since we've really talked," Ellie said. "Do you know what I mean? Not just exchanged little packets of information the way we do. Not a hit-and-run. Remember how we used to spend hours on the Hatchers' swing set, going back and forth on the glider, hanging upside from the rings, just talking and talking and talking? Remember . . ."

Ellie was launched into something now. Her father was shifting impatiently in his chair, tugging at his shirt collar. Maureen was trapped.

She decided just to carry on. She cradled the phone in her shoulder and picked up her trimmer. She held his face steady and evened off his sideburns. She took a can of talcum powder from the counter and sprinkled the back of his neck. It was easy if she just kept moving. She loosened the smock and brushed his shoulders off with a few quick strokes.

Ellie's voice was still coming at her. She was saying something about family now. Ellie spoke the word as if it were in italics, spun it somehow, managed to load it with layers of complexity, equal parts sadness and shame and longing, a tincture of nastiness.

"But you were the oldest," Ellie said. "It had to be worse for you. You got it both barrels. I can't imagine. What was it like? What was it like for you?"

"For me?" No one ever asked. She was supposed to begin now? "This is just not a good time."

"I'm sorry," Ellie said.

"Can I get back to you?"

"I hope so," Ellie said, and Maureen put the phone on the counter. The floor was littered with wet, lifeless clumps of his hair.

"What was that about?" her father wanted to know. His voice was scared and threatening, both.

"Nothing," she said.

"Nothing?"

"What do you call it?" she said. "A telephone solicitation." He was moving his head slowly, experimentally, from side to side. "Now where was I?"

She grabbed him around the neck. She pushed her thumbs hard into his flesh. He winced. She could feel muscle and bone, tendon and nerve, all the delicate wiring stretched across the human scaffold. She traced small, deep circles with the heel of her hand. She worked his shoulders up and down until something cracked. She kneaded him.

"Right there," he said. "That's the spot."

PART III

SPRING

12

THE NORMAL RHYTHM

OF THE HEART

THEY CAME WITH TAPE MEASURES AND BIG SMILES TO COURT HER, three realtors in three days, full of admiration for her woodwork and structural integrity, her copper pipes and generous storage. They laughed at her little jokes while they counted phone jacks and electrical outlets, measured rooms and assessed closet space while they heartily seconded her observations on the weather—winter *had* lasted too long, spring *was* definitely in the air. Phyllis appreciated their professionalism, not just their thoroughness and attentiveness to detail—tile and grout, wiring and insulation—but also their discretion, impeccably tactful as British valets in the presence of the master's impropriety, as remarkable for what they ignored as for what they noticed—Hal's closet in the master bedroom emptied save for a rack of outdated ties and a pair of bowling shoes, her antacids and pain relievers in the bathroom cabinet, the heaps of moldering trash in the basement.

Phyllis felt sorry for the first agent, a young man in tortoiseshell eyeglasses suffering with hay fever, reduced finally on the deck to a red-eyed paroxysm of apologetic sneezing. She ushered him inside, sat him on the couch, and brought him a fresh box of tissues and a glass of water.

The second agent was a woman named Loretta, whose face Phyllis recognized from the Saturday *Home Finder,* which she'd taken to studying in preparation for her sale. Loretta was a million-dollar seller. In person, she flashed the same practiced smile she displayed in her photograph. She was pleasant enough, but not sufficiently careful to disguise the effort she was making. She struck Phyllis as just too abrupt, a local sales celebrity with a fancy car and designer pumps and bigger fish to fry.

The third agent, she decided almost immediately, was the one. His name was Earl Bass. He had a gray crew cut and the bouncy, prowling energy of a high school coach. She called his office Thursday afternoon and he showed up first thing Friday morning, wearing a V-neck sweater and a crookedly knotted striped tie, a stack of computer printouts under his arm. He handed Phyllis his card, eyeballed the main floor, and headed down the basement. She caught up to him in front of the oil furnace, a hulking iron box, like the witch's oven in "Hansel and Gretel." He swung the door open and stared into the orange flame. It was the first day of spring, but the temperature had been below freezing most of the month, the furnace humming all night, just a few hours of sunshine in the afternoon sending rivers of melted snow down the driveways and street before they froze up again in the evening. "Whew," he said, and wrote something on a notepad.

Then he was upstairs, running water in the kitchen sink and testing the disposal, yanking sash cords in the living room, on his hands and knees peering up the fireplace flue. He described what he saw in a rich baritone, like a television commentator, whether talking to himself or to her, Phyllis wasn't sure. "Triple-track windows," he announced. "Ceiling fan and chandelier." He moved with long athletic strides, not a young man, but still trim and agile.

He walked through the bedrooms and upstairs bathroom quickly and finished in the attic. Phyllis turned on the light and stood halfway up the stairs and watched his brown shoes move back and forth across the floor, around the cardboard cartons in the boys' old bedroom. His shoes had little metal clips on the soles that made a happy clatter when he walked.

Afterward he sat at the kitchen table and made calculations while Phyllis put the coffee on. "You want to sell, right?" he said. "No fooling around."

That's exactly what she wanted. She wanted to get out of the house, the sooner the better. It felt dark and poisonous to her now, like a mine shaft, and no spring cleaning, no amount of elbow grease and air freshener, was ever going to reclaim it. She would have loved to just walk away. Hal had packed two suitcases and loaded a few cardboard boxes into his trunk and never looked back. After forty years. What about your stuff? she had asked. I don't care, he said. Throw it out. Part of her was envious. It was that simple. But she wanted to do it right. She wanted to put her house in order. It was biblical. It felt like an obligation, a duty, a responsibility she had avoided for too long. Time was running out. It was *her* house now, she had the deed, and she wanted to put it in order. And then sell it.

"No fooling around," she said. She leaned on the counter

and watched an aromatic stream issue forth from the purring coffeemaker.

"It's hard, isn't it?" he said, and looked up from his figures. One eye was fixed on her, the other wandering off a few degrees. His face was creased and supple, kindly well-worn leather. At that moment something toppled in Phyllis, all her tight-lipped bravery, constructed day upon day. There were tears in her eyes, and she nodded, rapid little spasms of agreement. She didn't dare say anything.

He stood and handed her a contract. Ninety days and seven percent. The price he had inked in was on the low side. She took the pen from his hand and signed next to the little X.

They drank coffee and Earl explained what she could do to help move the house—some paint in the entryways, a little yard work, haul the trash from the basement.

"But don't try to do it all by yourself," he said. "Get some help. Have a cleaning party."

"Trash bags and funny hats? Spic and Span and potato salad?"

He smiled. "That's the spirit."

On the way out he stopped in the living room to admire the grandchildren on the mantel. His calculations completed and the signed contract in hand, Earl, it seemed, was off-duty now, free to observe the human furniture. There was little Grace, brand new and wide-eyed, staring intently into Calvin's bleary face; Lucy with grease-pencil whiskers and homemade mouse ears; Becky at an amusement park with her arm draped so stiffly around Dylan he might have been a cardboard cutout; outdated school portraits of Terri and Rick.

Phyllis explained that Grace would be baptized later in the month and that Lucy would be in town with Phyllis's daughter and son-in-law. They would stay for a week, and then she could put the house on the market. "It will be nice to have them here," she said. "One last time."

Earl nodded as if he understood. He had a wallet full of grandchildren himself, it turned out, three boys, whose portraits he extracted from the plastic and laid out on the coffee table like grinning, buzz-cut kings in his own game of solitaire.

"Pain in the chest," Phyllis said and moved her finger down her list of definitions.

"So what's he look like?" Maureen wanted to know.

"What kind of question is that?" Phyllis said. "He's my real estate agent. What does your mailman look like? Angina Pectoris."

"He's all you talk about. Earl this, Earl that. Look—you're blushing. Is he cute?"

"Variation from the normal rhythm of the heart."

"Is he?"

"He's got hair like a hedgehog and a bad eye. He wears wing tips with metal cleats."

"Cleats?"

"Clippity-clop. Like a Clydesdale."

"I think you've got a love interest."

"Arrhythmia. You didn't study, did you?"

"You gotta write big, Mom, or I'm sunk."

It was Monday night, and they were in a windowless junior high school cafeteria, cramming for a medical terminology quiz, this week the cardiovascular system. The class had been Maureen's idea, a way to get Phyllis out of the house and prepared for a job in health care, as a doctor's receptionist, maybe.

Phyllis was reluctant at first, but before long, she began to

like it. Turned out, she couldn't get enough of medical terminology. She pored over her textbook, big as the white pages,
complete with pronunciation guides, self-tests, and little
games for practice: once you read forward, backward, up,
down, and diagonally and located all fifty words in the Word
Puzzle on Blood, the remaining unused letters spelled "red."
She memorized prefixes and suffixes, matched specialists with
their fields of practice, labeled glands and organs and systems
and named their accompanying disorders. There was so much
to learn.

What she was so intent on studying, she realized, was herself, hoping to discover among the definitions and diagrams
what it was that was going so terribly wrong in her own
insides. Her pains, hot abdominal piercings, dull throbbing in
her lower back, had grown more intense and more frequent.
She swigged liquid antacids right from the bottle and gulped
Extra Strength Tylenol, but still, between her pain and her
worry, there were nights she barely slept. She kept her textbook on her bedside and studied—pressed herself here and
there, matched symptoms, and pronounced the names of terrible diseases.

She was fascinated especially by the case studies included in
each chapter, little medical stories stripped to essentials: name
and admission date, present illness and past history, summary
and conclusion all on a single page, key terms in italics. Violet
Tucker, a thirty-six-year-old female with a history of *erythema-
tous papules* admitted with a burning sensation of her lips;
Melba Rose, a sixty-year-old woman presenting with *colonic
distention, hypertension,* headaches, and skin rash. Phyllis would
skip to the conclusion, like someone peeking at the last page
of a novel to learn the main character's fate, whether she
returned asymptomatic, or was readmitted, complaining, for

further treatment, or, like Alice White, a sixty-six-year-old widow suffering episodes of *edema,* fatigue, and *apprehension,* and diagnosed with *congestive heart failure,* died suddenly.

Sometimes, at night, alone in her creaking house, she tried to compose her own case study. She could imagine some evil malignancy nestled among her organs. But in the morning, she felt foolishly sound. "Hypochondria" was located between "hallucination" and "hysteria" among the psychiatric terms, defined as imaginary illness, and distinguished from "malingering," which was pretending to be ill. She would see a doctor before long, she knew, but not quite yet, not until after the baptism, and when she did, she wanted to be fluent at least in the language of disease.

On the quiz that night there was a long column of terms to match, a few fill-in-the-blank definitions, and a diagram of the heart with long curved arrows showing the direction of the blood flow, like a weather map. Phyllis wrote down the names of the chambers and valves, arteries and veins, and then turned her paper over while Maureen chewed her pencil and sighed.

For the next two weeks, Phyllis led a curious sort of underground existence, venturing out only to attend class with Maureen, reaching out once a day to grab the mail, bills and catalogs, which she piled unopened on the kitchen table, dividing her time between mastering medical terminology and sifting, like an archaeologist, through the artifacts of her family's history in the basement. She dragged boxes and bags into Hal's paneled office and sat for hours under a bare lightbulb, sorting.

It was hard to throw anything away. She started with two

piles, keep and throw, but after the first morning, she hadn't put anything at all in the throw pile, not Geoff's football scrapbooks full of ticket stubs and programs, not the picture postcards of gigantic leaping roadside fish and lonely Great Lakes lighthouses Hal used to send when he was on the road, not a single scuffed pair of skates or even one torn and taped board game leaking dice and markers and pastel currency.

There was a fat file folder full of glossy recipes for beautiful meals she never cooked. In a bag of old clothes there was a little blue sweatshirt covered with cardboard circles, taped in place, each one decorated with a hand-colored icon, a baseball bat, a glass of milk, a book, a sad-eyed hound—something Ellie must have concocted for little Calvin, who'd envied Geoff's Boy Scout merit badges. There was an odd lot of dirty, unmatched baby shoes in a grocery bag, the laces frayed and stiff with age. Cigar boxes full of crayons and toy soldiers. A pile of silver-spined Golden Books.

She swallowed her sobs at first, pressed tissues into the corners of her eyes, her chest heaving with sorrow. But when she turned the knob on a worn wooden music box and saw golden-haired Jack and Jill tumbling down a grassy slope while the melody chimed, delicate and pure as tiny church bells, she let go at last, abandoned herself finally to grief, and howled, filling the empty house with wailing lamentation.

Because they'd all grown up and the shoes were never bronzed. Because she remembered it all so dimly. Because it was her life, and she'd missed it. The truth was that she had been scared of the children, with one eye always on the clock, wanting the time to pass, waiting for naptime, for bedtime, for school to begin, and now, like a dupe in a cruel fairy tale or a bad joke, she had gotten exactly what she wished for.

If she ever did tell her story to the Partners of Offenders, she realized, that would be it. Fear was the story of her life. As a girl she had feared her father's drunken rage and her mother's silent severity. She had lain down with Hal the first time beneath a coarse green blanket on the narrow bed in his rented room only because she was afraid not to. She married him because she was pregnant and afraid what people would say, what would become of her. With Hal on the road five days a week, she drank because it dulled her fear, took the edge off her panic, though even then she was always afraid to be found out, and when she finally quit, after a nasty fall, a trip to the ER, and one hour with a psychiatrist, it was only because she was more afraid of what would happen if she didn't. Over the years she had grown obsessed with safety, deadbolts and chains on the door, the Club in her car, as if with the right hardware, the proper precautions—if she drove defensively, if she *lived* defensively—she could protect herself from the catastrophe she was forever glimpsing from the corner of her eye, only half-suspecting that it was going to be an inside job, that the prowler lay beside her. She had stayed with him for so long, after the affairs and the accusations and even after the sentencing, because she was still afraid to be alone. And now she was afraid that to discard a single miserable battered artifact would be to sever her connection, however frail, to what used to be her life, to forget the last scrap of that hazy and distant dream.

First to go were her cards from the children, Valentine's and Mother's Day, Christmas and Easter, her birthday, a pile of lopsided homemade hearts, paper plates and yarn and sequins and gobs of glue, signed in crayon with hugs and kisses and love, love, love, and always more love. She held each one again, read it over one more time, and like a spy, having committed the secret message to memory, she destroyed the thing itself—tore them in half and tossed them in a long green bag. It wasn't so hard.

Next she threw out a shoe box full of souvenirs from the last family vacation, a suffocating car trip out West, six of them crammed into the Lincoln, Maureen carsick and the boys bickering, Hal stopping to make sales calls while they roasted in the car. Phyllis dumped it all, beaded belts, postcards, Grand Canyon decals still on the cardboard backing. She tossed years of canceled checks rubber-banded together in their fat window envelopes, boxes and boxes of magazines, heaps of their clothes from over the years mixed crazily together—a tiny fringed cowboy shirt, tie-dyed swim shorts, somebody's yellow bridesmaid dress, plaid parochial school jumpers, mittens and stocking caps, grotesquely wide ties and narrow black belts, bell-bottomed jeans, a satin cummerbund.

It got easier and easier. She threw out an entire wicker basket of white shirts she was supposed to mend. She threw out yards of fabric and paper packets full of patterns. She threw out her whole sewing basket, thread, bobbins, thimbles, pin cushions, buttons. At times, with something substantial in the bag, a case of Hal's samples or her mother's flatware, she felt exhilarated, a little reckless, almost giddy. The more she threw out, the more she wanted to throw out.

She came up from time to time, it might be midnight, it might be noon, to warm something in the microwave or to put on a pot of coffee. In the basement, with no clocks, no television, and hardly any light, she lost track of time entirely. After one long session downstairs, she emerged, stiff, wrung out, blinking, tissues wadded in her pocket, dragging another bag up the stairs. She pushed open the side door and discovered dawn: a blast of cool air smelling of rain and fresh mud, the bright twitter of birds above her head, a bank of low billowy clouds in the east bathed in delicate pink light. Never had she seen anything so exquisitely colored. She shivered.

"Spring cleaning?" a voice croaked. It was leathery old Rose Terragnoli from across the street, wrapped in a plaid robe, standing in the driveway while her poodle nosed around the bushes. She had a mug of tea in her hand, steam rising as if from some magic brew. Phyllis added the bag to the growing mountain at the curb, her own heavy-duty, three-ply plastic monument. She waved. "Feels good," Rose said. "Doesn't it? Doesn't it feel good?"

Phyllis was staring into the freezer compartment when the doorbell rang. It was Earl Bass, standing on the steps with a boxy black camera hanging around his neck. He looked like a news photographer from an old movie. "Do you mind if I take some pictures?" he said.

Phyllis patted her head instinctively—she was a wreck—and then laughed. "Go ahead," she said. "I'll be right out."

She watched him from the living room window. He stood across the street, on Mrs. T.'s boulevard, looking up at Phyllis's house, then down through the viewfinder, fiddling with the lens, edging backward step by step. He was trying to get a shot of the house, she figured, without the garbage. Finally, he positioned himself, two houses down and three strides into the street. Phyllis liked the fact that, though indistinguishable, no doubt, in the *Home Finder,* she would know that she was in the picture. A school bus turned the corner and slowed down and stopped while Earl kept clicking. Then he looked up and waved, and before the bus passed by, the driver, a young fellow in a painter's cap, leaned out the window and chatted for a moment. Earl smiled and nodded, and then stepped across the street, glanced at the trash, and headed toward her front door.

She let him in. "You've been busy," he said. He was wearing a windbreaker and the same tie as the other day, blue and green stripes, held in place with a little circular black tie tack.

"Thank God for Hefty bags," she said.

"Amen," he said. When he smiled, his unfocused eye, which seemed to be gazing at a spot just over her left shoulder, still looked knowing and amused somehow. "Hey," he said. "I brought you a present." He pulled a paper bag from his jacket pocket and handed it to her.

"Really," she said. Inside there was a long coil of white rope and a sales slip. "Is this enough of the proverbial to hang myself?"

"For the windows," he said. "I had some extra. I'll show you."

She found him a screwdriver and watched him work. He turned a couple of screws and lifted off the oak window frame in the dining room, removing what she had always thought of as permanently fixed with startling ease. He pulled out a ratty broken cord and a massy, irregular cast-iron weight, like an anchor. It was filthy inside, and Phyllis cleaned up with a bottle of spray cleaner and paper towels, while he tied the new rope around the weight, cut it with a pocketknife, and ran it through the little pulley.

Phyllis liked his concentration, his confidence. He knew

what he was doing. And then a slow pain rippled through her innards and she waited it out, took a deep breath and focused on Earl's big hands moving the window up and down, testing the new sash.

"I was wondering," Phyllis said. This was it, her chance to be bold. "I've got all this frozen food. How about some dinner?"

He looked at his watch. It was three-thirty. She thought he was going to laugh. "Sure," he said. "Why not?"

So they sat in the kitchen and sampled stuffed shells, a deep-dish pot pie, teriyaki chicken, broccoli and cheese on the side, Sara Lee pound cake for dessert. Phyllis asked him about real estate. How was business? Did he like it? How long had he been with the company? Maureen had told her once that she asked too many questions. You interview people, she said. But men liked it, Phyllis was convinced, and it gave her a chance to chew. Earl said he was new to real estate. For years he had been a manager for a company that specialized in providing lighting to commercial properties, mostly grocery stores. Phyllis nodded. All those bulbs.

"What about you?" Earl asked. "What did you used to be?"

"A wife," Phyllis said. "But I got sacked."

"It happens," Earl said. "Times are tough."

"And a mother," Phyllis said. "I used to be a mother, too."

"You're still a mother," Earl said.

"Sometimes I wonder."

"No, that's for keeps. Look at me. My daughter is thirty-two years old. She hates my guts. Hasn't spoken to me in three years. When I called at Christmas to talk to the boys, she just laid the phone down. 'Merry Christmas, Liz,' I shouted, 'I love you.' Maybe she heard. Even so. But she still needs a father, maybe just to be mad at, and I'm it."

"That's terrible," Phyllis said. "Why is she so mad?"

"I've made some mistakes," Earl said.

"I know what that's like," Phyllis said.

"Big ones," Earl said.

"Tell me about it," Phyllis said, and they both laughed out loud, for no good reason, deep rolling belly laughs volleying back and forth between them, until he was doubled over, and she was weak and teary-eyed.

The baptism was going to be on Sunday, and Ellie and Walt, who were the godparents, were arriving late Saturday afternoon. Ellie had agreed to stay with Phyllis only after weeks of invitations, lobbying, and negotiations, more letters and phone calls than they'd exchanged in years. Phyllis assured her that if it didn't work out, they could pick up and move to Howard Johnson's, no hard feelings. She didn't mind if they rented a car—why should she?—and she didn't expect them to sit around the house all week and amuse her. She would give them a key, and they could come and go as they pleased. Phyllis liked the prospect of having all the children together again.

She got up that morning and went right to work. She mopped the kitchen floor. She went to the grocery for soda and crackers and stopped at a toy store to get some trinkets for Lucy. She laid out towels and bedding. For the first time in years, she baked cookies: she read the recipe off the back of the yellow bag of chocolate chips, and though she burned the first sheet, eventually she filled a plate with a respectable batch and the house with a pleasant smell.

Sometime around four, there was a knock at the door. Phyllis was standing at the kitchen sink. There were butterflies in her stomach. She didn't know what to expect. Lately she no longer knew what was going to happen, not even what she was going to say next. And now Ellie was standing on the other side of the door. Phyllis washed down two Advil with a glass of milk, checked her hair, and headed down the hall.

She heard voices. She paused, waited for a moment with her hand on the knob, savoring the muffled sound of Lucy's high-pitched questions, her own daughter's motherly, patient reply, in no hurry now, knowing that she was nearly ready, done with her work, almost.

13

COMMON PRAYER

AFTER GRACE WAS BORN, AFTER THE MIDNIGHT RUN-IN WITH HIS father on the front steps—his mother called it a fight, which it wasn't, but he didn't know the right word for it and didn't bother to correct her—Calvin started going to church again. As a boy, he had attended Sunday mass at St. Mark's regularly, into adolescence, long after it was required of him, but despite a kind of stirring that even off-key congregational singing inspired in him, despite the vague uplift he felt at the invocation of the saints, John and Paul, Cosmos and Damien, he was eventually driven away, by the stench of his father's white-shoed usher's hypocrisy, by the incessant pulpit-pounding about envelopes and capital expenditures, by all the rules and regulations and body-and-blood sacramental voodoo.

For six unspeakably strange weeks as a college sophomore, during his first semester away from home, under the influence of an intense red-haired beauty named Sharon, he had become a born-again Christian. It was mainly about lust, Calvin told himself—fervent women drove him wild. He attended classes and worked in the library by day, and at night read Scripture with Sharon.

He had accepted Jesus Christ as his personal savior. He had even spoken in tongues. At a prayer service in a shabby basement club room, he had stood up in front of the assembled, his vocal chords turned Ouija board, and like an inspired percolator, burbled forth a wild barrage of nonsense syllables, great strings of crackling consonants and low, yowling vowels. It had felt to him the way he'd heard the experience of being hypnotized described: you expect a radically, magically transformed consciousness, a glimpse of some new reality, then forgetfulness, perhaps, but in fact, he had felt absolutely, stunningly normal the whole time, except that his mouth was working automatically, as if he were singing the national anthem while he scanned the crowd at a ball game. He felt only a little curious about what he was spitting forth. It would have been less eerie if it had not been so ordinary. He had never told anyone about it, not even Kate, and rarely thought about it anymore. Until his window-peeping at his father's house, it had been the only completely irrational, inexplicable episode in his life, and he was embarrassed by it. When he read the phrase "youthful indiscretion," he sometimes thought of himself and his holy babble that night, and felt a hot stab of shame. Eventually his religious passion had just petered out. He skipped Bible study. He got interested in a girl at the circulation desk. It was as if his spiritual resources, capable of lasting a lifetime if husbanded carefully, had been squandered, spent like a sailor's pay in one idiotic binge.

Then, years later, Grace was born, and Calvin got desperate. Nothing he'd read in their baby books prepared him to be so thoroughly, numbingly, baffled by the baby, by his marriage, himself, everything. There had been one marvelous week of daily UPS deliveries for Grace and what Calvin called drive-by casseroles: self-contained little meals dropped off by beaming friends and neighbors, quiche, two lasagnas, a whole roasted chicken, with bread and pie and all the fixings. But after that, it was clear, once the dishes were washed and returned, once the thank-yous were written, they were on their own.

Grace was a beautiful baby, but she cried a lot, almost constantly and inconsolably in the evening, tearless, crimson-skulled wailing that to Calvin sounded electronically amplified. They tried everything the books recommended to comfort her—swaddled her, walked her, sang to her, even ran the vacuum for her—but nothing worked. Though he didn't dare speak the word, Calvin read and reread the sections on colic, matching symptoms and looking for a loophole, trying to find some reason to believe that it didn't apply to Grace.

She was nursing every two hours, and to feed and change her and get her settled seemed always to take so long that, at best, Kate was sleeping barely an hour at a stretch. Calvin had always known sleeplessness was a problem for new parents and used to make little jokes about it in his cards of congratulations to friends with babies. But now he understood why sleep deprivation could be a kind of torture. He did what he could—put in loads of dirty laundry, which multiplied mysteriously like never before, ran trays of food up the stairs to Kate—but it wasn't much. When he tried to give Grace a bottle, she rarely took it. He brought home an endless variety of nipples from the baby store, experimented with little airless bags of milk, even draped Kate's sweater around his shoulders and held the bottle to his own breast, but it didn't work. Grace screeched until Kate came and took her from him. He felt utterly worthless.

He was afraid that they were all getting a little crazy. Kate grew pale and hollow-eyed, wandering, dazed, through the house in a zip-up baseball jersey. Sometimes at night, when Calvin would wake up in bed alone, he would stick his head in the baby's room and see Kate, rocking spookily in the dark: fierce and possibly disoriented, she hissed requests—open a window, bring a glass of beer—that didn't seem entirely sensible. For days they ate out of boxes and talked only about nursing and sleep and bowel movements. He found himself guiltily looking forward to the end of his prized paternity leave, yearning for the orderly daytime world of his office.

Kate dressed Grace in her best outfit for their first Mommy and Me class and returned near despair. She had fussed the whole time, the only one. The other babies were angels, some of them already sleeping through the night. The mothers were radiant and well rested. Everything was perfect. When one of the women told a story about a mother who had thrown a crying infant out a second-story window in the middle of the night, they were horrified. "It's horrible," Kate said. "But I understand."

His mother, God bless her, was worthless. She would stop by, apologize for intruding, move through the house in a nervous flutter, and stand over the baby, finding resemblances between Grace and relatives he hardly remembered. She was consumed with her divorce, full of legal questions about procedures and timetables. It was a weird reversal: she was going to court now, and he was covered in baby spit. When Calvin got around to asking her what he wanted to know—did she burp on the lap or over the shoulder? what kind of sleeper had he been as a baby? had he taken a bottle?—she looked blank. "I can't remember," she said. "Can you imagine?"

Then one Sunday morning—he knew it was Sunday because the paper dropped in the door was a fat one—Calvin stumbled into the Church of the Good Shepherd. After an especially harrowing night, Calvin had promised Kate that she could sleep in, he would take care of Grace. It was brave talk. He carried her downstairs, put her in her bassinet, sipped instant coffee, and watched her sleep. He had a bottle of breast milk in the refrigerator and a pan of water simmering on the stove to warm it up. Asleep, she looked fragile and placid, too small to have brought such commotion into their lives. When she started to stir, Calvin warmed the milk, and had Grace cradled in his arm and latched onto the bottle before she was even fully awake. He admired her silken hair, her perfect fingers and nails, listened to her contented sucking. He was awash in warm feeling, proud of himself, proud of his daughter, calculating happily how many hours of consecutive sleep Kate was going to rack up.

Then, as if rousing herself by sheer force of will from her milk stupor, Grace opened her eyes, fixed Calvin in an unnerving gaze, and started to wail. He lifted her to his shoulder and rubbed her back. "Everything is all right," he said, "there's nothing to worry about." But he could feel himself starting to perspire. She brought forth one magnificent bubbling burp, gulped some air, and resumed her crying. He changed her diaper, and she cried the whole time. He offered her the bottle again, but nothing doing.

When he heard Kate moving around upstairs, he knew he

had to do something. Grace was almost purple, she was crying so hard. He picked up the wall phone in the kitchen and stared at the auto-dial buttons. His mother was preoccupied. Maureen was distracted. Geoff wasn't at home anymore, and Joan had never liked him much. Ellie was long-distance, but she was good with children. They'd talked a couple of times in the last month, and she had entertained him with stories of her own early bumbling with Lucy.

"Ellie," Calvin said when she answered. "This is Calvin. I need help." He explained what was going on.

"Okay," she said. "What's it like out?"

"You mean the weather?"

"How cold is it?"

Calvin pulled back the curtain and looked into the back-yard. The sun was shining, the sky was a brilliant blue. The neighbors' cat was crouched beneath their maple tree, staring up at a branch lined with sparrows. "Not bad," he said. "In the forties, I bet."

"All right," Ellie said. "Bundle her up, and take her out for a minute. A little fresh air is always good. Change of temperature. Sunshine. And you won't disturb Kate."

"It's worth a try," Calvin said.

"And if that doesn't work," she said, "try something else."

Calvin pulled a sweater over Grace's sleeper and tied a knit cap on her head. He zipped her into a quilted sack like a papoose and put her on his shoulder and headed out the door. He walked fast away from the house, Grace still wailing, feeling like he was perpetrating some unlikely infant abduction. He walked down the block, past his neighbors' sleepy houses, shades drawn, Sunday papers piled on the porch steps and advertising circulars stuck in the wrought-iron hand rails, a few scraggly bushes still wired with unlit strings of Christmas bulbs.

Two blocks down was a brick church and a day care center, Good Shepherd Episcopal, where in the summer, he used to see a yard full of kids with big wheels and jump ropes and a couple of women in shorts leaning on a fence talking. There was a sign out front: NO GOD, NO PEACE; KNOW GOD, KNOW PEACE. While Calvin stood in front pondering his next move, right, left, back home, Grace became suddenly, ominously quiet, and he got scared. He walked up the stairs of the church, pulled the wooden doors open, and in the vestibule, laid Grace on a table, and undid her sack. She was sound asleep. No sign of frostbite, just pleasantly pink cheeks and easy, regular breathing.

Inside the church, he could hear music, a few cascading organ chords and a swirling melody. He put Grace back on his shoulder and moved into the doorway. Standing near the altar was a white-gloved hand bell choir, ten men and women in red cassocks and starched white surplices, shiny golden bells in hand, throwing them forward on cue as if dousing the congregation with holy water. There were some older women, lumpy and silver-haired, a couple of fortyish men, studying their sheet music through reading glasses, a young man with a ponytail, all of them focused, intense.

They finished, the last note lingering in the air, while its ringer held her arm forward in statuesque follow-through, smiling shyly into the perfect silence of the congregation. Then the minister, an imposingly tall woman with oversized glasses, rose and announced the closing hymn and invited everyone to stay for coffee, and before Calvin knew it, they were headed down the center aisle straight for him, the singing minister and her entourage, carrying a cross and leather hymnals and lighted candles, then, a flood of parishioners, most of them wearing circular cardboard name tags around their necks held in place with colored yarn, like homemade Olympic medals. They surrounded him, smiling and cooing at Grace, and in a minute, he had been greeted and patted and slapped with his own adhesive name tag and led downstairs into a gleaming kitchen.

There was an enormous shiny metal coffee urn with a glowing red light and trays and trays full of pastries: doughnuts, crullers glazed with sugar, cinnamon rolls, muffins. He was overwhelmed with attention, and did his best with names and faces. There was Bob, who was one of the bell ringers; the pastor, Alice Something; an old codger with a cane who introduced himself as Dr. Powers. A woman named Ruth held Grace while Calvin filled a cup and grabbed a roll, and by the time he returned, a small crowd had gathered around her and someone had stuck a tag on the back of her sleeping sack: HELLO MY NAME IS—GRACE! They were all friendly and chatty and never quite seemed to grasp the fact that he was only a crasher. They were delighted and surprised that he lived right down the block, that the baby was only six weeks old, that she had a mother at home.

Finally Calvin got Grace back in hand and excused himself. They insisted he take something home, and like grandparents at Thanksgiving, they pressed a bag of food in his hand and followed him up the stairs and out the door, standing on the church steps in their shirtsleeves, waving to him while he backpedaled down the street, drenched in unearned goodwill and inexplicable kindness, sheepishly shouting his thanks.

Calvin came back the next week, and the week after that and the week after that, with Grace in her sack, and while she slept or stared serenely up at the spinning ceiling fans, he hung back in one of the rear pews, reading in the hymnal and Book of Common Prayer, moved stupidly almost to tears by each of the hand bell choir's performances, feeling for its members a glowing, inarticulable affection that he could locate almost precisely just behind his sternum. He listened not so much to the words as the music of the homilies and readings, the passionate rise and fall of the minister's mellifluous voice, the rich rhythm of sin and salvation. After services, he drank coffee in the kitchen and gobbled down pastries and made small talk with the regulars, astounded that people whom he could not recall ever having seen before greeted Grace and him by name, like old friends.

After Calvin was informed that anyone who had been baptized was welcome to take communion, it occurred to him that maybe Grace should be baptized. If it was a kind of lifetime free pass he possessed, shouldn't she have it too? Kate, who had seemed amused by Calvin's churchgoing—she laughed at him and his name tag and photocopied church bulletin, but loved the cinnamon rolls he always brought— thought it was a good idea, too. It would make her mother happy.

Arrangements were made. Calvin approached Pastor Alice after services one Sunday, and she seemed delighted by the idea of a baptism. She shook Calvin's hand, which was sticky with doughnut sugar, and stroked Grace's cheek. She took out her calendar and they settled on a date right then and there. Ellie and Walt agreed to be godparents, and Calvin was glad. He was a little unclear as to what exactly the job entailed, but they were good parents themselves, calm and sensible and decent. They held hands and prayed before meals, his mother said. And it was Ellie, after all, who'd sent him and Grace out to Good Shepherd that first Sunday.

Twenty minutes before the baptism, Calvin was so nervous that he couldn't remember his sister's name. He was standing on the front steps of the church chatting with old Dr. Powers. It was a fine spring morning in Minnesota: the snow was finally gone—knock on wood—and even though the lawns were still spongy, there were buds on the lilacs and the smell of baseball was in the air. Kate was sequestered in the sacristy giving Grace a last-minute feeding, and the bell choir was running through a new hymn in the church. Dr. Powers was telling him about tulips, the time he planted his bulbs upside down.

She came wobbling down the sidewalk and up the steps in red heels, digging through her purse, trailed by her kids, looking spiffy and shy, and Calvin said to Dr. Powers, "This is my sister—" and he drew a blank. Her name disappeared into his memory's blind spot. He could almost hear the sound of her name, see the shape of the letters, but he couldn't say it. They stood there, the two of them looking at him, eerily frozen, as if the film had stopped, and just when it might have started to burn at the edges, she spoke up. "I'm Maureen."

"My God, Calvin," she said. "You look terrified. They're not going to stick *your* head under water, are they? What's with you?" He couldn't say. It was a quarter to, and Ellie and Walter hadn't shown up yet, but that wasn't it. Maybe it was just the crazy confluence, Maureen and Dr. Powers, Geoff and the hand bell choir, his family and the Good Shepherd crowd, the desire not just that they get along but enjoy and appreciate each other, the fear that he wasn't exactly the same person in each camp and would be found out somehow. His enthusiasm felt exposed and vulnerable, too, an obvious target for his family's ridicule. He knew how easy it would be to make fun of them, how easy he had become to make fun of. But maybe you could make fun of anything someone cared about, maybe caring itself was laughable. And maybe there were worse things than being laughed at.

They arrived just in time, Walt looking impressive and uncomfortable in a suit and tie, like a football star at an awards dinner, Ellie wearing a yellow dress and a straw hat, hurrying up the sidewalk together while his mother and Lucy trailed leisurely behind, hand in hand, deep in conversation. Calvin hugged Ellie, and shook Walt's big hand and thumped his back and led them down the center aisle of the church, past the regular crowd and a cluster of family members: Kate's mother smiling beneath a black hat draped in some sort of netting, like a beekeeper; his sister-in-law Joan sitting stiffly between Becky and Dylan; Maureen doing something to Terri's hair while Rick fanned himself with a bulletin. Ellie scanned the congregation while they walked, warily glancing back and forth, it seemed to Calvin, squinting into the candle-lit corners, looking for someone. They found their seats in front with Kate and Grace, who was propped in the corner of the pew in a new white sleeper and her pink blanket. (His mother had offered the family baptismal gown, the yellowed relic she'd found in her basement, and Calvin had hemmed and hawed and finally said, "I don't think so," and his mother had said, "I understand," and maybe she did.)

When the first organ notes sounded, and they stood for the opening hymn, Calvin leaned over to Ellie and whispered, "He's not here." His father had become a kind of family fugitive soon after that night on the steps. Maureen, who fed the family tantalizing scraps about him like a paid informant, claimed he was injured, possibly disabled. Calvin felt only rare twinges of pity, nothing like remorse. "He's a broken man," Maureen announced. "Good," Calvin had blurted out, surprised at himself. No one talked about him or seemed to miss him very much. According to Maureen, he was living in the northern suburbs, paying alimony, making his rounds in a neck brace. Calvin seemed to feel nothing that his father had disappeared from his life, that he might never see him again, nothing at all. Except guilty relief.

They stood for the Gospel, the story of the five barley loaves and two small fishes, how Jesus fed the multitude and the disciples gathered up twelve baskets of leftovers, and sat for Pastor Alice's homily. She stood at the pulpit in a coarse hooded robe, and spoke from index cards, which she turned, one after another, sometimes without even looking down at them. Her voice was rich and resonant, like a Shakespearean actress. But she used ordinary words, a word like "food" or "bread," and somehow, through her patient, almost hypnotic repetition—daily bread, the bread of life, the bread of affliction, and the bread of tears—through her respectful, reverential pronunciation, she imbued them with new significance. We gather together each week, she said, a hungry multitude, and are nourished.

When it came time for the baptism itself, Kate handed Grace to Calvin. She was no longer the alien and inexplicable creature she'd seemed back in those early bewildering days.

Calvin had learned how to comfort her, how fast to rock and where to rub, how to pitch his voice to the special frequencies that made her smile. Back at work now during the days, he missed her sorely. He came to the office with milk stains on his suit coats and pacifiers in his pants pockets and called home every chance he got. Kate would hold the phone out so he could listen to her little squeakings and bulldog snuffling. And at six o'clock, stepping off the bus, two blocks from home, thinking only about her, imagining that he could already smell her sweet baby scent, he would start to run, his briefcase beating against his legs, his arms hungry to hold her.

Ellie and Walt stood solemnly beside them while Pastor Alice said a prayer over Grace and then, smiling, asked them to answer for her. They responded in unison. Together they renounced Satan and all his works, forsook the vain pomp and glory of the world, firmly, once and for all, as if they really meant it. Grace meanwhile lay in Calvin's arms, asleep, her mouth working slowly, lost in her milk dreams, blissfully un-aware of Satan's snares. Calvin would have liked to hold her there always, safely enfolded in his arms, sheltered, as they said each Sunday, from all anxiety. Alice ever so gently poured a tiny splash of water over the back of her head, just a cautious rinse, and quietly pronounced her baptized in the name of the Father, the Son, and the Holy Ghost. She made the sign of the cross on her forehead and blessed her.

Then Alice announced that Calvin and Kate would now bring Grace around so that the members of the congregation might add their own blessings and welcome. She took Calvin's elbow and turned him toward Ellie, who bent down and kissed Grace's head, and Walter, who patted her carefully, and then led Calvin and the baby to the front pew, where the family was sitting. Kate's mother bit her lip, pained with joy, and stroked Grace's head. Her eyes were open now, serenely watchful, the way she was in the hospital when every light was brand new, staring upward, entranced by a ceiling fan or the glimmer of stained glass. Phyllis ruffled her blanket with one hand and wiped a tear from her eye with the other, trying to save her makeup. "God bless you," she said. The kids, Grace's cousins, peeked in at her too, murmuring, touching her cheek, admiring her tiny hands, the boys stiff and self-conscious, the girls almost quivering with excitement.

Alice guided Calvin to the center aisle of the church, slowly down one side and back the other, Kate trailing behind, people gathering like on a parade route. He stopped at each pew, holding Grace out in her blanket, seeing just hands now, men's and women's, old and young, thick fingers and gold bands and glossy red nails, gently touching her, caressing her head like a downy softball, rubbing it like a charm, crossing her, blessing her. They were the multitude, and their reaching out to Grace, with battered knuckles and liver spots and nails chewed to the quick, seemed to Calvin something both common and wonderful, like bread, an ordinary miracle.

In the back of the church, Calvin spotted Geoff, who must have arrived late and found a spot comfortably distant from Joan. They had spoken only once since Grace's birth and Calvin's decking his father and Geoff's separation, a short call of congratulation their first day home from the hospital that turned imperceptibly into a discussion of the job offer Geoff was considering in California. Geoff said all the right things, his voice perfectly composed and balanced. Now he was standing alone, impeccably dressed, starched oxford cloth and herringbone, smiling, a picture of studied nonchalance, like a catalog model. As Calvin approached, his brother drew his hand from his coat pocket and raised it slowly, his long, curved fingers extending stiffly from the pale palm as if to grasp something.

At the reception afterward, Grace lay across Walter's lap and slept, undisturbed by the general din, the clanking of glasses and the cutting of the cake and the explosion of flashbulbs, her little hand wrapped around his thick index finger. Once Calvin had made sure that everyone had something to drink and there was enough ice and the kids got ice cream, he joined them on the couch. Walter's tie was loosened, his top button undone, his sleeves rolled above his elbows. He waggled his finger slowly back and forth, and Grace hung on. Ellie darted by the kitchen doorway, bent at the waist, in hot pursuit of Lucy, who seemed to be gleefully making off with something, and Walter smiled.

The fewness of Walter's words used to be the subject of great merriment at family gatherings. Geoff could take him off hilariously, clearing his throat as if in preparation for a grand speech, and then finally, whispering, after much ado, "Salt?" Calvin could remember vividly Walter sitting on someone's deck for what seemed like hours without saying a word, watching meat sizzle on the grill while Maureen's kids climbed up his back and fooled with his hair.

But Calvin was grateful now that Walter didn't talk. He was trying to hang onto something. He wanted to remember the feeling of the church, that blessing. People tried, but there was no way to say anything about it, about what mattered most. Outside the church, after the service, Grace had started to squawk a little, and somebody joked that it was the Holy Spirit. Then somebody else said the same thing. It was a neat service, Maureen said. Better not to talk at all. They sat there shoulder to shoulder in silence, like a couple of old farts on a park bench, Walter a reassuringly large mass, watching little Grace sleep.

Then Kate called his name. She was standing at the front door with Joan and the kids, saying good-bye. Calvin stood and joined them, thanked them for coming, trying to remember whether or not they'd brought a gift. He gave Dylan five, high and low, and kissed Becky's hand, smacking and slobbering until she blushed. He helped Joan with her coat. She was holding an unlit cigarette, gesturing to Maureen across the room. "Wednesday is D day," she said.

"I still say," Maureen shouted back, "get the patch. You won't regret it." Dylan made a face, his eyes rolling and mouth twisting in surly contempt, an expression of more than ordinary adolescent disgust, something downright hateful. Only Calvin saw it.

"Thanks," Calvin said. Joan was still talking. "Thanks for everything," he said, inching toward the door, gathering them up and moving them out like a sheepdog. Finally, after more thanks and more chitchat—his family spent more time planning their next get-together than they did actually visiting—they were out the door, in the car, and down the street.

Geoff showed up so soon after Joan's departure that Calvin wondered whether he had the place staked out or they were working carefully timed, predetermined shifts. Calvin looked up and saw his face pressed darkly against the front door screen. "Hello?" he said. "Anybody home?" Calvin let him in. He was wearing a white polo shirt and khakis now, his hair wet and combed back. He had a stuffed dog tucked under his arm. Calvin shook his hand and was startled by his brother's new angularity—he hadn't noticed it at church—by how slight he'd grown. It was the mania for exercise Maureen had told him about, his blading, biking, race walking, running, constant motion in fancy footgear, around and around the lakes. He was in terrific shape, she said. But his face seemed cancerously thin, his cheekbones protruding, and this, combined with his perfect clothes and nice tan and expensive haircut, produced a disturbing effect, like a dying Hollywood star on the cover of the *Enquirer*.

Calvin led him into the dining room and left him with his mother and Ellie chatting over a table full of plates smeared with frosting. When he returned with a cup of decaf, Geoff had just announced he was taking the job on the West Coast. "But she doesn't know yet," he said, "so don't say anything." Joan was always the understood antecedent; Geoff rarely spoke her name, even in good times. (Robert E. Lee, Calvin remembered, used to refer to the Union troops only as "those people.") Calvin said congratulations, and Ellie asked why California, and Phyllis asked when, and Geoff fielded their questions, coffee cup in hand, composed as an official spokesman at a press conference. It was a great opportunity, he said, giving special weight to the word "opportunity," as if they all understood some unspoken meaning it carried. He would start with the new fiscal year, the first of July. "I can't wait," he said. "Of course, it will be hard to be away from the kids." Ellie reached down and patted Lucy, who was on the floor at their feet, crouched on all fours in front of a bowl of Cheerios, studying her reflection in the glass door of the hutch. "Good kitty," she said, and Lucy started to purr.

Then Pastor Alice rang the doorbell, and by the time Calvin got her coffee and cake, and brought a fresh cup of tea to Kate's mother, his mother and Ellie and Walt were edging to the door. It was time for Lucy's nap. Calvin had hoped to spend more time with them, Ellie especially, and had imagined that without his father and his television, the black hole at the center of most family gatherings in the past, things would be calmer, more leisurely, not just the usual clamor of coming and going, kissed cheeks and handshakes. "We'll be here all week," Ellie said, and patted his arm. "Later, alligator," Lucy said, and hid her face in her mother's skirt.

After they pulled away, Kate handed Grace to Calvin and joined her mother on the porch. He walked slowly through the living room with Grace high on his shoulder, rubbing and patting, while Geoff watched from the couch. "You know who she really looks like, don't you?" he said, and Calvin's heart sank. He didn't want to hear. "She looks just like Popeye. All she needs is a little corncob pipe."

Once he got going, Geoff could be funny, but Calvin didn't want to hear it now, his constant flow of jokes and one-liners and comic voices, like a stand-up routine. There was an unpleasant undercurrent to Geoff's humor, a meanness, something a little nasty. He was always laughing at someone, seizing on something and turning them into characters. Like Walter, the paramedic from Buffalo, the source of endless Heimlich and Super Bowl jokes. Calvin was tired of it.

He walked Grace into the kitchen. Part of him just wanted to keep his distance from Geoff, to keep him away from Grace and everything he loved most, to lock up his heart's treasures as long as his brother was in the house. He strapped Grace in her bouncy chair and busied himself at the sink.

Geoff followed him into the kitchen, leaned on the table, and watched Calvin work. When he lived at home, Geoff never did housework. Calvin remembered him as defiantly lazy. If it bothers you, he used to say, you clean up. It doesn't bother me.

Calvin meticulously scraped a stack of plates, conscious of Geoff watching him, wondering what he wanted. Grace's eyes were starting to droop.

And then while Calvin rinsed, Geoff launched into a story about a family he saw in a pizza joint the other night. There were three kids in one booth, parents in another, all of them wearing identical sweatshirts. "With fancy lettering," he said, "and some kind of logo, tablets and a Latin inscription, like an Ivy League college.

"At first I see one of the kids' shirts—CHRIS. And I think, okay, they're wearing their names. But then I see the T. All of them are wearing shirts that say CHRIST. In big beautiful block letters."

Calvin put the stopper in the sink and turned on the hot water. He squirted soap under the tap. "So, I'm waiting for my sub," Geoff said. "I'm curious. I mean, it's the middle of the week. I figure, I'll watch them, Team Christ. The kids have a bag of potato chips and a carton of dip on the table along with the pizza."

Calvin watched the sink fill, suds roiling, steam rising. "So what do you think, Calvin? How does a family of true believers eat their pizza? It's interesting, don't you think? Calvin?"

Geoff wanted him to turn around, but Calvin promised himself he wasn't going to do it, not this time. He closed his eyes and plunged his hands into the scalding water.

14

VIAL OF LIFE

HAL WAS LIVING NORTH OF THE CITIES NOW, NO PARTICULAR PLACE.
The mailing address was a numbered county road in a munici-
pality he had never heard of. It was near the freeway. He had
his own parking space in a back lot. He mailed his rent checks
to a corporation based in Dallas. When there was a problem, a
guy with a walkie-talkie showed up, like the auto club, within
the hour, always someone different. There was an expansive
lawn in front of the complex with a built-in sprinkler system
and a series of recessed floodlights that illuminated the building at night, like the White House. There were no sidewalks,
no trees, no dogs, no kids in the street, nobody washing a car
in the driveway. There was a golf course across the road, an
office complex—doctors and dentists and physical therapists—
and a video store, big as Kmart.

In his apartment, Hal felt self-sufficient. He had everything he needed. There was a dishwasher and a garbage disposal. There was an air-conditioner. He had a sleek new television with a built-in VCR. He had a cable connection and a new box. There was a microwave oven and a refrigerator stocked with frozen gourmet dinners in boxes. There was a black telephone parked on his butcher block kitchen table, where he would sit and drink coffee and make his calls.

Hal liked the anonymity, the solitude. Most of the other residents got into their cars with their coffee cups and briefcases early in the morning and didn't return until after dark. A few were retired, older women mainly, but they kept to themselves for the most part, watched their game shows and waited for the mail, carried out tiny sacks of trash to the dumpster in the back. Only one, Leona Birch from across the hall, introduced herself. She was an elfish woman with spiky orange hair, jaggedly cut, like one of the black-leather punks at McDonald's. Except she was lined with wrinkles and her mouth was filled with unnervingly large, ill-fitting false teeth. She advised him about laundry room etiquette and asked him a lot of personal questions, which he dodged the best he could. On St. Patrick's Day she left a piece of green cake outside his door. Through the peephole, Hal watched her shuffle across the hall and set it on his mat. She was wearing a green plastic derby with glittery silver letters: THANK GOD I'M IRISH. She was just being friendly, a nosy but basically harmless old lady. But she spooked Hal. The hair. Even her skin was a little off, another unnatural shade, tending toward orange too, not tanned but like it was stained or dyed. There was a big sticker plastered on her door: VIAL OF LIFE. Hal had no idea what it meant. It gave him the creeps. It made him think of something ghoulish floating in a test tube. If he were headed out the door, and he heard Leona in the hall, he would hang back, instinctively, until she was gone and the coast was clear.

It was Wednesday morning. Outside Hal's back window, it was gray and hazy. There were puddles in the parking lot from a thunderstorm the night before, which Hal remembered only vaguely—a cracking overhead, loud as gunfire, sheets of rain beating against the window. He was on the couch now watching two guys on CNN rehashing Waco, talking about David Koresh and Janet Reno, suicide drills, tear gas, ATF, and the Seventh Seal. When Hal heard the door, he was puzzled. At first he thought it was part of the program. Then he thought it was somebody on the floor making repairs or hanging a picture. He muted the set and listened. It came again, three fast knocks, like a coded message. It was supposed to be a security building, but someone was out there, banging on his door.

Hal took his glasses off and put his right eye to the peephole. It was a dark-haired young woman with fancy dangling earrings. Though only a few inches away, she looked weirdly distant, as if she were standing at the end of a tunnel instead of on the other side of an oak-veneer door. Her face was so serious, she might have been another policewoman or a new probation officer. Except she was good-looking. There were the beginnings of lines around her eyes, and her lips were tight with purpose, but she was appealingly intent. She looked like the kind who collects signatures for a good cause. Hal switched eyes, and the woman took a step back so that he could see her whole. That's when he recognized her. His daughter. Eleanor.

Hal pulled away. He felt sick to his stomach. It didn't matter that he was unlisted. She had come all the way from New York and found him out somehow. He had known this day was coming, surprised only that it had come now, that this was the day. He looked again. Unobserved, like a customer in the bank's camera eye, she looked serenely determined, wrapped in a sort of fierce, missionary calm. She wasn't going to go away. She just kept knocking, not angry, not sharp, just relentlessly patient. Hal put his hand on the knob.

He tried to imagine it. He knew what she wanted; he knew the script. She would sit on the couch and make small talk. He'd offer her something, and she'd refuse. You look great, he would say. How was your trip? But sooner or later, she would be in his face, fangs bared, like an attack dog, spewing hot froth and venom. She would have a list of grievances, another indictment. He was supposed to listen. While she spit her resentment at him.

How much humiliation did he need to eat? He'd been arrested, frisked, fingerprinted. He had pleaded to a judge. Paid a fine. Recited his sexual history to a smirking social worker. Been knocked around by his son. Now his daughter was here to get her licks in. Hal took his hand away. Enough was enough.

He heard something in the hall. Again, Hal put his eye to the peephole. He saw Leona Birch standing in the hall with Eleanor. She was wearing a terry cloth robe, her head wrapped turban-style in a white towel. They were talking. Hal put his ear to the door. "His daughter?" Leona was saying. "You don t say. I didn't know he had a daughter."

They huddled together in the hall for a moment, their voices low and conspiratorial, and then stepped into Leona's apartment. They left the door open. Hal rubbed his eye and squinted, but his view through his peephole was out of focus, distorted and distant, like the world seen through the wrong end of binoculars: he could see his daughter's back in the doorway, some floral furniture, a glittering table of picture frames and knickknacks. It occurred to him then that Leona was retrieving a key to his place that she had stashed somewhere. Hal looked around his apartment, and for one fleeting, crazy moment considered prying off the back window. But it was three stories down, nothing but concrete below. He was no high-flying television hero, no Tom Selleck. He had arthritis and a bad back. He felt like Koresh in his compound now, wounded and trapped.

Eleanor stood in the entry to Leona's apartment for what seemed like forever. Hal could hear the murmuring of their voices, nothing distinct, maybe the sound of his name, maybe not. He caught glimpses of Leona scurrying back and forth in her robe.

Finally Eleanor stepped back into the hall with something black in her hand. "Thank you," she said as Leona closed the door. "I will." It was sleek and sharp. Hal thought at first it was a weapon or a tool of some kind, a screwdriver, maybe, a jimmy, or even a knife. But it was just a pen. She had some paper, too. She leaned against the wall, like a student between classes, and started writing, the paper balanced on the inside bend of her forearm.

She bit her lower lip in concentration, as she had always done, even as a little girl, sweating over her homework. Hal could remember how she struggled with long division, spelling words, even the catechism questions required at confirmation. Nothing came easy for her. But she kept at it. She had her mother's elegant hands and long fingers, and his own plodding tenacity. He used to chew his lip, too. She never paused, never lifted her pen, never looked up. She just kept writing, page after page.

Finally she stopped. Capped the pen and folded her pages. A little pleased with herself, Hal imagined, at least relieved. She approached his door one more time, looking so intently into the center of it—right at him—that he was afraid that she could see him there in the hole, one terrified eyeball, like the back of a dollar bill.

Hal stepped back and watched it come nosing slowly under the door like a living thing. He didn't want to touch it. But it just lay there, a packet of purple paper. It was harmless, he told himself. Sticks and stones. He looked into the hall one more time, but she had disappeared. There was just the door, closed now, and its unimaginable message. VIAL OF LIFE. Words can never hurt me.

He bent down and picked it up. Held it in his hand. Took a deep breath and unfolded it. "Dear Dad," it started. Ellie's handwriting was strong, her letters perfectly formed, and Hal, who hated his own childish scrawl, found it beautiful.

Hal couldn't read straight through. There were spots of white light dancing in the corners of his eyes, like flashbulbs. He jumped from word to word and phrase to phrase, like a stone skipping across the surface of a lake. He was looking for something dreadful he never found. It seemed to tell a story. *Once, a long time ago . . .* She talked about the house, the old tree out front, saltwater taffy. There wasn't any mention of him. He didn't see the point of it, her rambling. *Things happened,* she wrote. *You know what I'm talking about. But not just to me. I know that now. There was enough heartache to go around. So here's the point: I don't hate you anymore.* At the end, there were some wishes for him, a long list, like the prayer of the faithful. *May you find peace.* On and on. May this, may that.

She signed her name at the bottom of the last page, and below that, wrote, "God bless us all." Like Tiny Tim. So he was Scrooge now, unredeemed, the vision fled. But that wasn't it either. He was nothing to her now. Not a father, not a villain. Nothing. She had traveled a thousand miles, slipped past the locked front door, and nullified him. He was nothing now, and she was gone for good. He knew that. He was guilty—he'd known that always, lived in it for as long as he could remember it, the guilt inexplicably preceding any shameful acts, the medium and the raw material, their soul and substance, making them possible, driving them. But now he had been forgiven, and that was worse, left behind, a stinking carcass doused in holy water. She could keep her paltry forgiveness. He didn't want it.

15

INSTANT PARTY

"Love you," her mother said, her mouth full of Juicy Fruit, the car already starting to roll. Becky stood on the curb in front of her grandmother's house and watched her mother drive away, tugging unhappily at her earring in the rearview mirror. It was a drizzly Saturday morning. Becky was dressed in grubby jeans and had her baby-sitting bag slung over her shoulder. She was there to help with the house, which was going on sale Monday. Aunt Ellie said she would pay her to watch Lucy, but that wasn't necessary, Becky told her, and she meant it.

Her mother couldn't stay, she said, because she had a long list of things to do, errands to run. Part of Becky was relieved, glad to get away just for a day. Her mother had quit smoking on Wednesday—one last drag at the stroke of midnight and the rest of the pack crumpled dramatically into the garbage—and she was still fidgety and irritable. Becky had spent the last hour and a half listening to her bitch about her dad, who, they'd just learned, was moving to California.

It was what her mother imagined therapy to be, how she thought Becky talked to Dr. Reston while she read her magazines in the waiting room. They would sit together for hours in the breakfast nook, her mother drinking black coffee and talking, talking, talking. When Becky went to the bathroom, her mother waited outside and started in again as soon as she opened the door. Always about him, what he was doing, what he'd done, what he was going to do. "A hundred dollars an hour," her mother would say as she cleared the table when one of their sessions broke up. But really, even though Becky herself tried to mimic Dr. Reston—she listened with her hands in her lap, nodded, asked, "How do *you* feel?"—it was just complaining. It was the same way Becky and her friends talked in the lunchroom about their teachers. Afterward, her mother always claimed to feel better. "I just needed some relief," she said once, red-faced, like someone on a daytime TV commercial suffering with constipation or blocked sinuses or feminine itching. Becky always felt worse. The heady feeling of grown-up confidentiality wore off soon enough, and she would be left newly anxious, exhausted, and burdened with the grim business of adults. It was as if her mother had sloughed off some emotional queen of spades in a game of hearts, and Becky was left holding it, thirteen points.

The front door was open. As a little girl, she had loved her grandmother's house, which was itself like a quirky old relative, eccentric, a little scary, full of musty surprises. There was a back servants' staircase to the second floor, like something out of Nancy Drew, and a wooden shelf and little square door, shoulder-high, that opened between the kitchen and front hall, originally for a telephone, where Becky, perched on a bench, used to talk to her grandmother while she made dinner. There was an attic full of books and old clothes, and a paneled office in the basement with a spinning chair. In the bathroom there were old-fashioned faucets and pull-chain lights and a big medicine cabinet with a smoky beveled-glass mirror that was warmer somehow, more forgiving, than the antiseptic glare of their brand-new bathrooms at home.

"Hello?" Becky said. She could hear music playing somewhere in the house, rock and roll. "Hello?" she said again, but no one answered. She opened the storm door and stepped inside. Across the living room's dirty expanse of beige carpeting, she could see his chair—rusty plaid upholstery, the wooden handle like a throttle, the pockets bulging with newspapers and *TV Guide*s and remote controls. As if he'd be right back. She felt the cold dread spreading in her gut. But she started moving, taking slow steps, like someone crossing a frozen lake, like a soldier on patrol, expecting the worst but afraid to stand still.

The room was not quite the way she'd remembered it, as if things had been moved around and put back just slightly off kilter. The couch was pushed against the front windows, the pillows all piled on one side. The family pictures above the mantel looked as if they had been rearranged, the picture of her and Dylan angled toward the chimney. There were voices in the kitchen, people laughing. Becky walked past the chair toward them, past the hulking, unplugged television, around the corner and into the dining room, where the chairs had been stacked onto the table, like a restaurant after hours.

In the kitchen, it was happy, purposeful chaos, like an Amish barn-raising. Uncle Walter was standing on a step stool, two streaks of white paint in his hair, touching up the kitchen door frame with a narrow brush, daubing and leaning back, considering, daubing again, like a great artist at work, bopping to the tinny music, "Domino," which was coming from a transistor radio on his ladder, the horns swelling, the singer growling, "Lord have mercy." Grandma Phyllis was polishing the scarred oak kitchen table with a thick white cloth. Aunt Kate was on a ladder outside looking in, washing windows intently, and Uncle Calvin was kneeling in front of the refrigerator with Grace beside him in a bouncy chair, fishing for something under the refrigerator with a long-handled brush.

Becky stood for a moment in the doorway, invisibly, inhaling the smell of fresh paint and lemon wax. She felt glad to see them, grateful for their presence. Aunt Ellie, wearing jeans and a denim shirt, her hair tied up in a red bandana, was standing on the counter, rummaging through the top cupboard shelves. She turned, two bottles in her hand, black liquid rolling behind the clear glass, like hard stuff in an old western movie. "Two more," she shouted over her shoulder. "How much molasses have you got, Mom?" Then she saw her. "Becky," she said. "We were just talking about you. Welcome to the cleaning party." She eased herself off the counter and onto the floor, like someone getting into a pool, and gave Becky a big hug.

Becky had long wanted to be like Ellie. Pretty and artistic and full of confidence. A mother who kneeled down to talk to little ones. And stood up to the police for her. Becky knew all about her statement, even though she never said anything about it. She had written Ellie a few letters over the winter, just stupid chat about the weather and school, and hoped she understood. Ellie always wrote back, on creamy stationery in her gorgeous handwriting, which Becky spent her study halls trying her best to imitate.

And now she seemed so genuinely happy to see her, patting her arm, smiling, announcing her arrival, looking at her— really *looking* at her—as if she were somebody special. Becky didn't know what to say.

''What can I do?'' she said.

''Have a cookie,'' Grandma Phyllis said, and held out a plate.

''Really,'' Becky said.

Lucy was lying on the floor beneath the kitchen table with a coloring book and a fat red crayon in hand, watching. Becky opened her bag and brought out the contents, one by one, books, puzzles, a roll of stickers, little bags of dinosaur treats, her *Beauty and the Beast* videotape. She lined them up on the floor, and watched while Lucy approached, cautious but curious, warily determined as a chipmunk approaching a campsite.

They spent most of the afternoon together surrounded by the commotion of cleaning and home repair. They sat on the floor side by side and read every book in the bag twice over, Lucy completely transfixed by Becky's own well-worn childhood favorites, some of them coverless, Madeline and Frances the Badger and Lyle, Lyle Crocodile, her hand resting lightly on Becky's arm, Becky shouting over Ellie's hammering and the roar of the rented carpet cleaner Uncle Walter drove through the living room like a runaway Zamboni machine.

When Becky tried to get up, Lucy threw her arms around her neck and grinned like a little fiend. ''You can't leave,'' she said. ''You have to stay *forever*.''

She was like the little sister Becky had long ago ceased to pester her mother for. She loved her, no questions asked. When everyone else was nothing but questions. What are you gonna wear? her friends at school would demand. What did you get on the history quiz? What's the significance of this or that, her English teacher would ask, and if no one said anything, she went down the list. Her mother asked, Why didn't you tell *me?* Like it was something that happened to her. Was there penetration? the policeman had wanted to know. He had bad breath and needed a shave. Becky thought he might be enjoying himself. But no penetration, and they lose interest. She shook her head and blushed. But it wasn't that simple. That night, Becky looked the word up in the dictionary again, studied all its meanings: the act or process of entering or forcing a way into something, piercing, permeating; affecting deeply as by piercing the consciousness or emotions. *Everyfuckingday turdbreath,* she wrote in her diary that night. *That's how I feel.*

"Forever is a long time," Becky said, but Lucy just tightened her grip. "Okay," Becky said. "Okay."

Later in the afternoon, an older man in a crew cut showed up with a for-sale sign. It was yellow and black, like a generic label. On the bottom was a name, Earl Bass, and a telephone number. Becky wasn't in the room when he arrived and didn't catch his name, but she figured he had to be Earl Bass. They followed him outside and watched him pound the sign into the lawn with a rubber mallet. The sign made the house look completely different somehow. Vacant and unloved. They stood back in silence and looked at it. Somebody coughed. It was like a little ceremony. Grandma

Phyllis's eyes seemed watery, but it might have been the wind. Becky wanted to say something to her, but she didn't know the words. Then she saw Earl Bass touch her arm, and they headed back inside.

After that, everyone went back to work. Ellie and Kate headed down the basement loaded with cleaning supplies, torn T-shirts, rubber gloves. Walter and Calvin went into the backyard with a pruner and a box of leaf bags. In the living room, Becky built a Duplo house with Lucy—a front door, two windows, and a landing pad on the roof for the Duplo helicopter. Grandma Phyllis and Earl Bass stayed in the kitchen. Becky could hear the buzz of the can opener, drawers shutting, the refrigerator door, and the confidential hum of their conversation. Before long she heard sizzling and spattering, and the whirring of her grandmother's beaters, and the downstairs was filled with the smell of garlic and onions and strange spices.

She stood on her toes and studied herself in the bathroom mirror. Already she had forgotten what she used to look like, before, when her skin was clear. Lucy's complexion was perfect, like all little girls'. Becky had taken it for granted, and now it was gone. There was a red swath of pimples on her right cheek, angry and volcanic, hard nodules beneath her skin waiting to erupt. Her forehead was covered, too, and her chin. She no longer felt as if her face was a part of her. She felt now as if she were peering out from behind it, wearing it like a mask.

In the pamphlet they gave her at the doctor's office it was called *Acne Vulgaris*. Becky read about the causes—something involving bacteria, invisible things living on her skin, clogging her pores. She learned the terminology and studied the varieties—blackheads and white heads, papules, pustules and cysts, which caused scars. "They are permanent," the pamphlet said. Period. The hideous cutaway diagrams of normal skin were bad enough—the peeling layers, the oil glands and hair follicles—but there were photographs of diseased faces, too, their eyes hidden by black rectangles, their cheeks covered with pustules. She noticed them nowadays, the scarred ones, always working lousy jobs—in greasy coveralls at service stations, behind the counter at 7-Eleven—and they looked to her inexplicably related, like scattered members of a single family. It dawned on her finally that what they shared, their only kinship, was a kind of surly shyness and the scarred terrain of their red faces.

She washed her face gently with soap and water, the way she was supposed to. Then, in the medicine cabinet, she found a pack of Wilkinson Sword blades. She imagined slicing her face clean, a neat surgical removal, once and for all. It was crazy, she knew, but it seemed so easy. She picked up a pumice stone from the ledge of the tub instead. It was a rough little block of concrete. She took the stone to her face, moved it slowly back and forth across the skin of her cheek. Red lines appeared, a spot of blood. Downstairs she could hear the clatter of dishes, the sound of muffled laughter. She leaned forward and watched herself work. She pressed harder. It was ugly, but she couldn't stop looking. It was painful, but she couldn't stop scraping.

They gathered later around the dining room table for dinner, Aunt Ellie and Uncle Walter, his hair still streaked with paint, Lucy on a phone book at Becky's side, baby Grace bundled in a pink blanket fast asleep on Aunt Kate's shoulder. Becky thought Ellie might be looking at her face, but she didn't say anything. Grandma Phyllis shuttled back and forth to the kitchen with serving dishes, her hands wrapped in big oven mitts, happily harried, like it was Thanksgiving. Earl Bass ladled out big chunky bowls full of steaming chili and Grandma Phyllis passed a salad bowl and handed around little squares of corn bread.

"Looks great, Earl," Calvin said, and doused his bowl with great globs of sour cream. Uncle Walter leaned down over his bowl and took one slow spoonful, then another, and another. He leaned back and wiped his mouth. His face was red, and there were little beads of sweat forming on his forehead. He extended his hand across the table to Earl Bass, who looked surprised, a little scared. Walter grabbed his hand and they shook and shook. "Now that's chili," Walter said.

When Becky looked down on her plate, a sandwich had appeared there. Grilled cheese with sliced tomato, cut diagonally, the way her grandmother had fixed sandwiches for as long as she could remember. Becky wanted to thank her, but she was already gone, back in the kitchen, rattling through the silverware drawer.

Then there was a knock at the front door. It was a heavyset guy in dirty jeans and a baseball cap come to take the big television away. He counted out some bills and handed them to Grandma Phyllis, who jammed them in her purse. She seemed embarrassed. "I sold it through the Thrifties," she said to no one in particular. "What do I need with that?"

The man squatted in front of the set and ran his fingers lightly over the screen, the speakers, the controls. He seemed delighted. But he needed some help getting it into his van. He and Walter took one end, Calvin and Earl grabbed the other, and Ellie and Becky got their hands on it, too. Phyllis cleared the way and propped the door. "I can't believe he didn't take it with him," Calvin said, inching backward out the door, grimacing with effort, ropy veins standing out on his forearms.

They moved carefully down the stairs, controlled but still straining, making a slow procession to the street, where the fellow's van was parked. On the count of three, they lifted and pushed it into the back next to a ladder, two yellow hard hats, and a metal thermos. The man covered it with a quilted drop cloth. "Thank you," he said. "It's been a pleasure." They stood at the curb and watched him drive off, waving like old friends.

Inside there was a creased rectangle of bright carpet where the television had been. The room felt cavernously big. They sat down again, and Earl Bass tried to tell a joke. It was about a preacher, his wife, bad sermons, and eggs. He went on and on, but he couldn't get it right. He kept doubling back, changing things, adding details. Then he just stopped. It was so not-funny they couldn't stop laughing. He pretended to be flustered and annoyed with them, but Becky could tell he was enjoying himself.

Then Grandma Phyllis cleared the dishes, and they moved into the living room, the grown-ups settling in with their coffee, Calvin and Kate on the couch, Grandma Phyllis in the rocker, Aunt Ellie on the floor with Becky and Lucy. Earl and Walter stayed behind in the dining room to discuss car travel between Minneapolis and Buffalo, the two of them bent over a map, like generals planning a campaign, tracing the lines with their fingers, reciting the names of highways like secret codes, comparing routes across Canada. Nobody sat in the big recliner.

"I can't believe it," Grandma Phyllis said, and everybody nodded. In the rocker, wrapped in a sweater, she looked small and tired. Even her skin looked gray.

"Hey," Ellie said. She was poking around in a wooden stereo cabinet along the wall, what Becky had always thought of as just another doily-covered surface. "Look at these," she said. She held up a big stack of long-playing record albums. The covers were faded, the big circle of the record showing through, but to Becky, used to cassette tapes and CD's, the art seemed huge, like posters. There was Carole King barefoot with her cat. The Kingston Trio in matching green button-downs, their heads thrown back and mouths open, whooping it up big time. Young Nat King Cole with two grinning pals. It was like a time capsule. Ellie held up the Everly Brothers, all pudgy peach-fuzz. *"Instant Party,"* she said. "My God."

"Just add water," Calvin said.

"More of the Monkees," Ellie said. "This is mine. Can you believe it? I loved the Monkees. Geoff and I had a big argument once about who was better, the Monkees or the Beatles. Do you remember, Mom, when you took us to the Beatles concert?"

"I never."

"You sure did. We didn't have tickets or anything. But Dad was out of town, and everyone was nuts about the Beatles, so we all piled in the car and parked outside the stadium and rolled down the windows and listened. It was like a drive-in. Calvin was just a baby, all bundled with blankets. Maureen stood on the hood of the car and gyrated. Come on, Mom. You really don't remember?"

"Maybe," she said. "What did it sound like?"

"All I remember is screaming. A hundred thousand watts of echoing adolescent hysteria. It was weird. But we ate some Milk Duds or something and then went home. We were part of history."

Ellie lifted the lid of the cabinet and peered inside, like a mechanic inspecting a car engine. "Does this thing work?" There was some clicking and a clunk and then the scratchy tinkling of a piano joined by a bass and the brush of a drum. Calvin raised his index fingers and swept them back and forth in time to the music, like jazzy little windshield wipers. Grandma Phyllis just smiled. This was her music.

The music pulled Walter and Earl Bass into the room. Earl Bass made a compact little bow in front of Grandma Phyllis's chair, and held out his hand. She took it, and just like that, they were dancing, doing what Becky recognized from the ballroom unit in Phys Ed as the jitterbug. But compared to her own self-conscious and mechanical steps across the gym floor with Tresa Bailey as a partner—step-touch-step-touch-back-and-step-touch—their movement was graceful and fluid, like something from an old movie. Earl Bass held up his arm, and Grandma Phyllis twirled, first one way and then another, laughing, surprised and exhilarated, like someone on a roller coaster. Earl Bass's shoes thumped rhythmically across the floor in time to the music, and Grandma Phyllis, though bent and weathered—"You're kind of wrinkly," Lucy had said at dinner and she was right—glided across the floor smiling, looking pleased and dignified, like the good queen at a fairy tale ball. Only people who were really in love could dance like that.

It was weird to think of her grandmother with a boyfriend.

Becky's mother, who could be nasty and insinuating, said she'd heard that she was going around with a man, as if her grandmother was lurking down a dark alley with some kind of hoodlum. Becky didn't blame her. Grandma Phyllis always used to seem so fluttery and nervous. She and Grandpa Hal had lived in the same house, but they were never really *together*. They weren't a couple. Now she was dancing across the living room floor in big white sneakers and anklets with her arms locked around a gray-haired realtor. Becky could just imagine what her mother would say. But so what? She was happy, maybe it was simple as that. Didn't people deserve to be happy?

Then Walter and Ellie started dancing too, more cautious, holding each other a little tentatively, like a nervous first date. Kate, sitting alone on the couch, scooped the baby from her seat, hoisted her, blankets and all, to her shoulder, and grabbed Calvin. They shuffled back and forth slowly in place while little Grace reared up from time to time for a wobbly, bug-eyed look around.

Lucy, practically exploding with excitement—grown-ups dancing!—pulled Becky up and out onto the floor. They held hands and swayed back and forth, and then Lucy stepped carefully onto Becky's feet for a free ride. She wasn't very heavy. Lucy closed her eyes and held on while Becky whisked her around and around the floor, steering clear of the grown-ups, moving in energetic orbits, like skaters on a rink, until the room started to spin.

When the music stopped, Earl Bass took orders all around, Coke, coffee, water. Calvin and Walter collapsed on the couch, and the ladies loitered in a little group, pink in the face, breathing heavy, a little sheepish. Talking about good dancers, who really knew how to lead. Earl Bass came back with a tray full of drinks, like a waiter. He held out a tall glass of ice water to Becky. "Can you give this to your mother, please?" he said. He motioned with his head toward Ellie.

She was standing right across from her, huddled with Kate and Grandma Phyllis, looking down, watching her mother demonstrate a fancy maneuver. Becky couldn't tell if she'd heard or not. Earl Bass was mixed up, and now was the time to set him straight. But she didn't. "Yes," she said, and took the glass. "I'd be glad to." And felt a rush of being bad. The glass tinkled merrily in her hand.

"Here," Becky said, and Ellie reached out and took it, her eyes shining with conspiracy. She must have heard. "Thank you," she said. She took Becky's arm and pulled her into the circle. Held on tight. Becky wanted to stand there in the iron grip of her affection forever, watching her grandmother's feet make little shuffling steps, some old-time variation of the fox-trot, breathing the smell of her antique perfume, watching her blue-veined ankles, her white sneakers, dancing like there was no tomorrow.

It was Ellie who suggested that Becky stay overnight. Earl Bass had gone home, and they were sitting around the living room, looking at the clock, talking about how late it was, how tired they were. Lucy, still attached to Becky, clapped her hands. Grandma Phyllis brought down a pile of bedding and opened the fold-out couch. "I'll make pancakes tomorrow," Walter said.

"I can come by and take you to church," Calvin said.

"I have to ask," Becky said.

Her mother answered the phone, and Becky knew right away that she was mad. No one else could condense so much unhappiness into just two syllables. She'd run into a stupid checkout or been caught in traffic. Something had boiled over. Maybe Aunt Maureen called. It always happened when Becky was away. She would call during lunch from a pay phone at school and get the blow-by-blow. Underneath it all, Becky heard her mother's old grinding resentment, her suspicion that she might be having a good time. Fun was a betrayal of her mother and her frozen-faced misery.

Becky was supposed to ask what was wrong, but she didn't do it. She told her that Grandma wanted her to stay over, her voice as flat, as uninterested, as she could make it. There was a pause. She heard her mother inhale. ''Fine,'' she said finally. ''Go ahead.''

16

SPIRITS

THE FIRE STARTED IN THE BASEMENT. A SLOW SMOLDERING IN THE dark. Then, a warm red glowing. Finally, dancing orange and blue flames, licking at the plywood paneling in the office, casting flickering shadows across a neat line of cardboard boxes, turning a plastic wastebasket stuffed with papers into a melting, collapsing torch. When the fire ignited the pegboard doors to the storage cabinet under the stairs, the flames popped and crackled like pine cones in a campfire. The flames lapped at the joists and the floorboards, and moved hungrily up the stairs.

Later that morning, the fire inspector, who had spent most of Saturday night dealing blackjack at his little brother's stag, desperate for a glass of water and an aspirin, in no mood to pick nits, would find a blackened can of linseed oil and the charred handle of a mop next to the ancient furnace and put two and two together. He would write it up and that was that. Cleaning products. The appalling, combustible stupidity of everyday life. Exposed wire, drunks smoking in bed, overloaded circuits, kids with matches, space heaters left unattended for days, paint thinner and oily rags. Nothing surprised him anymore. He saw it every day.

Becky lay in the unfamiliar dark, watching headlights flicker across the ceiling, studying a square of marbled light on the wall from a window she couldn't see, like a ghostly framed picture. Her dream: a low-slung boat moving slowly back and forth across black waters, while a crowd looks on, humming with disaster, the barge dredging, dragging something, churning up a horrible debris—a child's black shoe, a twisted doll. Then suddenly at the wheel of a car, her hands encased in thick gloves, the dashboard alive with manic light, like a pinball machine, looking up into grotesquely flattened faces pressed against the glass, grinning. Clogged voices calling her name. She had willed herself awake, as she had learned to do, rising slowly, through the sheer force of her concentrated longing, like an act of levitation.

In the kitchen, Becky turned on all the lights. She found a square of corn bread wrapped in wax paper on the bread box and poured herself a glass of milk. She sat at the table and listened to the nighttime noise of her grandmother's house, its creak and rattle, the electric buzz and hum of its appliances. The kitchen smelled of Spic and Span and something warm, a lingering cooking smell, like fried eggs or popcorn. Becky thought about their cleaning party, Ellie standing on the counter arranging and polishing, about the fast one they pulled on Earl Bass. She thought about her mother at home, falling asleep to the flickering light of her bedroom television, the phony talk-show laughter seeping into her dreams.

Then she heard something, a dry crackling, like static. She stood and stalked it across the kitchen. Something was burning. She checked the stove, peered inside the dishwasher, studied the radiator. The noise was getting louder, revving like a motor, coming, she realized at last, from the basement. When she opened the door, it came billowing out—thick, suffocating black smoke.

She took the stairs two at a time, crying and choking, her lungs filled with smoke and terror. It was another nightmare. The house was on fire, and she needed to make a noise, but she couldn't do it. She opened her mouth but no words came.

Her grandmother was sitting upright in bed, ghostly and frightened in the dim glow of a street lamp, her hair undone, her face foreign and pinched without her glasses. *What is it? What's going on?*

The child was standing in front of her, wild-eyed, sputtering desperation. Years ago, her own children had stood in the same doorway, one by one, clutching stuffed animals, disoriented and frightened, thirsty and sick, lonely, reeling from bad dreams, wanting something. "What is it?" Phyllis said. "What's going on?" The girl just sobbed, quivering mutely with something too horrible for words. "Becky," Phyllis said sharply, a command. "Becky," she said, her voice rising louder and louder, "Becky," she said, a reprimand, a warning, a plea. "Say it." And then she did. Coughed up one word: *Fire.*

Only later were they able to piece together what happened next. There were two 911 calls, ninety seconds apart. Phyllis made the first from her bedside phone. "My house is on fire," she said, and recited the address, two times, spelled it, said "Thank you," and hung up. Becky charged into the guest room and stepped on Lucy, asleep in a bag on the floor. Ellie, roused immediately by Lucy's startled shout, scooped her off the floor, clamped her under her arm, and didn't let go. She herded Becky and Phyllis down the stairs, pushing so hard she raised a perfect bruise—a thumb and four fingers—on her mother's upper arm.

Walter, shirtless, striped boxers billowing out of his un-zipped jeans, made the second call from downstairs, then moved calmly through the house opening windows. He stood at the front door while they exited, distributing jackets and footgear from the hall closet, like a coat check: a black wind-breaker for Ellie, a roll-collared cardigan for Lucy, a plastic raincoat for Phyllis, a pair of fur-lined boots for Becky, a hooded sweatshirt for himself.

Always polite, Walter patiently helped Phyllis on with her coat while flames crackled in the kitchen and the downstairs filled with smoke. Her arm got tangled in the sleeve, and she tried again. She took one last look around. The carpet finally was spotless. The windows sparkled and the wood-work gleamed. She felt glad about that, a ridiculous old woman's pleasure, the satisfaction of clean underwear in a car accident.

She buttoned her coat, and Walter raised an eyebrow. It was time to go. So this was it, the famous parlor game: your house is on fire and you're headed out the door. What do you take with you? What do you salvage? Photographs? Jewelry? Stock certificates? There was an empty glass on the mantel, a pile of unopened mail, yesterday's newspaper, a sickly fern. And now that it was no game, now that her eyes were stinging with real smoke, she knew the answer. Nothing. Not a god-damned thing.

Ellie stood on the front lawn, staring at the house, Lucy clutched tight in her arms. Sirens wailed in the distance. There was a light shining upstairs, and through the half-opened curtain, she could glimpse a sliver of her mother's bedroom— a white bathrobe draped over the closet door, a serene domestic still-life. Downstairs, an orange light glowed ominously in the kitchen.

Phyllis stood with Becky at the curb, the two of them talking quietly, looking up and down the street. Walter was prowling in the shrubbery on the north side of the house.

"Walt," Ellie hissed. "What is it? What happened?"

"I don't know," he said. His face was impassive. He was on duty. "It's something in the basement. Something started down there."

Then Ellie remembered. She had been down the basement the day before. Kate sweeping the floor with meticulous short strokes. In her father's work room, his office, rubbing her knuckles raw on the paneled walls, scouring the scarred desk, emptied at last, the smell of spirits in her nostrils. A warning on the label, for chrissake. She could see herself with a handful of grimy rags—careful with those, Kate said—her skin crawling with her father's touch, wanting fresh air, wanting to scream, and pitching them in the direction of the humming furnace.

"Look, Mommy, look," Lucy said. Suddenly the house was bathed in flashing red light, and the street filled with rumbling trucks, polished chrome and rubber, the crackling of radios. There was a swarm of black-coated men, helmeted and visored, grim with purpose. Three firefighters, gold reflective strips gleaming on their coats like unearthly vestments, approached the house with axes and crowbars. They paused, and then, as if on some silent cue, like uniformed vandals, they smashed the basement windows with short, powerful blows. The glass exploded, and thick streams of smoke came pouring out, like exhaust from a downed plane.

Ellie stood on the lawn, transfixed, watching, drawn closer, feeling the heat now on her face, sweating in it, breathing the smoke of it, this fire she started.

A few passing cars slowed at the intersection, and once they seemed to realize that it was a real fire, not just a stroke or a gas leak, they pulled over to watch. The firefighters unrolled great lengths of flattened white hose, opened a hydrant with a red wrench, mounted ladders. The chief, in white shirtsleeves and a baseball cap, carrying a bullhorn he never used, paced and shouted instructions like a coach. Three times he asked Phyllis whether everyone was out of the house, and three times she took a head count: Ellie, Walter, Lucy, Becky. "Very good," he said. "Very good. Any pets?"

The man left his car running down the block with the flashers on. He was wearing a string tie and stinking of patchouli oil. He sidled up to Phyllis and shook her hand. He handed her a creased business card. When Walter came over, he was talking, and she was still studying the card in the flashing lights of the engines, looking perplexed. Walter took it from her:

JIM KEENE

INDEPENDENT CLAIMS ADJUSTER AND CONSULTANT

"Serving the Policy Holder"

There was more glass shattering, more black smoke pouring from the house. The man kept right on talking, selling his greasy service like an undertaker. Walter hated these guys. "Excuse us," Walter said, and put his arm around Jim Keene's shoulder. He grabbed his tie, twisted and shortened it like a dog's leash, and pulled him down the sidewalk, past two more firefighters jangling by in their turnout gear with extinguishers, to where his vinyl-roofed Olds was rumbling. Walter opened the car door and deposited him in the driver's seat, hard. "No thank you," he said.

Mrs. Terragnoli, wrapped in a plaid bathrobe, a green kerchief over head, came out of her house, and, making little clucks of disapproval, cleared a scruffy bunch of beery young men off her boulevard. They scattered like pigeons. Across the street, the firefighters went about their work, and the family stood together on the sidewalk watching. The air was thick with smoke, like a battlefield. She put her head down and crossed over.

"I'm so sorry," Phyllis said, as if it were her fault. The little girl was shivering.

"She should come with me," Mrs. T. said, and Ellie nodded. Mrs. T. took Phyllis by the arm, turned the girl away from the burning house, and brought them both inside.

The old woman's house was crowded with photographs and statues, baskets of newspapers and magazines, the furniture covered with afghans, thick pillows, knitted things. Everything smelled like mothballs. Lucy sat in the front room and played with a little white dog named Moon, who knew how to shake hands. Again and again, Moon raised a paw, and Lucy would seize it, give it a robust shaking, and say, "Pleaztomeetcha." Grandma's house was burning down, and she was in the kitchen talking on the telephone about it.

Outside she could see her father standing at the curb with a group of firemen, talking and pointing at the house, telling them what to do. Her mother was standing next to Becky on the sidewalk, wrapped in a black jacket. The collar was turned up and her hands were jammed in the pockets. She flickered red in the lights of the engines. Her long black hair looked wild and pretty, but her shoulders were sad.

Earl Bass answered on the first ring. It was four in the morning, but he sounded wide awake. When Phyllis heard his voice, she started to cry. "Earl," she sobbed. She had heard the crackling in her kitchen, seen sparks flying, wallpaper peeling in fiery strips. Mrs. T. busied herself at the sink, rinsing cups with steaming water. "I'll be right over," Earl said.

Phyllis took a deep breath, and called Calvin, only because she knew he would scold her if she didn't. He dropped the phone and remained politely noncommittal for a good minute until he realized who it was. "Mom," he shouted, "for chrissake," and then Kate started to murmur in the background.

"I'm okay," Phyllis said. Mrs. T. set a faintly flowered cup and saucer in front of her, a spoon, a three-legged creamer. She filled her cup from a teapot wrapped in a frayed blue cozy, and Phyllis mouthed her thanks. "She's okay," Calvin was saying.

Phyllis hung up and sipped her tea. Enough calls. She thought for just a moment about Hal, the dull ache of her lost limb. But it wasn't his house anymore, and she wasn't his wife.

Lucy sat at the kitchen table and drank hot chocolate made on the stove from milk and syrup from a can. On the table playing softly there was a white plastic radio, big as a toaster, and resting on it, three bottles of pills, black beads spilling out of a leather pouch, a worn deck of playing cards. Mrs. T. scrubbed a saucepan with a green sponge she pulled from the gaping mouth of a ceramic frog squatting on the edge of the sink. Phyllis sipped hot tea and cleaned her glasses with a paper napkin and told Lucy again and again that everything was going to be all right.

On the side of the van it said, "EMERGENCY ENCLOSURES, 24-HOUR SERVICE SINCE 1974." According to the ad in the yellow pages, they offered complete disaster cleaning, smoke and odor eradication, flood damage repair, utility restoration, and debris removal. Two fellows dressed in matching brown jackets got out, stretched, and warily looked the place over. Most of the windows were gone, the back door was shot. The frames in the basement were burned out. Everything was blackened and sopping, everything smelled like wet ashes.

They unloaded plywood panels from the van and piled them on the front lawn. They filled their aprons with nails. One of the guys tipped back a Styrofoam coffee cup, drained it, and flattened it under his boot. The other stuffed his mouth with tobacco from a pouch he carried in his hip pocket. Then with utility bars they broke out the rest of the glass from the windows and piled the shards in five-gallon buckets, and while one crazy bird down the block started to chirp and the street lamp on the boulevard began to flicker, they grabbed brooms and swept up the broken glass.

17

REMEMBER

THE EMBERS

EARL BASS HAD BEEN SOBER FOR FIVE MONTHS, TWO WEEKS, AND three days. By the grace of God, his sponsor Lyle would remind him. Lyle, a crusty old-timer, who spoke in slogans, who loved black coffee and the big book, who hated yuppies and whiners. "Fuck your bad day," he would growl under his breath. "Talk about the steps." Lyle had been encouraging him to cultivate what he called an attitude of gratitude, and Earl *was* grateful. He had a new job, and he liked it. He had a new apartment and a new used car. He had Phyllis, a new friend.

But he still wasn't sleeping right. He laid off coffee in the evening, drank a glass of milk after the news, put on pajamas, and, good and tired by eleven, he would fall easily asleep. Then an hour later he'd be bolt-upright awake, his heart pounding, his gut leaden with the icy, creeping dread of half-remembered dreams. He would lie in bed and try to think about pleasant things, favorite golf courses, the layout of particular holes, how he'd play each one. He'd alphabetize the states, the capitals, the presidents. But he couldn't lie still. He twisted and thrashed in the bedclothes, wired with anxious electricity. He thought about his daughter, who hated him. He remembered things he'd said to her mother.

Earl made a vague reference to sleeping pills, maybe something over the counter, but Lyle said no, absolutely not. Sober is sober. So Earl had taken finally to reading—newspapers, magazines, anything he could get his hands on, paperbacks from the spinning racks just inside the door of his local branch library, Zane Grey, guides to personal finance, a book about angels. When Phyllis called, he was sitting at the kitchen table with a fat history of the Civil War propped open to a map of the western campaign, the tangled red and blue lines and arrows, Grant and Buell and Bragg, like the web of veins and arteries in her textbook. "I'll be right over," he said.

When Earl got there, the fire was under control, and Phyllis's neighbor was handing out warm clothes. He helped her arrange to get the place closed up. They talked to someone on her insurance company's toll-free line who spoke with the practiced compassion and studied calm of a crisis counselor, and promised an agent would be there in just a couple of hours. In the meantime, Earl suggested, why not get something to eat. Phyllis shrugged. "Why not?" she said.

Walter couldn't get over it, the name of the restaurant, Embers. For the longest time he couldn't say what was so funny.

He just sat there, shaking his head and chuckling, pointing to the big red letters on the place mat, REMEMBER THE EMBERS, to the menu full of flame-broiled Emburgers. Earl thought maybe he was in shock. Finally Walter spit it out. "Embers," he said. *"Embers.* Get it? Like glowing embers?"

Earl had never given the name a second thought. He'd grown up with Embers. It was an all-night restaurant. A chain. It was where, truth be told, he had boozily shoveled up his share of late night eggs. Where he had eaten his dinner last Thanksgiving—a turkey club in honor of the holiday. It was just the only place open.

"It's not that funny," Ellie said.

"It's ironic," Phyllis said. "That's what it is."

Walter was turning the pages of his menu, still chuckling. "It's not that ironic," Ellie said.

They were sitting together in a semicircular corner booth near the register, Earl and Phyllis, Walter and Ellie. The girls were standing at the glass dessert case, studying the rotating cakes and pies like connoisseurs in a museum, Becky patiently pointing out the bunnies and baby chicks and tiny colored eggs half-concealed among the doilies and whipped cream, while Lucy nodded solemnly, her mouth round with wonder.

The place was practically empty. There was a booth full of glassy-eyed kids, and one big smiling woman sitting alone at the counter, her head wrapped in a scarf and a billed cap, like a member of the French Foreign Legion, spinning back and forth slowly on her stool, her lips moving silently. She got up from time to time and wiped the counter with a wad of paper napkins, lined up the salt and pepper shakers, straightened the menus. She was a demented volunteer, harmless and happy.

Their waitress brought water, coffee and tea, cream and

sugar, extra hot water, lemon slices. She was an Asian girl with a stunning mouthful of silver braces and wires that glittered when she smiled like exotic jewelry. "Do you need some more time?" she wanted to know, and they nodded.

"What looks good?" Phyllis asked. Everything *looked* good. Menus always looked good—glossy as soft-core porn, perfect omelets and salads and steaks, fresh glistening vegetables and grated cheese tumbling down the margins. But what arrived on the plate always disappointed.

They ordered big. Pancakes and French toast. Fried potatoes and sausage on the side. Large juice all around. Walter, after making some inquiries about peppers and onions, went for the everything omelet. Becky ordered a strawberry waffle. The waitress just kept flipping the pages of her pad, scribbling and smiling, like she was on commission. Lucy ordered for herself, pointing to the buttermilk pancakes on the children's menu. "With maple syrup, please," she said. Earl got pancakes too, the tall stack.

Just as the waitress was heading toward the kitchen with their order, Phyllis called her back. She asked for a milkshake, chocolate, very thick. "You only live once," she said. "Isn't that right, Earl?"

"Right as rain," Earl said. Other people said it, but Phyllis knew it. That's why he loved her.

"Every time my house burns," she said, "I drink a milkshake, okay?"

"Me too," Lucy said. "Please?"

Ellie wrinkled her nose, considering. "Walter?"

"Sure, Walter said. "Why not? And," he said, pointing to Becky, who'd been absently touching her chin, and perked right up, "she needs a milkshake, too."

"Wait," Earl said, suddenly inspired. "One for everybody.

A round. Extra thick.'' The waitress counted with her finger and grinned, and Phyllis, under cover of the table, gave his leg a good hard squeeze.

Earl saw it coming, like a car accident. One of the kids at the booth across the room, a girl wearing jeans and a baggy sweater, a ponytail protruding from a golf cap, got up and headed toward the rest rooms. She moved with a weirdly mechanical energy, stiff and swift, as if she'd been wound up. She never slowed, never broke stride. She missed the turn into the ladies' room, and walked full-tilt into the back wall. Her head made a dull thud on the paneling, and she crumpled.

Somebody screamed. They bolted from their booths, napkins flying, and bent over her like an injured player. When Walter lifted her eyelid, Earl saw only sickeningly vacant white. ''Call somebody,'' Ellie was saying. ''Call an ambulance.'' The girl's friends, a boy with a wispy mustache, another girl in a sweatshirt, stood back, stricken. A little pockmarked man in a greasy white apron emerged from the back wiping his hands on a striped towel. He squatted on his heels and muttered something softly in another language, some passionate formula, maybe a prayer, maybe a curse. The girl was so pale, so still, Earl was afraid that she was dead.

But then she opened her eyes. She was embarrassed, apologetic. ''I'm okay,'' she said. ''Really.'' The big woman with the cap fetched a glass of water, and the waitress held the girl's head while she slurped from a tall hinged straw. Walter held up fingers and made her count. ''I'm fine,'' the girl said. ''I just blacked out. I'm really sorry. I haven't eaten all day, that's the problem. I'm okay.''

They helped her to her feet. Had she been an injured

player, they would have applauded now, and she would have limped down a tunnel, waving bravely. Instead, the cook brought a lumpy towel full of ice, which she clamped to her head, and with more assistance than she needed, she made her way back to her seat. ''Thanks a mil,'' she said. When she was unconscious, they could be urgently and passionately concerned, but now she was watching them, and they assumed once again attitudes of polite reserve.

''You're welcome,'' Ellie said.

''Take care,'' Phyllis said.

''Easy does it,'' Earl said.

''I'm fine,'' the girl said. ''Really.''

They returned to their booth, and repositioned place mats, filled coffee cups. Ellie took Lucy, who was full of loud questions, to the rest room. Earl tried very hard not to look over at the girl, but he couldn't help it. What was it like, he wondered, to open your eyes into a circle of strange faces? Did she see stars? A warm light? She was chomping french fries dipped in ketchup now, two and three at a time. Their eyes met for a moment, and she raised her water glass in his direction, ever so slightly, a sheepish long-distance toast.

The milkshakes came in frosty silver cups, topped with whipped cream and cherries. Walter blew the paper off his straw, and Becky followed suit. ''Walter,'' Ellie said, but Earl could tell she really wasn't mad. She filled a soda glass for Lucy, who was sitting between them, kneeling on her seat, long spoon in hand, ready. Earl, who rarely ate sweets, tasted his milkshake. It wasn't bad.

''We have to do this more often,'' Phyllis said.

"Here's to Becky," Ellie said, and raised her glass. "The hero of the day."

"She's a jolly good fellow," Walter said.

Just then Phyllis's son, Calvin, the lawyer, came through the door. Earl didn't recognize him at first. He was wearing a leather-sleeved letterman's jacket and a pair of horn-rimmed glasses he hadn't had on the day before. His hair was sticking up in back. He looked apprehensive.

"Hey, Cal," Walter said. "Over here."

Ellie grabbed a chair from another table, and they pushed their place mats together. They squeezed him in, and Earl waved down their waitress. "Bring this young man a chocolate shake," he said. Calvin patted his pants pockets, front and back, reached into the pockets of his jacket.

"Stop," Earl told him. "Your money's no good here."

Earl watched Calvin clean his glasses with a paper napkin. He pushed them up his nose and looked them over, a little wary still. Phyllis had a tiny bit of ice cream on her upper lip, a chocolate mustache. Walter, red-eyed and unshaven, was reading his place mat, squinting at the map of other locations, smiling vacantly to himself, probably still thinking about embers. Lucy was methodically piling whipped cream on a saucer.

"Knock knock," she said, without looking up from her work.

"Who's there?" Walter said, suddenly animated.

"Knock knock," she said again.

The woman at the counter was wiping it down again. "Who's there?" Earl said. They were happy idiots, every one.

The waitress brought their food on a tremendous round tray and unloaded it plate by plate. Walter's omelet. A side of toast. Becky's waffle buried under a mountain of strawberries. Earl's tall stack. Somebody's bacon. Calvin had to move a bowl of half-and-half and the salt and pepper to make room for it all.

Lucy's pancakes arrived arranged as a bear, a big face, two little ears, whipped cream eyes and nose. She studied her plate, her eyes shining with excitement. Earl could just imagine. It was the middle of the night, and here she was, at Embers, sipping a chocolate milkshake, looking at a plate of pancakes. In her pajamas. He could remember taking Liz out for Sunday breakfast when she was a little girl, hatted and ribboned after Sunday services, all girlish lace and shy smiles. She loved pancakes, too.

"Do you need some help?" Earl asked Lucy. Her mother was busy spreading jam on a piece of toast. "Would you like me to cut your pancakes?" Lucy nodded and stared at her plate expectantly. Earl picked up his knife and fork, and minding his elbows, cut, as precisely and carefully as he could, little regular pancake squares. He felt crude and awkward, like an oversized crasher at a girl's tea party, but he took his time and did a good job. "There," he said. "How's that?"

"Good," she said. "Now pray." An order. She seized his hand, clutched two thick fingers tight in her little palm, took her mother's hand on the opposite side, and lowered her head. Ellie took Becky's hand, and Becky reached over to Walter, who had a forkful of food halfway to his mouth, but put it down. Phyllis and Calvin closed the circle.

Lucy began and the others joined in. "Thank you for the food we eat. Thank you for the birds that sing." Earl didn't really know the words. But he moved his lips and made some noise anyway. *"Thank you, God, for everything."*

Earl doused his cakes in syrup and dug in. There was some passing and reaching, a clatter of silver. The waitress came back to their table. ''Is everything all right?'' she wanted to know.

Earl just nodded.

18

ONE MORE THING

Walter and Lucy flew back to Buffalo on Sunday night after the fire. Ellie decided to stay on for a few days to help her mother get settled. Phyllis said it wasn't necessary, but Ellie insisted, and Phyllis seemed grateful. It was the right thing to do. Still, it was hard to be away from Lucy and Walter even for a little while, hard just to say good-bye. Even strangers' leave-taking filled her with inexplicable sadness, and that's all the airport was. While they waited to board, Walter listened patiently to her list of instructions, who to call, what to water. "No problem," he kept saying. Tonight, she loved the massy warmth of him, his solidity. She hugged him tight and held on.

Lucy, always in the present tense, said, "I'm missing you, Mommy." Then their row was called, and practically sick with grief, Ellie watched them disappear, waving, down the airline's tunnel. It was death in miniature, and she didn't want to look. But she made herself stand at the terminal window, waving vaguely into the darkness and her own teary reflection, until the plane taxied away, and she headed down the escalators to the parking lot, her mood dark with irrational forebodings of death and disaster.

The insurance company was putting Phyllis up in a furnished apartment downtown. The building was a fancy high-rise that catered to out-of-town executives and wealthy senior citizens, complete with a smiling, uniformed doorman, leather furniture, and a picture-window view of the river and the Minneapolis skyline. Ellie peeked into the dishwasher, swiveled in the cushioned executive chair. "Very impressive, Mom," she said.

"I'm in good hands," Phyllis said.

Her agent was a young man named Jared, who called several times a day to make sure that she was all right, to see if she needed anything. "He's very earnest," Phyllis said. "I have this feeling he's working toward a merit badge—helped old lady in distress, something like that." He provided detailed résumés of the contractor and workmen he was hiring to repair the house and cut her a big check to cover incidental expenses. "I'm loaded," Phyllis said when Ellie offered to pay for groceries. "Never been better off."

But there was work to be done. In order to be reimbursed for her possessions damaged or destroyed in the fire, the insurance company required that Phyllis perform a complete inventory: a precise description of every item, date of purchase and price, estimated current value. Phyllis told Ellie that Jared

seemed disappointed that she didn't have documentary photographs of every room stashed away in a safe deposit box somewhere. He instructed her to record everything—appliances,
furniture, clothes, knickknacks, the contents of closets and
cupboards and even the refrigerator. Phyllis made a little joke
about the difficulty of depreciating dairy products, and Jared
arranged his face into something like a smile, but she could
tell he was not really amused.

First thing Tuesday morning, Ellie, clipboard and pen in hand,
watched her mother open a shiny, oversized padlock and push
the front door open. Inside, the house was both familiar and
utterly transformed, and Ellie felt the betrayed disbelief and
confused recognition of a mourner at a wake. It was unnaturally dark, the windows boarded, the walls blackened. There
was makeshift plywood flooring, but there were gaps and crevices: she could peer from the front hall directly into the basement at the water heater below her. Even though the hall was
littered with big cans of something labeled "MALODOR COUNTER-
ACTANT," the house smelled so purely, so intensely of
smoke—its very essence, concentrated like perfume—that Ellie couldn't even recognize or name it immediately.

They moved cautiously and silently from room to room,
holding hands suddenly, scared kids in a haunted house. In the
kitchen, four wicker chairs stood with no wicker, just the
smoky curved gold bars of the frames, like something ultra-
modern. The handset of the wall phone had melted into its
holder, the whole telephone reconfigured into something
nightmarishly ill-proportioned and misshapen, like a Dali
painting. The basement door was charred and flaking black.
The stairs were gone entirely: Phyllis gasped and stopped

short and grabbed Ellie at the edge, and together they looked down into the murky, wet darkness. "Oh my God," Ellie said.

It was like an archaeological site, a frozen glimpse of every-day life, only this wasn't Pompeii, it was her mother's life, her own life. In the guest room upstairs, Ellie found Lucy's sleeping bag in the middle of the floor, inside out, a discarded cocoon. The paperback mystery she had been reading on Saturday night was still face down on the nightstand, its pages blackened, and when she picked it up, there was a perfect white rectangle on the tabletop. In her mother's room, there was a glass of water on her dresser, a layer of ash floating on its surface. The sweater Phyllis wore the day of the cleaning party was hanging on the closet doorknob, the same lifeless gray now as the walls and sheets, not so much stained as drained of color.

Phyllis picked up a book from her nightstand. "Okay," she said. "Let's begin." She blew a film of gray dust from it. She sniffed it. "One Holy Bible," she said. Ellie took up her pen and started to write. "King James Version, red-letter, self-pronouncing." Phyllis opened it, ruffled the pages. "Purchased in 1954," she said. "Four dollars? Five dollars?"

"What's the current value?" Ellie said. "I have to fill that in."

Phyllis looked at her, hopeless and amused.

"Make something up," Ellie told her.

They worked dutifully through the house, item by item and room by room. Phyllis would hold something up and dictate. Dresses, shoes, picture frames, towels, magazines, makeup.

Ellie recorded plausible prices. It wasn't easy finding words to describe the most ordinary object—what you hung coffee mugs on, the wooden thing near the front door where Phyllis put keys and letters and spare change—and in the kitchen especially, it wasn't always clear or obvious what some things were or used to be.

After a while, it started to get funny. They grew giddy, punch-drunk. They played Name-That-Burnt-Vegetable in the kitchen. Phyllis started to inflate and embellish her descriptions, turning everything into an antique, a rarity, something collectible. "Let me see," she said, holding up the cup where she kept paper clips and thumbtacks. It was a converted ashtray, somebody's lopsided art project. "One handmade, decorative pottery urn, possibly imported. Priceless."

Late in the morning, they sat outside on the front steps and talked. "Isn't this a breath of the proverbial," Phyllis said. The sky was full of what Lucy called morning clouds, faint white wisps, like a jet stream. There were glittering nails scattered in the lawn, wood shavings on the sidewalk.

Ellie sniffed her sleeve. "Do you think we'll smell like ashtrays for the rest of our lives?"

Mrs. T. was digging in her front lawn across the street. Phyllis waved, and the old woman raised her trowel in salute. "When I used to smoke," Phyllis said, "I was a walking ashtray. But I couldn't smell anything at all, including myself. Then I quit, and I could smell everything. Like a bloodhound. Isn't that funny?"

"I'd almost forgotten," Ellie said. "Benson and Hedges, the long ones. You used to send me to the corner store with a note to buy them for you." Ellie could still recall Harry, the man behind the counter, his acrid breath and flickering portable black-and-white television.

"I was a bad mother," Phyllis said. Her forehead and cheeks were smudged with gray ash. There was black under her fingernails, dark streaks on her sleeve. "Not like you with Lucy. I smoked and drank and didn't protect my daughter."

"Forget it," Ellie said. But the word "protect" caught in her innards somewhere, a glittering golden lure.

"I want to make amends."

"You let me burn your house down, didn't you?" She had truly felt it, the arsonist's hot thrill.

"Go on. It was spontaneous combustion. That's what the firemen said."

"Spontaneous combustion? That's impossible, isn't it? Like perpetual motion." Ellie had heard the stories. Old ladies popping off like hand grenades, going up in flames with their shopping bags. It happened in a Dickens novel. "That's urban folklore, like cats in the microwave and alligators in the sewer. You don't believe in that, do you?"

"Nowadays," Phyllis said, "I believe in everything." She picked up a handful of stones from the sidewalk and shook them in her hand. "But if you burned my house down, you're entitled. I'm glad."

"I'm glad, too, I think," Ellie said. "Isn't that awful?"

"What's so awful? It was a swell fire. It was the most exciting thing that ever happened to me."

"You're different, Mom," Ellie said. "You're a different person." Ellie had noticed it right away, had whispered it to Walter the first night in the guest room. *She's changed.*

"Good thing," Phyllis said.

"What was it like?" Ellie said. "Being married to him all those years?"

"We had some times," Phyllis said. "He wasn't Hitler."

"Did you love him?" Ellie said. "Ever?"

"We had an arrangement."

"Did you love him?"

"Love is never arranged, is it? When you children were little and we were busy, we worked together, we stood over your cribs side by side. But running a small business together isn't love either."

"How about Jack Brady? Did you love him?"

"Oh yes. How did you know that?"

"I remember all the time he spent in our kitchen, sipping his beer and playing cards with us. You used to talk to him in a special voice, sort of bright, not phony, just fuller somehow, like stereo instead of mono. And when he died, you went to pieces."

"He was so *decent*. And so lonely. We were kindred spirits."

"I used to wish he was my dad."

"I used to wish he was my husband." Phyllis paused and lowered her voice. "But there was never anything physical between us," she said. "Wait," she said. "I take that back. It *was* physical." She laughed. "Are you sure you want to hear this?"

"I think so."

"I remember once he was at the kitchen table, telling me a story, something funny, and he reached over and touched my arm, the way you do, smiling, *Now get this, Phyllis,* he said, and my heart just melted. Something got rearranged inside me. I was so grateful. From that moment, I loved him. Because I was real to him. Your father never touched me, not that way. *Now get this, Phyllis.* I thought about it all the time. It was sad. Because it was so rare, and not very much really, just a touch. But it was everything to me.''

Ellie studied her mother's profile, angular again now in her gaunt old age, and she could see the outlines of that young woman, hungry for affection, aching to be touched, in love with a sad, decent, doomed man. She wanted to protect *her*. But it was too late now.

''We kissed just once, at a New Year's Eve party, in the Kruks' paneled basement. Like teenagers. Hal was out of town, and Maggie had gone home early with a migraine. We drank champagne from plastic glasses and danced, and then, at the stroke of midnight, we kissed. That's when we both knew it, we were dangerous.''

Ellie couldn't help but smile. She felt glad to be the daughter of a dangerous mother.

''I used to feel so guilty,'' Phyllis said. ''But no more. There was something in me Jack kept alive. My heart's pilot light. Do you know what I'm talking about?''

Ellie nodded. She knew.

''As long as I'm telling you my secrets,'' Phyllis said, ''there's something else. There's one more thing.''

In her mysteries, Ellie knew, there was always one more thing. A horsehair from a violin bow. A cigarette butt. A single enigmatic word scribbled on a scrap of paper. It explained everything, if you knew what you were looking for.

''I haven't been feeling well, not for a long time. Something inside. I thought it was indigestion. I thought it was Hal.

When I was taking my class with Maureen, I thought it was beriberi. I guess I thought it would go away, or clear up, or dissolve by itself, without intervention, as they say. Anyway, I finally went to see Dr. Dorsher.''

"What?'' Ellie said. She knew what was coming.

"Now don't be alarmed. It's nothing, really. Well, it's something.''

"What is it?'' Her mother was dying. How long had she known?

"Not so good, maybe. I need more tests. There's definitely something there, he said. Not necessarily benign, if you know what I mean.''

"I know what you mean,'' Ellie said.

"I'm going back tomorrow. There's no time to lose, the doctor said. Amen, I said.''

"Amen,'' Ellie said.

"I'm not telling the other kids, I don't know why. But you're flying back tomorrow night, and I wanted to tell you.''

"Okay. You told me.''

"Just so you know.''

"Thank you.''

"You're welcome.''

Ellie put her arm around her mother's shoulder. She felt sharp-boned and frail. They sat on the step together, trembling in unison with muted sobs, watching Mrs. T. work methodically across her lawn on her hands and knees, digging, digging, digging.

Just then Earl Bass pulled up in a blue sedan, something boxy and nondescript, like a rental or a priest's car. He got out of the car and walked slowly up the front walk carrying a cardboard tray full of tall, wax paper cups, the breast pocket of his shirt full of plastic straws and spoons.

He looked them over, mother and daughter, their faces streaked with tears and ashes.

''Holy smoke,'' he said softly. ''What have we here?''

EPILOGUE

PHYLLIS HAD NON-HODGKIN'S LYMPHOMA, CANCER OF THE IMMUNE system. It was what Jacqueline Onassis had, and like her, Phyllis suffered from what the doctor called an aggressive form. Phyllis understood his tone of voice even before she looked up the words in her medical companion: the cells they biopsied were "anaplastic," which meant they were primitive-looking, highly malignant. It had spread to her spleen, possibly her liver. They ordered aggressive treatment—chemotherapy, radiation, antibiotics. In June, when she toured her restored house with Jared and Earl, she needed to stop and rest after climbing the stairs. She found jokes to make, about being on steroids, about her affinities with Jackie O. But she knew what she knew, and couldn't keep it a secret any longer.

Back in Buffalo, Ellie talked to her mother on the telephone daily through the summer, sometimes two and even three times a day, long rambling conversations at odd hours. Late at night, when rates were low. Early in the morning, when it was quiet and the sky was pink. In the middle of the day when Phyllis remembered something she had wanted to say earlier. Sometimes her mother called, sometimes Ellie called. They lost track. It cost a fortune, but Walter, who paid the bills and generally fretted about money, never said a word. While emptying the trash, Ellie found a bill he had paid, four pages of itemized long-distance charges, the amount due as big as their car payment, and she teared up, over her phone bill, her heart wrenched by the computerized record of her late intimacy with her mother: forty-three minutes one night, $9.27 worth of talk the next day.

When Ellie wasn't talking to her mother, it seemed, she was painting, sometimes doing both at once. In the community education catalog, she found among the crafts and computer training and cooking classes a course in painting and drawing, one night a week. After years of furniture restoration, a decade having passed since her last real art class, Ellie decided, she was ready for a change.

Her teacher was a little elderly man named Piccone. That's what he called himself, how he signed the one work of his Ellie located in a local gallery, a gigantic hallucinatory oil painting. He was a last-minute substitute for the regular teacher, who had been hospitalized with gallstones. He wore olive-green work clothes, matching shirt and trousers, like a janitor or a Communist laborer. One of his legs was substantially shorter than the other. His left shoe was built up into a thick black slab, like a club, and he walked with a swaying, swaggering limp. While the class worked, he would often lean against a wall, and standing on his good leg, fold the other behind him, like a runner stretching hamstrings, and pull and tug and grimace, his face contorted in pain, shaking his head in sad contempt, whether in response to their artistic efforts or his own frailty, Ellie wasn't sure.

The first night they did contour drawings for three hours— the door, a window, a cornice. It was difficult to draw without looking, but that was the point, so even though Ellie's sketches were painfully ragged, barely recognizable, she kept at it. She gradually got absorbed in the movement itself, the exercise of her arm, its own muscular freestyle dance.

The man working next to Ellie, meanwhile, produced a series of technically perfect drawings, so painstakingly precise she assumed he had to be an engineer or a draftsman. Making his rounds at the end of the class, Piccone stood for a long time staring at the man's work while he looked on shyly.

Piccone pulled at his face, as if he were dissatisfied with the configuration of his flesh, stretching, reshaping. "You're good, aren't you?" he said. "A real artist." The man smiled.

"Idiot," Piccone muttered, only half to himself, and shuffled over to Ellie's woolly, irregular sketches. His eyebrows seemed to raise ever so slightly. He yanked his chin. "Big strokes," he said.

There was some grumbling after class. You shouldn't insult students, not in community ed. Drop the first week and you could get a full refund. Maybe this Piccone was not a nice man. So what? Ellie was surprised to discover that she didn't care. She kept coming back.

It had always been Phyllis's nature to make lists, and now that her worldly possessions had been disposed of, her house sold finally to a nice young couple, she took repeated inventory of her children. She went down the line. Maureen was talking up alternative treatments, pushing herbs, extract of garlic, little pills that arrived wrapped in plain paper from Mexico. "No thanks, I told her," Phyllis said. "But it's the thought that counts." Maureen was flighty and bad with money and needed to pay more attention to her kids, but she would be all right, Phyllis was convinced, because she was really good at heart. (Ellie sometimes wondered, but never asked, what her mother said about her to the others. Was she good at heart? She would have liked to know.)

Geoff, newly relocated on the West Coast, sent her funny get-well cards and extravagant floral arrangements. "I feel like I won the Kentucky Derby," Phyllis told Ellie, who sometimes wondered about her older brother's heart. Nothing concrete, just inklings, intuitions. Something about his jawline she distrusted, the number of exclamation points in his annual Christmas letter, the way he spoke to his children.

Joan, now her ex-daughter-in-law, still called Phyllis from time to time. After some preliminary inquiries about her health, she spent the rest of the time doing what she called "venting." She was a cauldron of unhappiness, resentment, complaint. "This is what I'm like now," she announced. "The real me at last." She was unpleasant and proud of it. She seemed jealous of Phyllis, the fire, possibly her cancer. "Must be nice," she said when Phyllis mentioned she needed to replace her smoke-damaged and ill-fitting wardrobe. About Geoff she was by turns petty—he was a day late with the child support, had forgotten something or other he'd promised—

and vaguely, darkly global in her indictments. "If you only knew," she said more than once.

Of course the kids were affected, Phyllis said. Dylan had become sullen and hard, and Becky, wearily resigned to playing sidekick to her mother, temporarily compliant, like an indentured servant. She went clothes shopping and drank coffee with her but was already sending off for college catalogs, marking time at home. Becky told Phyllis that she wanted to go to school in New York and live with Ellie. A specialist was treating her skin now, but nothing seemed to work. It was bad and getting worse.

Calvin, meanwhile, had been a godsend. He wrote Phyllis's will, which she signed solemnly in his conference room one afternoon, witnessed by an owlish paralegal and sealed away by Calvin, who had his own safe right in the office. It was an act of love, Phyllis said, all this paperwork. Every Sunday, on his way home from church, he stopped over to see her with Grace, who found her grandmother inexplicably and endlessly amusing. Just on the verge of crawling now, she would look up at her from the floor, on all fours, her legs revving, about to engage, and cackle with glee. All it took was a look from Phyllis to set off her baby hysterics.

"So," Phyllis would say, having gone through her list, "that's that." Next day, she would do it again. Only once did Phyllis say anything about Hal. "He didn't just happen to me, you know," she told Ellie. "I chose him. That's the difference between you and me. I don't despise him now, I don't regret him. But I don't feel sorry for him, either. I don't think about him that much, to be honest, and I don't want to see him. I just accept him, I guess, because I have no choice in the matter. Just like you know what."

Ellie used to be obsessed with the idea of private work space, a room of one's own, a loft, a studio, with a sign that read DO NOT DISTURB, where, protected from telephones and the meter man and Lucy's and Walter's constant demands, she would, undistracted, reach deep within herself, and *create*. Now she worked right in the kitchen, in the middle of things, garbage trucks rumbling on the street, a lawn mower cranking down the block, her paper clipped to Lucy's orange Little Tikes easel. The idea of "interruption" just didn't apply anymore. She would sit in Lucy's squat school chair and paint. Step back and have a look at what she'd done while she fixed a sandwich or stirred something on the stove. Go back and daub a little. Lucy seemed tickled by her mother's newfound interest in paints, her unexpected discovery of the joys of messy play. More than once Ellie let her add something of her own, a line here and there, always bold, always an improvement. She could just imagine what Piccone would say.

She tried some portraits, rough pencil sketches of her family from snapshots, Walter and Lucy, her mother and father, Maureen and Geoff, but too often they came out looking like police artists' composite drawings of fugitive criminals, grim and shifty and not quite fully human somehow. So she turned her attention to ordinary, everyday things, what was right in front of her. Lucy's crumpled rain slicker hanging on a doorknob. An oatmeal box. Her coffee cup and a pitcher of cream. A tangle of mismatched shoes piled near the back door. First India ink, then watercolors on school paper, black and white mostly, with little splashes of gray. She loved the rough, irregular way cheap paper took paint.

In July, Phyllis and Earl got married. "It was either that or the last rites, you know," Phyllis told Ellie. They had been living together in the downtown high-rise, defiantly and radically, Phyllis imagined, a scandal in the eyes of the elderly permanent residents of the complex. Biddies and clucks, she called them, geezers and fogies. Phyllis and Earl certainly didn't need their approval, but Calvin advised them that marriage made sense, legally speaking, and they had their own reasons.

They did it on a sweltering Wednesday afternoon in the downtown chambers of a jowly district judge. "It's so corny," Phyllis told Ellie. "I don't know if I want to discuss it. You have to promise not to laugh."

"I promise," Ellie said.

Phyllis wore a plain gray dress, black pumps, and a new string of artificial pearls. Earl wore a new blue suit. They were the last of three couples, the only ones without a photographer or well-wishers. The telephone sounded right before the vows, three shrill rings, and its red light flashed, like an alarm. They smiled and ignored it. Earl kissed the bride, and a secretary daintily threw rice. Earl brought his own bottle of sparkling grape juice, which the judge himself opened and poured for them. "To life," he said.

Phyllis declined the court's offer of a free name change. "Phyllis Bass sounds like a tropical fish, don't you think?" she told Ellie. She kept her maiden name, Wheeler, which she had assumed once again after the divorce. It was the name she had written on her homework papers as a girl, and now, she told Ellie, just signing a check could send her back. Somehow, her hand remembered, the loops and curves of her former signature, the contours of her old and new name, familiar and strange at once.

Ellie's friend from college, Mavis, the jewelry maker, stood in the kitchen and surveyed Ellie's work. The paintings were hung on masking tape loops, on the cupboards, the walls, the appliances. "Ellie," she said, "I'm surprised at you." As if she'd discovered something a little unseemly. "You're living large, El," she said.

She went right to Ellie's favorite, Lucy's rumpled raincoat. "Now this is a slicker with an attitude," she said. "It's a slicker that's been places, done things. It knows things." She took a step back and studied. "It says, I'm weary but still waterproof."

Ellie just laughed. "Inanimate objects don't talk to *me*," she said.

"Oh, but they do," Mavis said. "Don't deny it."

They sat at the kitchen table and drank iced tea. Mavis told Ellie what she'd heard about Piccone, that he had had polio, was European-trained, brilliant and irascible, prolific and unappreciated, a lecherous old goat, maybe a little mad. Ellie talked about her mother, her prognosis, her marriage, her phone calls, her will.

"I see," Mavis said.

On the way out, Mavis asked if she could have a painting or two.

"Help yourself," Ellie said. "There's more where that came from." Mavis took the raincoat, one of her best coffee cups, and an ill-proportioned view of the kitchen wall phone, all tangled, twisted loops of cord. She carefully removed the tape and rolled them up. She left with them tucked under her arm, like an architect or a general with big plans. Only much later, after puzzling over a mysterious letter of congratulations, would Ellie discover that Mavis had forged her signature and entered them in the annual upstate art show.

Walter took a real interest in Ellie's art, too. He would stand in front of a new piece for the longest time, squinting. He'd move way up close and study particular brush strokes. Sometimes he'd point to his favorites, but mostly he just asked questions. How'd you do that? He understood craft, appreciated technique. At night, Ellie took a renewed passionate interest in him. He was surprised and grateful. He'd lie back on his pillow and sigh, full of contented, exhausted astonishment. How'd you do *that?*

Late in August, the doctors told Phyllis there was no more to be done. Things had spread too far. They gave her painkillers, which, for a couple of days, made her manic and distracted and irritable. She chewed Ellie out one morning in a high-pitched voice completely unlike her own, for something, for nothing, and then called back ten minutes later sobbing. "I'm not doing this very well," she said.

"Nobody does, Mom," Ellie said. "Nobody does it well."

Ellie had a ticket to Minneapolis, and Walter thought now was the time to use it. But something told Ellie to wait. Before long, Phyllis was almost herself again. She thanked Ellie for the painting she'd sent as a wedding present, watercolor pots and pans. "I put it on the refrigerator with magnets, just like old times. Earl loves it, too. He stands at the fridge admiring so long he forgets what he came for." And Phyllis enjoyed the little joke. "I don't have to scrub these, and the bottoms will never tarnish. The perfect gift."

Phyllis was comfortable, she said, she had everything she needed. "Earl makes me ice cream treats, and sits on the bed and fluffs my pillows. We talk. All we do is talk, Earl and I. About everything. Our first kiss, our favorite dogs. Things I haven't thought about in years. It's all there. Old movies, who you voted for. How do we remember this stuff? Where does it come from? We just keep talking. Tell each other stories about when we were young and strong. All lies." Ellie heard Earl say something in the background. "Okay," Phyllis said. "Mostly lies."

As the days passed, her voice grew weaker, the pauses longer, her breathing more labored. At some point, Ellie realized, there was no more old ground to cover, no more exposition, no more background. Everything was used up. She understood that there was no need for any last-minute frantic motions of grief and consolation, no need for bedside scenes. They were simply together now, clutching their telephones a thousand miles apart, in the present moment, listening to the quiet, rhythmic sound of each other's breathing.

"Early, early in the morning," Phyllis told her, "in the city, wherever you are, you can always smell a bakery, the sweet burnt-sugar smell, and you can hear trains rumbling and whistling in the distance. It's lovely and it's true, and no one ever mentions it. Why is that? Don't they notice?"

"I don't know," Ellie said.

"The world is so beautiful, Ellie, I ache. That's the only word for it. When I was at the doctor's office last, I was waiting in an examination room on the eighth floor, tugging at my gown, and all of a sudden, boom, a pigeon landed on the ledge outside the window. Its neck was the most beautiful green, and the purple on its wings just sparkled in the sunshine. We stared at each other, both of us stupid and scared, and then it flew off, and I thought, this is it, the meaning of life, don't ask me why.''

The last time Phyllis called, Earl had to hold the phone. She spoke in an urgent whisper, insistent and impatient, like a frustrated child trying to be understood, crazed and holy, muddled with morphine, full of oracular enigmas. There was something she wanted to say but she may have only been thinking it, speaking just bits and pieces, garbled riddles. There were great leaps and missed connections in what she said. Ellie was standing in the kitchen, watching Lucy in the backyard, the telephone held to her ear with all her might, trying to make sense.

Phyllis moaned. "The first page," she said finally, "and the last page. They're already written." Ellie could see Lucy outside in her ruffle-bottomed suit leaning into the spray of the lawn sprinkler with her hand out, cautiously testing the water. Ellie waited.

"And the rest," Phyllis said at last, her voice calm now, full of weary wonder.

"And the rest?" Ellie said. "The rest?" She needed to know.

There was a long pause. Lucy put her head down and charged.

"Love," her mother said dreamily.

ABOUT THE AUTHOR

MICK COCHRANE was born and raised in St. Paul, Minnesota, and holds an undergraduate degree from the College of St. Thomas, and a Ph.D. in English from the University of Minnesota. Currently, he is professor of English at Canisius College in Buffalo, New York, where he teaches writing and literature. His short stories have appeared in *Minnesota Monthly, Northwest Review,* and *Kansas Quarterly*. He lives outside of Buffalo with his wife and two sons, and is currently at work on his second novel.